GW01157808

M
P

The Walk to the Paradise Garden

Leon Arden

Muswell Press Ltd

The Walk to the Paradise Garden by **Leon Arden**

First published in June 2011
by **Muswell Press Ltd**

ISBN 978-0-9565575-9-9

Book design by **THIS IS Studio**
Printed and bound by **Shortrun Press Ltd.**

www.leonarden.com
www.muswell-press.co.uk

Also by Leon Arden:

Novels:

The Savage Place

Seesaw Sunday

The Twilight's Last Gleaming

One Fine Day

Plays:

The Midnight Ride of Alvin Blum (with Donal Honig)

TO FRANKIE

With all my love through all the past and coming years.

The Walk to the Paradise Garden

Leon Arden

The Story So Far

In the beginning there was nothing and then it exploded. Galaxies went flying every which way until, in the outskirts of one of these cosmic cartwheels, a small planet cooled down, life started up and the rest was pre-history. Millions of years later civilization began and gave us, from the outset, social inequality and shameless slaughter. It was near the middle of an over-populated and war-savaged century that I was pushed rather clumsily onto the stage.

This event went unnoticed except by my parents. From the very start they made a point of warning me of the numerous and ever-present dangers in life. My mother said not to go off with strangers or out with wet hair. My father told me not to play in the road or run sucking a lollipop. Most important, I was not to touch electricity. This was especially dangerous because it was in the house all the time - unlike lollipops. If I had my way they *and* electricity would be in the house all the time. Sadly, this was not to be for candy, I was told, was bad for the teeth. Another worry.

My father, whose name was Jacob, ruled the household like a king on guard against rebellion. He had married a woman whose attempts to challenge him, he well knew, would always be ineffectual, and he had a son whom he tried, as best he could, to keep from growing up. He failed at this but for a while it was a damned close run thing. Friends he kept at a minimum and at a distance as if they, more than family, might find him out. What he feared people might discover was that he was not omnipotent or omniscient or even skilled at keeping these shortcomings hidden. If a subject was introduced that he knew nothing about, he would commandeer the conversation to one he was familiar with. If this was not possible, the drawbridge went up and, as far as he was concerned, the subject was closed. He was hard working, successful, oppressively loving, quickly frightened, smotheringly helpful, increasingly corpulent and, whenever he had a free moment, charming.

He had a great influence on me and it was all I could do to get free of it.

And then, one mild day in early spring, he looked into my eyes and asked softly, "Will you help?"

He looked thin. He needed a shave.

Many days earlier I had said, "Let me speak to Sol."

"That bum. He's worthless."

"Perhaps if I..."

"You're wasting your time."

Now, in his bedroom, a seagull hovered beyond the window wondering who we were. Then it dropped away leaving, as far as the eye could see, the suburban prairie of New Jersey.

When I had first come into the room and told him what I had, he asked, "How many are there?"

"Twenty. It's unopened."

"Is that enough?"

"I think so."

"Are you going to give them to me?"

"Are you saying... are you really saying you want to go ahead with it?"

And that's when he asked, softly, "Will you help?"

The question hung there like carbon monoxide. Would I help? From the window I could see a white yacht in the Hudson as though it were a child's boat in the bath. I could see white, flat-bottomed clouds like shipments of eternal peace. I could see my father's reflection in the window as he sat in his wheelchair, wearing his white bathrobe and slippers, waiting for my answer.

Years have passed since then. But before I get into what happened, there are a few things I would like to touch upon first. It won't take long. Just a few things I need to say so that I'll be able to do justice to the injustice of it all.

Enter Exiting

My life almost ended the day I was born, an example of my parents' infinite capacity for misadventure. If a tendency toward catastrophe dwells in the genes, ours are chockablock. Anyway, I was yanked clumsily into this world and nearly slipped right out again. The first time I heard about it, I was eight years old. My father had mentioned at dinner that the Polish woman across the street was pregnant.

"Want to hear what happened when I gave birth to you?" my mother asked. "I was in labor for three days."

I had an idea what being in labor meant for I had seen a western in which a farmer's wife, about to give birth, was biting on a piece of wood to stifle her screams, her face glowing with sweat.

"How long does labor last?" I wanted to know.

"A few hours," my father said. When he saw me take more bread, he took some too. He often did that.

"Three whole days," my mother said. "Oh, that was something, I'm telling you. And you know what happened then? In the middle of it all he turned to him and he said..."

"Who turned?" I asked quickly, "and who did he turn to?"

"Whom did he turn to," my father corrected. "Anyway, he didn't turn to me because I was in the hall at the time."

"OK, he went into the hall and then he said..."

"Who said?"

"She means the *doctor* said," my father growled.

"Yes, the doctor said..."

We waited for her to continue. She looked at my father. "What were his words again?"

"He said who shall I save, your wife or the child?"

There was now a dizzying pause.

"Was that something?" she asked, "or was that something?"

My father was cutting a boiled potato in half.

"And you said save my wife," I told him. He nodded and I was relieved that he had done the right thing.

"Boy, oh boy." She shook her head.

"Yet they saved us both," I said.

"Oh, you were a mess," she told me. "Black eye, swollen cheek. They used forceps. That's how you got those scars. He said to bring you back for checks."

"For what?"

"For medical tests," my father explained. "We did that for a couple of months."

"No," my mother said, "for twelve months. A whole year."

"Why?" I asked.

"The umbilical cord had become detached and the doctor was certain you were... ...that it had affected your brain," my father explained.

"And he was right." She rocked with pleasure at her little joke. "But what's-her-name saved you. A wonderful woman."

"*Who* saved me?"

"The nurse. What was her name?"

"Gibbs," said my father.

"I mean her first name?"

"Jenny?"

"No, no, it wasn't Jenny."

"What happened? Was I too big?"

My father said the doctor had made a mistake by waiting too late to perform the Caesarean. When I looked puzzled, he added: "The name was derived from Julius Caesar because that's how he was born."

"They take them from the stomach," she explained.

"It's an operation."

I stared into the ghastly past, frozen with fascination.

"When the doctor finally pulled you out, he signaled to Nurse Gibbs not to touch you."

"He wanted her to let you die," my mother announced, "can you imagine that? Luckily she was new."

"Miss Gibbs had just started her medical training and it was the first time she had witnessed a birth."

"No, no, she had witnessed a birth before," corrected my mother with great certainty.

"She just started. What are you talking about?"

"OK, you know everything."

"And I suppose you do?"

"OK, forget it."

"So what happened, Dad?"

"Nurse Gibbs couldn't keep herself from doing her job. She cleaned you off and got you breathing. The doctor was so furious he..."

"A wonderful woman," my mother interrupted. "What was her first name?"

"I don't know."

"Just wonderful."

"The doctor was so furious, 'Young woman, do you realize this child will be retarded for life? That he'll be a burden to his family, to himself, and to the City of New York?'"

My mother frowned. "He didn't say that."

"What are you talking about? Gibbs said so."

"Gibbs told you that?"

"Yes."

"Boy that whole business was something."

I am on a beautiful beach sitting astride a corrugated suitcase. I rub sand with my palm over a wide area of the dark, serrated surface of wrinkled cardboard. Decades later, sifting through a box of old black and white photographs I came across a small, glossy image of thin, tousled-haired me in the shade of a beach umbrella wearing bulky bathing trunks and sitting on a suitcase. I am rubbing sand with the palm of my hand on the dark, serrated surface of the wrinkled cardboard. Who else, I wonder, has an actual photograph of his earliest memory?

Another snapshot taken perhaps that same day shows my mother in a dark dress lounging stiffly on a blanket, my toy boat nearby. In those early days we went to the beach often and I was always a little annoyed that she was the only person there fully clothed. She promised to buy a bathing suit when she found one she liked. I finally realized she would never find one she liked because she never shopped for one. I knew that much because, when she went shopping, she took me with her. So then she promised to buy one as soon as she lost weight. She lost weight, all right. She must have lost as much as two thousand pounds and just as quickly put it all back on again. It finally hit home that she was unhappy with the way she would look in a bathing suit. Hell, I wasn't too crazy about my figure either. Stick-like, all head plus a face like a first draft. And, after all, every time we went to that beach we saw all around us the stocky, the bulging, the corpulent and, that most popular American size, the triumphantly gross.

Yet in the scheme of things, the fact that my mother came to the beach as though dressed for the theatre was unimportant.

In general, she was endlessly cheerful and frequently humming, though one never could tell quite what. I don't think she actually knew a melody. She hummed as though trying and failing to invent one. My father never hummed or needed to. He was, himself, a symphony by Mahler, brooding, ominous, strident, mawkish and frequently explosive. In my early years he was late Mahler. The 8th in E Flat had 7 solo vocalists, 2 mixed choruses and boy's chorus and organ. My father was all of them rolled into one. A busy man, he came and went. When he went, I was left alone with my mother and was happy. When he came back, he sat distracted and brooding, brass and kettle drums at the ready. Dinner was always a final exam on the subject of table manners. Mine, never his. If I knocked over a glass of milk, my mother would mop it up without saying a word. With my father present, the dining room became Carnegie Hall during a Beethoven choral finale with full orchestra, an apocalyptic ode to angst. These outbursts of *Sturm und Drang* so knotted my stomach, I would gobble down my food and flee. "Don't eat so fast," my mother would say. She never made the connection and she never intervened.

I know many tales about myself as a child because my mother was a poor but tireless storyteller. She had one to relate for almost every occasion. There was an aspect of my early childhood that she never ceased talking about. It was how much I perspired in the cradle. I would soak the sheets, the pillow, the blankets, everything all the time. She told this with amazement, almost awe. My capacity to sweat became legend. Ever since I was little, I would listen to this story utterly bemused. Finally, when I was fifteen, I figured it out. How ironic that I almost didn't solve it because I see myself as someone with a problem-solving mind. But having a problem-solving mind means there are some simple challenges that one cannot imagine not solving at once.

"You slept so poorly as a baby." That was another of her offerings. "You kept waking up all the time."

"Ma, you know why? Because you piled too many blankets on me."

"Don't be silly."

"Then why did I sweat so much?"
"It was your nature."
"To soak the bedclothes?"
"Of course."
"And I slept badly, right?"
"I'll say. You kept waking up."
"'Cause you piled too many blankets on."
"Don't be silly."
"You did."
"Tsh, stop that."
"Well, it's a miracle I'm here at all."
"You're telling me. Oh, you were something. One time..." And off she went with yet another reminiscence, causing turbulence with each illogical jump to another subject. "One time when I was pushing you across the street..."

This involved four-year-old me in a stroller after a heavy rain. We set off across the road the moment the light turned red. A driver, trying to stop, hit the brakes and then the stroller, knocking it and me across the intersection. I was unconscious. We were bundled into his car and rushed to the hospital. When my mother finally thought to thank the man, he had gone.

That adventure was always described thus, for she could remember nothing else about it. How long we stayed or what my injuries were: all that was lost. Always I wondered at my mother when I heard her tell this story because the horror of what she went through was never conveyed. In this drama, she, like Chekhov, did not take sides. She was a lofty and dispassionate observer. The event was a curious mishap. An act of God, albeit a clumsy one. And the next time she told it, she told it exactly the same way.

So all the signs were there and still I did not yet understand. During those early years when one is too young to remember much, only as bits and snippets of things, she was the best mother a child could have. She offered warmth, good cheer, devotion and uncritical love. What more does one need? Then a day came that changed everything. I'm not sure myself but I think I was about ten when it happened. A discussion was taking place. It was about Sol, my father's younger brother, and Nanna, who was my father's mother. Now this woman was a granny from hell. She would phone my mother and scream, "Oi, something terrible..."

"What?"

"Just now it happened."

"What?"

"The hot iron, it fell..."

"Yes."

"Burning hot and it fell hard. Oi, God."

"And what, what?"

"And it..."

"Yes, yes."

"Just missed my foot."

When she came to visit, she would sit like a witch in an armchair and say, "No kiss for Nanna?" I approached reluctantly. It must have been clear to her that I had no intention of giving what she really wanted. So she presented her cheek to receive my offering. As I leaned over to do the deed, she would swiftly turn her head and give me a treacherous kiss with those lips of hers like a pair of caterpillars.

My father usually defended the woman, and did so in the teeth of her most appalling behavior. But whenever relatives gathered in the forum of family gossip and Nanna was again, like mighty Caesar, quickly dispatched, my father did not play Mark Anthony and speak in her defense. Instead, he fell silent as would a menial, with mop and pail, who was there to clean the marble floor knowing that all those knives would not make his job any easier.

The discussion I referred to involved a claim by Nanna that my father's brother, Sol, had insulted her. There were few people in his life whom Sol had not insulted. He was as abrasive as Brillo and with all the sensitivity of a rockslide. But to dear Nanna he had always been ostensibly deferential, if not actually considerate. Nanna was a rampant neurotic who lived a fraught existence of bubbling paranoia which she heightened with melodrama, self-pity and unceasing and heavy-handed deviousness whose long term objective was to place all those around her under an emotional state of marshal law. When accused of any of this, she brought the issue to a close with a heart attack. If she were the victim of murder, no one who even vaguely knew her would have been without motive. But was it credible that my Uncle Sol, gruff as he was, would actually go so far as to call his own mother a putz?

This was discussed at dinner, my father remarking that if Nanna claimed it was so then it was so. My mother shook her head in disagreement while I asked if Uncle Sol had denied saying it.

"I don't know," my father grumbled. "I can't get him on the phone."

"But it's not a bad word, is it?" I asked, and reached for more bread. "Doesn't it mean a fool?"

"Putz also means penis." He reached for more bread.

"Yeah," I conceded, "sometimes Sol can be really insulting."

My father spooned out some horseradish. "He certainly can."

"Of course." My mother shrugged as if that goes without saying.

"But I never heard him use actual dirty words," I said.

"He calls everyone an idiot."

"But that's not a dirty word."

"He called Governor Dewey a schmuck. And once during Rosh Hashanah he shouted some really unrepeatable things at your Aunt Nadine."

Suppressing a smile. "Did he, really? Well, most people use dirty words sometimes."

My mother shrugged again. "Of course."

"Well, it's a mystery," I decided.
"No, it's not. He did it," said my father.
"You sure?"
"Yes, he did it. I know him."
"Who?" my mother asked, frowning.

At that moment something in me was cut down and never grew again. There was a loud noise. It was my father shouting. He finished and turned back to me, ready to continue our talk. But I stared at my mother as memories came alive like a cloud of startled birds. They wheeled about in the limited space of my young life, each a frightening event whose meaning I had avoided, whose insistence I had turned away from. Even now I catch myself turning away, losing patience, becoming angry, as though convinced if she would only make that extra effort, try one more time, she would somehow cease to be --oh, how I hated to say the word even to myself-- subnormal.

Let Those That Play Your Fools

Seated low and happy in the back of our two-door Ford, I was being taken by my parents along the blur of Queens Boulevard on our way to see what my father was about to buy for us. We finally entered the tranquil side streets of Rego Park and stopped. A fresh wind blew across the tall grass and scrub land of Flushing Meadow as I climbed out and swung round to behold the future.

There sat our newly built ranch house atop a groundswell of lawn. An inlaid stone stairway climbed languidly, curving gently, to the front door. I ran as fast as I could right at and up the hill of grass. Our voices ballooned inside the empty house where all was stark and clean with a wealth of light. There was a split-level living room at the far end of which stood, wide and waiting, a fireplace. Logs would spit and blaze this winter as I lay, book in hand, dog nearby, with approving parents looking on as I studied hard and, with luck, became learned. No more cramped apartment with people walking heavily on the other side of our ceiling. We now had grass in back that you couldn't see from in front and little lawns at either side between our house and the next house. The subway was a short walk up a hill with Manhattan only twenty-five minutes away.

That night Uncle Sol came to dinner and lifted from my hands a novel I was reading about Robin Hood and placed the volume out of reach on the top shelf of the bookcase. He slipped it into the space he had just vacated by pulling out a book called *Microbe Hunters* which he handed to me with the admonition that here was reading material I could benefit from. He admired a new vase my mother had bought, moving it to a table near the window where he said it would be seen to better advantage. Persuaded to sit down, he chose the couch which he announced was lumpy and needed replacement. He liked the scotch and soda my father brought him but asked if it could be made stronger.

Uncle Sol was a short, bald bull of a man who did not initiate or respond to humor. He seemed ill at ease as if forever worried that some day there might be a shortage of assholes to do battle with, resulting in his well-developed belligerence losing essential muscle tone. He was a pharmacist who, at the dinner table, told us a number of horror stories in which other pharmacists poisoned customers and escaped prosecution. He thought that Beryl's roast chicken was a bit dry.

Then my father told him all about our proposed move to Rego Park, tapping his fingers on the table as he always did when pleased with himself.

"How's the location, Jacob?"

"Short walk to the subway," my mother chirped.

"How short, Beryl?"

"Five minutes," she told him.

"And we have a view of the Meadow." Dad's fingers started tapping again.

"I should hope so. Without a view, a house is worthless."

"Of course." My mother shrugged as if dismissing the blatantly obvious. I felt sure that if, a moment later, someone had marveled at Einstein's equation: "$E=MC^2$," her response, here too, would have been, "Of course."

Sol turned to me. "Russell, what's the school situation?"

"If I don't go they send me to jail."

My father laughed.

"High school is, what, five years away? Is there one near you?"

"Yeah, close enough to walk."

"Does it have a name?"

"Forest Hills."

He seemed affronted. "Forest Hills High School?"

We offered a tentative, "Yes."

With lifted eyebrows: "Top science department," he conceded.

We were pleased. He had handed down a rare approval. As an afterthought he asked, "What about heating?"

"They have to have it," my mother said, "with all those children."

Almost shouting. "I mean the house you're moving into."

Dad looked puzzled. "We have central heating."

Sol laughed at him. "Of course you have central heating. But what is it, Jacob? Oil or what?"

"Gas. It's cheaper."

"Gas? You have gas?"

"Yes."

"Christ, don't you ever read the papers? In Jersey last year a house with gas blew up like a bomb. In White Plains, just months ago, in the middle of the night --Bam-- everybody dead. Gas? You got to be crazy. I'd never let them stick me with gas, the bastards. Oil, OK. Gas, never."

"I'll look into it," Dad said.

But he didn't. He went straight to the real estate office and demanded they return his down payment. He reported afterward how the shysters tried to squirm out of it. But he argued them into the ground and walked out triumphant.

Some months later my father did buy a house. I remember sitting low and bored in the back of our car as we drove out to claim the run-down, semi-attached brick dwelling that he had acquired from, of all people, my grandparents. I knew it well. Whenever we paid a visit I would have to kiss Nanna and play silly games with my cousins and eat at a table with relatives who shouted at each other as if they were deaf. In the midst of this fracas sat the only member of that household I actually liked: my grandfather, whom they called Pop.

He was bald to perfection. His splendid dome, except for a vestigial fringe for decoration, seemed to me an achievement the rest of us, if we lost our hair, should aspire to. Here was a placid man on the brink of a smile. If all the old timers in Odessa looked anything like him, it must have seemed like a summer resort for kindly judges and peace-loving generals. In truth, his impressive Russian face belonged not to someone of power but to a struggling sign painter. He had rented a shop just south of Jamaica Avenue and whenever I entered the place all of life became enhanced with the perfume of glossy oils, snappy varnish and tangy turpentine. Everywhere, in punchy primary colors, were stacked great lettered constructs and neon entanglements. He never said much but I could always make him laugh. All I had to do was mention W. C. Fields and he would bubble up with remembered pleasure. There he sat at dinner, spooning his matzo ball soup in the center of this unholy hullabaloo like a turtle amid a frenzy of fish. Years later I learned he had been an artist who once displayed his work in a Manhattan gallery and even sold a number of seascapes and shipwrecks. Yet he gave all that up to support a wife and five children.

The hullabaloo was over now, the rooms old and empty with dark smudges at every light switch. I was thrilled to discover a fireplace where the couch had been, until I was told it was fake. My father said later he bought the place because it only cost 6,000 dollars. But the money he sank into it afterward is never mentioned. Entire walls were knocked down. The front porch vanished. A new kitchen was installed and where a pantry had been, a toilet appeared. The bathroom, on the second floor, was retiled, walls and all. Storm windows were fitted like unflattering eyeglasses. Massive locks were embedded in the doors.

For all this to be done, builders, plumbers and electricians moved in, apparently for good. The only place to be alone was on the front stoop. When each room was painted twice, the floors stripped and stained and our old and some new furniture moved in, we were at last finished. Until one thunderous night when my mother opened the hall closet for some Vicks Vapour Rub to be confronted with a waterfall. A new roof was needed and, since there was a persistent leak in the basement that defied replastering, we also hired the builders to dig a six-foot trench along the side of the house to repair the failed wall.

But these upheavals were as nothing compared to what originally had awaited us in the cellar. Here, surely, was the control room for the ninth circle of hell. All it lacked was a sign on the door that read STAFF ONLY. Down there everything was black. Three wooden stalls, each large enough to house a horse, were filled with glistening mounds of crumbling coal. In one of these a black shovel stood upright. The growling furnace seemed near to bursting as it sent forth angry waves of oppressive heat. Small, grimy windows blocked out the sun while a smoky bulb in the ceiling gave off thin tubercular light.

When the cellar was emptied, we scrubbed it with disinfectant using a brush as hard as nails. The coal dust retreated, regrouped and fought back. We scrubbed for days until mother said, "My god, we'll never get this clean." Reinforcements were brought in from the Salvation Army at a dollar an hour until at last the place was pacified.

Then a tall black man in an unblocked felt hat appeared at our door and announced, "CON-version." We let him in. "How you folks?" We were fine. We led him down stairs. "Coal dust," he said, after two sniffs. "Dat stuff really hangs on, don't it? OK, let's see now." He examined a clipboard. "You folks are CON-vertin' to oil, am I rat? That would be real nass," he replied to my mother's offer of coffee. She always treated workmen as guests, sometimes causing embarrassment by asking them to sit down.

She wanted to chat, to put them at their ease, to offer cookies.

The Conversion Man had no trouble with my mother's passion to socialize. He sipped his drink and talked while he worked. "Lots a folks CON-vertin' to oil. Nobody is CON-vertin' to coal, I can tell you dat."

"Of course." My mother was proud to be part of a trend.

"Some folks changin' to gas 'cause it's cheaper. But we does all kinds of CON-versions. Oil to gas. Gas to oil. And from coal to each of dem both. Yes, sir."

We stared at him. My mother spoke first. "Did you hear that?"

"You mean if a house is heated by gas," I asked him, "and you want to change that, you can simply convert to oil?"

"No trouble a-tall. Real cheap too. Dis here coal CON-vertin' is the tough one. Soon though there ain't gorna be none of these here coal jobs left. Yes, sir."

In time I settled more or less happily into that dim, cheerless building where the lights were kept on all day and we had to travel by bus and train for an hour and a quarter to get to Manhattan. I never forgot the ranch house on that hill of blissful grass with its working fireplace and view of the meadow, a house I frequently found myself glancing at with longing as I went past on my way to visit a chum who, years later, with his family, moved in nearby.

Such a blunder by my father amazes me even now for he was a successful businessman who ran his own book advertising firm. Occasionally my mother and I joined him in his office in Manhattan after the others had gone home, desks empty, phones silent, each typewriter covered for the night like a birdcage. Nothing remained of the day's struggle except the smell in the art department of rubber cement. His private office was magnificent with vast windows looking down on the public library at 42nd Street.

He often told stories at dinner involving battles with clients, or with his own staff, that I would have loved to witness. I was thrilled by how fervent and articulate he was in debate, how he always found that perfect riposte, that deft squelch.

There was the time when, needing a shave and wearing casual clothes, he was returning at night from a weekend business conference when he was caught in a speed trap while passing through a small town in Pennsylvania. He said to the officer, "Don't make the mistake of assuming by the way I'm dressed that I am someone without influence. I was driving under the speed limit and you know it. I wish to make it clear that I have friends in the press and in publishing. *The New York Times* is preparing a series on this sort of outrage and I will personally see to it that you, and whatever judge you bring me in front of, will be mentioned by name in these articles." He was let go with a caution.

And there was the time in the office when a business associate given to imprecise language grew impatient when, on the phone, my father kept asking him what he meant by this or that phrase. "Jacob, perhaps I should conduct the rest of this conversation in baby talk?"

"Certainly," my father replied, "if it'll make it any easier for you."

Once or twice a year, he brought home a manuscript that a client, as a favor, had asked him to read. One of these, I remember, was a novel translated from French. A publisher's letter said it was the latest offering from a *nouuveaux romancier* dealing with the meaning of reality as seen through the eyes of a lame, mute, love-sick dwarf who worked in a traveling circus and who yearned to possess a beautiful, six-foot nymphomaniac and trapeze artist who was also his half-sister. I glanced through it and came across a long description of a roller-coaster ride filled with screaming nudists. I was astounded when my father handed it to my mother and said,

"Beryl, would you read this and give me your opinion?"

Sure enough, she put on her glasses and struggled through it. As always in these cases, when asked what she thought, she nodded and said, "Yes, very good."

I couldn't restrain myself.

"Dad, why did you give it to *her*?"

"She has excellent judgment about these things. I have never known her to be wrong."

"Don't you have to read a lot of books first to judge any one book properly?"

"That's right."

"But except for the one or two you give her, she never reads books."

"What do you mean? She often reads books."

"I've never seen her with a book."

"You're not always here."

"Like which ones?"

"I can't recall off hand. She reads *Life* and *Look* and *The Reader's Digest*. Yesterday I saw her looking up a word to check its meaning."

"Well, then a dictionary is one book we know she reads."

"That woman," he said, not hearing me, "has such a thirst for knowledge."

Delusional generosity was how I rationalized his opinion of her. Otherwise I steered my thoughts away from the subject as from those shady places where spiders live. In fact, exaggerated praise was more up his street than anything as tepid and balanced as everyday generosity. I have often stood bewildered when, on occasion, he would inform me of how wonderfully analytical I was, how thorough and trenchant, how admirable for reaching to the bottom of any subject I tackled and how expert at it I became. Pleased as I was to be pummeled by accolades, I never had the courage to offer a tempering corrective like the modest, "Come off it, Dad," or a bracing if ungenerous, "Bullshit." Instead I held back. To kick a hole in his image of my mother or even of me might bring down for good his miraculously levitating self-deception. What would become of him then?

A counterbalance to such embarrassing adulation he provided himself in the form of sadistic bullying. Let my mother do something truly dumb, like fail to follow the subject of a simple conversation, and he would lash out like a man who had married a brilliant wife only to find she had suddenly become embarrassingly stupid. I, too, suffered bullying. If I came home later than expected, he made it clear what such lack of consideration did to my mother, poor woman, who was worried sick over my absence (this was news to me) and who wasn't a well woman anyway (he meant her frequent headaches which were due, of course, to her having married him) and that I must not cause her to suffer such selfishness again.

Whenever he wished to control me, he did so in her name. Yet this embodiment of over-kill was the most patient tutor imaginable when I needed help with my homework. However late he would arrive from the office and however much work he had brought home with him, he gave me all the time I needed and never complained.

Sunday morning was a time I both looked forward to and dreaded. It was then that he and I drove to the Queens Borough Court House across the street from which was a bakery to die for. We pulled a ticket from the machine, stood in the crowd, studied the goodies tempting us from behind glass and waited for our number to appear on the wall. When our turn came, my father stepped forward like a potentate.

"An onion rye sliced."

"And what else?"

"A white bread sliced."

"And what else?"

"A dozen seeded rolls."

"And what else?"

"A dozen brown rolls."

"And what else?"

"A dozen plain Danish."

"And what else?"

"A dozen prune Danish."

"And what else?"

"A pound of Rugula."

"And what else?"

I tugged at his sleeve. "Dad, we have enough. *Dad*!"

"Oh, yes, an apple pie."

"And what else?"

"Dad, Dad."

"Yes," he said, turning to me, "and what would you like?"

When we returned with our cargo, my mother would touch her head as if suddenly in pain and call out, "Oh, my God. It'll all go stale."

"No it won't," he said.

"There's just three of us," she pleaded. "We'll never finish it all."

"We will."

"Why didn't you stop him?"

"How?" I asked, "There wasn't a cop in sight."

After one of these visits to the bakery, we staggered into the street with boxes of cakes and bags of bread to find our Ford trapped by a double-parked Cadillac. My father blew our car horn, fumed, climbed out, looked around, leaned in and pressed the horn again. At last a man appeared in a silver sport jacket and wearing a shirt that might have been cut from a pizza.

"This your car?" Jacob demanded.

"Make me an offer and it could be your car."

"You're double-parked. That's illegal."

"Sue me." The man climbed in and slammed his door.

"I'll call the police."

"Call."

"What's your name? I demand to know your name."

But the man waved us away and drove off. My father fumed and stayed glum all day. Later that evening I was climbing the stairs to bed when I heard him on the phone in his den.

"It's double-parked, I said, which is a civil offence and can result in your being ticketed and towed away. Then he got cute saying I should sue him. I'll do better than that, I said. I'll make a citizen's arrest right now and, believe me, I'll press charges. I've made a note of your license plate. You see that courthouse over there? That's where you're heading if you don't move your car right now. You should have seen his face. He took off like a rabbit."

I couldn't bear to hear any more. Down the stairs and into the backyard I went to hide in the blind night as remembered triumphs fell to dust. All he had told me about his past would be suspect. All I would learn of his life would be tainted. The truth of all things having to do with him, was now forever beyond reach. I looked up. There were no stars. Nothing. Though I lived at home with caring parents, making my clumsy way through the masquerade of a normal childhood, I felt for the first time the cold, uncaring and empty presence of the cosmos.

If Music Be The Food Of Love

The most bizarre character I ever met, outside my immediate family, was also the worst teacher I ever had. And in those days there was no lack of competition.

For example, Mr. McTavish, who taught biology, held the view that repetition was the key to learning and so the entire class found itself chanting such simple truths as, "Egg plus sperm equals fertilized egg, egg plus sperm equals fertilized egg." Mr. Lebeau, our French instructor, purposely made screeching sounds with blackboard chalk and, when we groaned, he held up his hand, the middle finger bent out of sight, and said, "What are you complaining about? Look what happened to me." Economics was taught by "Mr. What" due to his constant questions. "Bad money drives out what? The direction of a Bull Market is what? Inflation is what? Depression is what?" Soon "what? what? what?" was all we heard. And Mr. Rickman, our gym teacher, advised the boys in hygiene class that if we ever met up with a "fairy" we were to put things right by giving him a severe beating.

We had no opinion of our School Principal because his lofty position elevated him far above the mundane concerns of education. Rarely seen in the halls, he dwelt in a large room with a desktop as polished as a ballroom floor. Within arm's reach was a microphone into which he occasionally made solemn pronouncements that were broadcast with biblical portentousness throughout the school. "This is Mr. Tinworth. I would like to speak to you this morning on the proper way to salute your country's flag."

High School was simply a place we were forced to inhabit until the last bell set us free. Yet there was one class I couldn't wait to attend. On the top floor, in room 305, Mr. Itzkowitz taught a class called Enjoying Classical Music and his lucky students, I was told, listened to Toscanini conducting Beethoven and Beecham doing Mozart. Itzkowitz also compared renditions by various pianists as they played Schubert, Chopin and Brahms.

To me, an only child, classical music was like having an assortment of dear friends. Tchaikovsky, Schubert and I went back for so many years I couldn't remember when we first met. Much later, I discovered that the first two records my father owned were the *"Pathétique"* and *"Death and The Maiden"* which he played over and over while I crawled about on the living room floor. Chopin soon became an intimate while Dvorak never failed to cheer me up. Bach withheld his great secret until I went to high school. But Beethoven was the very model of manhood while Brahms offered autumnal wisdom. Haydn was weighty, witty, ground-breaking and indispensable. Mozart, who at first seemed quaint, slowly rose to almost unbearable perfection.

So I walked into my first music class as into a cathedral. I was ready. I was never more ready. It was then I discovered that the legendary Mr. Itzkowitz was no longer with us (he had been snapped up by a private school and carried off to Boston) and in his place stood a Mr. E. Trundel whom none of us had ever seen before. His bald head had a semi-circular fringe of hair that stood up like grass. He wore a Hitler mustache, Heinrich Himmler glasses and, when he smiled, displayed a tooth-gapped half grimace perfect for a horror film.

The students filed in quietly, trying to get the measure of the man. It didn't take long. One of the last to enter was the lovely Francene Swick who reminded me of the meaning of life whenever she appeared. She was forever exuding good will in generous, sweeping smiles. I knew well that toss of blonde hair, her soundless laugh, her blight of braces over which her beauty triumphed. I also knew how absorbed she was in music, unaware of how others were absorbed in her. It wasn't that she eclipsed the other girls. It was more like what other girls?

Mr. Trundle stood up, adjusted his glasses, introduced himself, and said: "Welcome. I hope in time we will really get to know each other. But now we must move right along because we have a lot of ground to cover. Today we will study music by a man some consider the greatest composer who ever lived. The three Rasoumovsky Quartets, or Razumoffsky, as it is sometimes spelled" (he wrote this out on the blackboard) "or 'ovsky' or even 'owsky'" he wrote this out, too. Before he turned to face us, a paper glider, thrown at Francene Swick, third row, fourth seat, dove into the open desk of "Fat" Biggs, seated next to her, which he closed and leaned on, none the wiser. "The three Rasoumovsky Quartets were composed by Ludwig von Beethoven and dedicated to Count Rasoumovsky, the Russian Ambasssador in Vienna, who was a keen quartet player himself." Trundle clasped his hands behind his back and rocked on his heels. "They are among the most noble creations in the pantheon of great chamber music and we will explore them together today and for the next several weeks."

It was not to be.

"Rats are what?" asked Pete Castilano.

"Rats are muffsky," someone shouted from the rear, evoking poisonous laughter. Mr. Trundle looked as if he had been slapped. He then panicked, announcing a demerit for "The boy in seat 7D no 7C, no I mean, 8C" as he indicated to a girl, who had been assigned to check the attendance with the class chart, that she should here and now enter this punishment into the ledger.

It was like firing demerits at Attila the Hun.

"Aw, I want a demerit, too," some lout protested.

"Me, too, teach."

A disapproving, "Tsh," came from Francene who, to my delight, also wanted this music to be appreciated, not desecrated. I caught her eye, something I had never been able to do before and we shook our heads in mutual despair. I was thrilled.

Mr. Trundle looked much as the captain must have when he first understood that the *Titanic* was doomed. With a good deal of foot stamping and ugly bellowing the class was finally subdued. Then, clearing his throat, a careful Mr. Trundle stepped ever so gingerly into the breech.

"A quartet is any body of four performers, vocal or instrumental. A piano quartet, for example, is a piano joined with three stringed instruments. Joseph Haydn, born in 1732, invented the symphony and also the string quartet. Indeed, he invented chamber music as we know it."

Francene scribbled notes, her shining hair guarding the page from wayward glances, while I kept an eye on our teacher as I would on an inexperienced member of a bomb disposal unit. Our room on the top floor overlooking the playing field had one of its three windows open. Trundle ceased talking and looked horrified. Louie Bruno was crouched on the sill. "Good bye world, I'm gorna end it all." He jumped into space. Trundle screamed and Bruno fell the entire two feet to the balcony below. An explosion of laughter. Trundle engaged in yet more screaming and foot stamping until the door flew open and in burst Mr. Rickman as if hot on the trail of fairies.

"WHAT'S GOING ON HERE?" he boomed, like the top Sergeant he once was. The class went as cold as a corpse. "Bruno, what in devil's hell are you doing outside that window?"

"Fell, sir."

"Then you must be even more stupid than I thought. Get your ass in here. The noise of this... this zoo... can be heard all the way across the hall. If I have to come in here again I'm banging heads, do you read me?"

The room became void of sound. An ominous breeze chilled us. Then Mr. Rickman departed behind a slammed door. Not once had he looked at Mr. Trundle who stood there as chastised as the rest of us. He blinked. Adjusted his glasses. I thought he might cry.

Instead he put a record on the Victrola and wound the crank. He said he would introduce us first to the slow movement of I forget which Rasoumovsk. We listened. A heart-rending meditation swelled softly into that barbaric room. Francene and I and the traumatized Mr. Trundle were drawn into another place.

"It is enough to make one cry," he had said before allowing the fat silver arm to rest on the turning record with its rotating dog on its rotating label. And sure enough Pete Castilano was rubbing his fist into his eye and soon "Fat" Biggs, hands over face, was shaking in misery and Louie Bruno had his hankie out and began sobbing audibly while several of the other guys were rocking as if at the wailing wall. Mr. Trundle killed the music and burst out with, "5F no 6F, I mean 7G and you, too, 3E, no I mean F, yes, 3F and also..."

When the bell rang. Mr. Trundle said: "Now, class, please listen class, because next Tuesday I want you all to consider..." But the room had already emptied as if at the start of a cross country run. Mr. Trundle did nothing. He just stared into those awful rows of vacant seats.

"I just loved the Beethoven," Francene said, like someone who had flown in on white wings to make an annunciation.

He looked wildly at her as if she had seen right through him and, desperate for something kind to say, had praised his underwear.

As I left the room, trying not to think of what had happened and, worse, would continue to happen, I rested my eyes on her bouncing hair and the sheathed metronome of her hips as she carried her books down the hall. Then she halted, turned, spoke.

"Isn't it terrible, what they're doing?"

"Yes, terrible."

"Someone should stop them."

"Someone should."

"Those awful, awful boys."

"Awful."

"I'm glad you agree."

She shook her head and walked off, leaving me with a dry throat and a resolution to improve my conversational skills.

But next week Francene was absent, the class a disaster, Mr. Trundle once more transformed into a fool. I was depressed for the rest of the day. The following Tuesday Francene swept back in looking more lovely than I had remembered and gave me a lingering smile, having no idea, I'm sure, what that could do to some poor lad stretched out on the rack of youth. Once more Mr. Rickman burst in and kicked ass while Mr. Trundle seemed to shrink as if hoping his entire life would go away and a far, far better one would take its place.

When the class ended and Mr. Trundle had fled, a few of the ring leaders stayed behind, drawn not to Francene's warmth and smile but to the persistent mystery of her snuggly clothed body.

"Why don't you behave yourselves?"she scolded, deciding to confront them at last. Louie Bruno knocked her books from under her arm and Pete Castilano stole her pen when it rolled away. As she sought to retrieve it, trying not to seem angry, he tossed it to "Fat" Biggs and, when she approached him, he lobbed it to someone else.

As I tried to put a stop to this substitution for a gang bang, Castilano wrestled me to the floor from behind while Bruno pulled off my left shoe and tossed this around as well. Francene, coming to my aid, called out, "Stop that," and, after giving a yelp, shouted, "YOU TAKE YOUR HANDS OFF ME," as someone pinched her rump. Now the door burst opened to the almighty shout of "WHAT IN HELL'S GOING ON IN HERE?" Pete Bruno pointed at me and said, "He's hitting us with his shoe."

Mr. Rickman took most accusations at face value for it greatly simplified things, particularly if one refused to listen to a second opinion as he refused now to listen to Francene's. So he pronounced me guilty and, in a loud voice, ordered me on detention.

This meant that for one week I had to get up at seven, when it was creepy dark, instead of eight when healthy sunlight was everywhere. I had to rush to school at seven fifty-five, instead of ambling in just this side of nine. Once there I was expected to sit and study in the empty auditorium; empty except in the back where could be found that little knot of boys who were well on their way to becoming tomorrow's drunks, felons and muggers.

That month, a sour-faced Mr. Hellerstein, who taught history, had the assignment of guarding these early-hour inmates and seeing to it that they didn't slide even further into trouble. Often, he stepped out into the hall to sneak a smoke, stepped back to peer at us, his hand behind his back, then furtively disappeared again trailing a cloud of white vapor.

It was a grim thing, detention. We slumped in our seats, yawning and disgruntled, or sat bent over our unyielding school books or, like the boy next to me, sketched on a note pad an assortment of buxom babes. Then it happened.

Far away and at the very bottom of the auditorium, a door opened and in came a small man who walked as though hoping to be unobserved. He stopped, stooped, opened the lid baring its teeth, sat, paused and played. In Mr. Trundle's hands the grand piano filled every inch of that vast place with first one and then another and finally all of Chopin's *Preludes*.

He had a delicacy of touch that filled the music with painful slivers of bliss. There was thoughtful sadness, restrained exultation and then those final, devilish, base notes of doom.

Silence.

Mr. Trundle stood, stooped, closed the mouth on those gleaming teeth and walked off.

When he had begun to play, the prisoners in the back rows looked up, then down again in boredom. Mr. Hellerstein glanced over at the pianist, looked back at his prisoners and slipped out into the hallway. I couldn't believe my luck. When I returned the next morning, Mr. Trundle reappeared to fill the place with Brahms. On Wednesday there was an hour of angry Beethoven. Next, Debussy, with his sunken cathedrals and reflections in water. And on Friday which was, sadly, my last day of punishment, I was treated to Scarlatti, Clementi, Schubert and Liszt.

Just think, I had only to be bad again to enjoy five more such mornings. The only trouble was every Tuesday afternoon I would have to watch another 45 minutes of his humiliation. I wanted to apologize for his pain, to agitate for his salvation. But what I did was go to my next class and conjugate the verb 'to be'.

Ten minutes later, Mr. Lebeau chose me, out of all the others in French class, to deliver an envelope to Mr. Rickman. At first I felt fortunate to be free of French. As I made my way into the depths of the building, toward my destination, I passed the echo chamber of the gymnasium where came a voice I recognized all too well. Poor Mr. Trundle was rehearsing the orchestra.

It was a spirited ensemble of determined tunelessness, of rhythmic derangement. Sometimes they became a platoon of dentists drilling in unison. At other times, a musical vacuum where Vivaldi should have been. They would deliver a chorus of razor cuts; then a discernable tune; then, not. It was Vivaldi, all right, but with Alban Berg struggling to get out.

Mr. Trundle conducted and shouted and stamped and conducted. I stood with my head against the wall grimacing. I managed to stay there until the bell brought an end to the nightmare. Then came healthy noises as the children fled from their calamity. I peeked in.

The gym was empty. Four rows of chairs were empty. The boxed podium underneath the basketball hoop was empty. I walked to a door that led to the locker rooms.

He was seated on one of the long benches resting a leather-bound flask on his left knee. The fringe of his bald head was upswept, as usual, and his rimless glasses were like transparent growths on his face. His tie was loose, his lips open.

He saw me and swung the flask behind him.

"Ah," he cried, as if stabbed. Straightening slightly: "Yes? You forgot something?"

"I'm not in the orchestra, sir. Just... passing by."

"You wish to get to your locker, perhaps."

"No, sir."

"You don't?" This with mounting suspicion.

"I, well... I was in the auditorium all this week and heard you play."

He peered at me as if to ready himself for a new humiliation. "You were in detention, then. One of *those* boys." He glanced at the doorway for possible cohorts.

"Well, yes."

"Ah, ha." I was clearly the enemy.

"No but I just wanted to say how wonderful it was. The Chopin. Everything. Someday I'd love to hear you play the four *Ballades*." Although a sophomore, I was trying hard not to be sophomoric. "And the Debussy was magical. At home we have records of Rubinstein and Serkin. I couldn't tell the difference. Between them and you, I mean. I just wanted you to know this."

He stood up and was at a loss for having done so. "Very kind. Very kind. What's that?"

I looked at the envelope in my hand. "Oh, this is for Mr. Rickman."

"You had better give it to him."

"Yes."

He was still holding his left hand behind his back. My praise seemed to have dropped into a void. I said goodbye and he nodded, still puzzling over me.

"Were you ever a concert pianist?" I asked.

"Yes, well... no, not really. Wanted to be. But no." He shook his head.

"What... happened?"

He looked away. "You see... it was a case of nerves." He looked back at me. "A bad case of nerves." He brightened. "Schnabel was my teacher for a time."

"Was he really?"

"Oh, yes. Had high hopes. Others too. A condition of the nervous system... made it impossible, you see."

"I'm sorry."

"Oh, well." He made light of it all with a tooth-gapped smile. "Never mind. Gave it a try. Have my memories."

"Ah, right."

"Played for Tureck, once, in London."

"Wow, did you?"

He stopped, as if ashamed by some indiscretion. I didn't know how to continue, either.

"Well, thanks again," I said.

"No. I thank you."

After I left, I was cheered by the thought of seeing him in class next week. But by then he was gone from the school. Nothing was said and Music Appreciation was discontinued until next term.

Francene Swick stunned me in the hall one day by speaking my name. Since we no longer shared a class, I hadn't seen her in weeks. Her braces were gone. She seemed to have acquired a new mouth, erotic and ready, bracketed as it was with those charming character lines near those slightly sunken cheeks. Her eyes became enlarged as if to draw me into all that cornflower blue.

"He's gone. They drove him away."

"I know." And I managed to tell her of our talk in the locker room.

"Oh, that's good. Oh, I'm really glad you did that."

I swallowed and gave it a try. "Look, I'm thinking of asking Mr. Tinworth to give me Trundle's address. To write to him. We can both write to him. Together, I mean. Compose a letter after school, if that's ok. And both sign it."

She smiled. I was certain she could see right through this little proposal of mine, right down to my boxer shorts. She spoke as through an erotic turbulence that let in the words but delayed their meaning.

"I'm taking typing lessons," she said. "If you come to my house, I can practice as we write it."

We agreed on a day. We agreed on a time. Here was a cue for a song. Her place, I said, was fine.

The "late" bell rang through the empty halls. She touched my arm and hurried off, her hips in jaunty four four time.

When the last class that day had ended, I went to the Principal's Office and carefully knocked. Told to enter, I stepped into a large room where, at its center, was a polished desk with a microphone of gleaming silver. Mr. Tinworth, well dressed and with a dark mustache, stood by an open file cabinet as if posing for his picture. He gave me a disapproving, "Yes?"

I tumbled out my mumbled request. Mr. Tinworth closed the cabinet and turned to face me. He had an actor's voice.

"That is kind and thoughtful. I will take note and inform your homeroom teacher of your concern. I will do the same for Miss Swick."

I waited. He waited. It was warm in there. He pulled slightly at each white shirt cuff of his dark blue double-breasted suit.

"I regret I must inform you that Mr. Trundle passed away last week."

Laughter rose up to us from the front steps of the school.

"What happened?"

"It is inappropriate for me to say more than that."

"Did he kill himself?"

"Now, now, these private matters are no concern of yours."

"He did, didn't he?"

"Did you hear what I just said, young man? Remember to pray for him. Tell Miss Swick to pray as well. And please close the door when you leave."

Early Man Exhibition

On mother's birthday I took my parents to dinner by way of celebrating another addition to that accumulation of years whose number she would rather die than admit to. "I'm eighteen," she said, answering a question no one asked, pleased by her display of devilish wit. My father told me to take Queens Boulevard. I told him I knew how to drive to Manhattan.

"Did you bring the umbrellas?" he asked.

"I brought the umbrellas."

"Both of them?"

"Both of them."

Then, as always, I suggested they buckle up and, as always, they refused. Since we were stuck in the car for a while, I decided to explore in depth the reason for this irrational fear.

My mother was against safety belts because, in the event of an accident, she wanted, as she put it, "to be thrown clear."

"You mean like a motorcyclist is thrown clear," I said, for I knew she disapproved of those "stupid madmen" who sped about forever thundering within inches of death.

She paused to think. "I don't want to drown," she burst out.

"Pardon?" I said.

"One time, in the paper, this man, his car went into the water and he drowned. It was his safety belt."

"It jammed," my father said.

"It was in the paper."

"Look, Ma, the only time you come anywhere near water is when we take the Queens Borough Bridge over the East River. So why don't you unbuckle on Long Island, when we approach the bridge, and buckle up again when we land safely in Manhattan?"

My mother said nothing. My father said nothing. When they shared an irrational fear, he let her do the talking.

Finally, she spoke. "You know about Phyllis Watts?"

"Yes," I said. She had told me the story of Mrs. Watts many times. The poor woman was an old friend of ours who, years ago, had been in a serious car crash. She was buckled up at the time and suffered internal injuries which were caused by her safety belt.

"She was badly hurt."

"Very badly hurt," Jacob added.

"She was never the same."

"Never."

"First of all," I said, "this accident happened when safety belts secured passengers across the waist and not, as now, across the chest as well. Two, Mrs. Watts incurred no other injury except those resulting from her belt. Three, Mrs Watts must have been going at a great speed to have suffered such injuries. Four, the safety belt she was wearing, despite the harm it caused her, actually saved her life. Without it she would have been thrown through the windshield and killed."

I could see them in the rear-view mirror grimacing and shaking their heads.

"Oh, go on. Killed? Don't be silly," my mother said.

"That's nonsense," added my father.

"Tell me, what happens to someone in the death seat when a car hits a wall at fifty miles per hour?"

Silence. I soon found myself chanting, as we did in Mr. McTavish's class, that a body in motion tends to continue in motion and a body at rest tends to remain at rest. Silence.

"Ma, when I was small and you were driving me places, what did you do when you suddenly had to apply the brakes? You threw your arm out in front of me, right?"

"Of course." She beamed, proudly.

"You're damaging your argument," my father growled.

"Why did you throw your arm out?" I asked, and again answered for her. "To prevent me from slamming into the dashboard, right?"

Silence. I assumed they were thinking and stopped at an Esso Station while they did so. My father thrust a ten dollar bill into my hand before I could even open the door. Although the evening was on me, I took it, to keep the peace.

The little numbers, that today mount up with subliminal speed, then moved at a more compassionate rate. The abrasive fumes recalled Grandpa's paint shop and still do. Leaving the nozzle pumping on its own, the attendant washed the windshield and checked the oil and water. I gave him ten dollars and got back four. All the while, I could see my parents conferring in the backseat. When I climbed in, my father looked modestly triumphant.

"We've decided why we won't wear safety belts," he announced.

As if out of sheer politeness, I tossed off a casual, "Oh, why is that?"

"It's due to irrational fear."

While winning the argument, I had somehow lost it. A bad sign, for we still had the dinner to traverse with its many landmines.

Before us was a white tablecloth, the gleaming silverware and the promising assortment of pristine wine glasses that to Proust looked like frozen daylight. It was as lovely as the fields of Gettysburg must have looked prior to the dispute that famously took place there.

The opening shot, of course, was ordering drinks. As always, my father requested for himself and my mother Finlandia vodka with soda and lemon. This odd drink had been created by committee. My father once heard, from God knows who, that Finlandia was the best of all vodkas. My mother had read that tonic was more fattening than soda and my father requested lemon with everything. A short essay could be written on how various waiters reacted. Suffice it to say, our man didn't flinch. I ordered what I needed: a double scotch on the rocks.

When the drinks arrived, we touched glasses.

"Happy birthday, Beryl."

"Eighteen today," she replied.

Then came the first complaint.

"I asked for lemon."

"It's in your drink, Dad."

"Oh." He looked with suspicion at what appeared to be a piece of twisted cardboard floating in his glass. In his mounting anxiety that he was not getting what he had ordered, might never get what he ordered, might never get what was due to him in this life or the next, he realized at the same time that this twisted cardboard might actually prove to be, against all appearances, a piece of lemon. So he bided his time.

We all studied the menu.

When the waiter arrived, my father looked up. "I asked for lemon."

Displaying the patience of one who worked in the dining room of a mental institution, our waiter intoned, "You have a twist of lemon, Sir." His manner suggested he would brook no disagreement. In fact, with his glinting lenses he gave off such an air of authority I didn't doubt that if he ordered my father to leave, he would do so at once.

"Oh," Jacob replied.

The waiter departed to give us more time to ponder our choice.

"I already told you there was lemon in it."

"But not enough."

"Not enough? What did you want, two twists?"

"I wanted a slice!"

"Then why didn't you ask for one?"

"Because you stopped me."

Whether it was meant to or not, this assault of semi-madness certainly stopped *me*. I longed to declare war. Considering my mother's blood pressure, I said nothing.

Silence for a bit. Then Jacob asked:

"What's that word, that sickness where you shake?"

"No," my mother answered, "Selma doesn't have that."

"How do you know?"

"I know."

"Well, what's the word? I ask a question and I get a debate."

"What's what word?"

"The name of the sickness where you shake."

"I don't know."

"Well, why didn't you say so?"

"Why do you ask?" I put in.

"Maybe it's catching."

"You know what's catching?" my mother told him. "You are."

"Me?"

"Always so nervous."

"What are you talking about? I'm not always nervous."

"Oh, forget it. What's sautéed?" she asked.

"You always ask that," he grumbled. "It means fried."

"Then why don't they say so?"

"Because it's fried in a fancy way."

"Well, they should explain themselves."

"You had sautéed potatoes when you were here last," I told her.

"Me? I was never here before."

With her poor memory, she was often struck by the novelty of places she had been to many times.

My father looked around. "Where's that damn waiter?"

"Dad, what's the rush?"

"They hide when you want them."

"Relax, we have all evening."

"I'm hungry."

At last the man came and my mother ordered a melon and then the liver. I went for the pâté, followed by the trout. My father chose the avocado and the shrimps. I settled for the house white. The waiter left. I relaxed. It seemed a good sign that Jacob hadn't changed his order, giving in, as usual, to that sudden lust for someone else's preference.

Silence descended. Beryl tapped my hand. "Well, tell me something."

"Cassius said that Caesar was ambitious."

"Oh, stop it."

"Well, you asked Russell to tell you something," Jacob said, not without some pleasure.

"I mean what's new? Tell me what's new."

This question from her never failed to annoy me. Like my father, she had little real interest in my life, so long as I was safe and not short of money. The truth was, they were born before conversation was invented. A small selection of grunts and gestures saw them through the day. For eloquence there was always the sudden scream or the slammed door. Yet here was my poor mother trying as best she could to introduce civilized discussion. To my shame, I answered as always, "Nothing much, what's new with you?"

The first course arrived not a moment too soon. When the waiter left, my father voiced a complaint. There were no shrimps in his avocado vinaigrette.

"Avocado vinaigrette with shrimps is not on the menu," I informed him.

"They often give you what's not on the menu."

"I see what happened. When you said shrimps, he thought you meant the Shrimps *Fra Diabolo*. I did too. You didn't order a main meal."

"I planned to order Chicken Kiev."

"You *planned* to? When?"

"After the appetizer."

"Did you plan to wait until he brought our entrées before telling him what your choice of an entrée was?"

Seeing that his refusal to admit error was sinking us into serious lunacy, Jacob said, "I decided not to have a main meal."

"What? I have never seen you skip the main meal."

"That's because you don't always eat with me."

"Mom, do you remember him not eating a main meal?"

"I don't pay attention to what he eats."

"She isn't always with me."

I asked if he was prepared to accept the Shrimp *Fra Diabolo* or did he want to cancel the order? Sinking into disgruntled self-pity, he said he'd have the shrimps.

We were getting low on wine and since this birthday celebration was in desperate need of cheering up, I decided not to worry about cost and ordered another bottle. A few more glasses each and the conversation finally got going, after a fashion.

My father complained about a lady who yesterday dragged a stroller onto a bus, blocked the exit and almost made him miss his stop. This gave my mother a chance to retell the story of how I was hit by a car as she was rolling me across the street. When I told them I intended to clean out the garage for it was cluttered and filthy, my mother retold the story of the struggle to rid our basement of coal dust as if we hadn't been involved in it too. When Jacob bitched about one of his employees who, for three days now, still hadn't returned to work, claiming to have dropped a record player on his toe, my mother began talking about the time Nanna phoned to tell of how a hot iron had fallen to the floor and not hit her foot.

"We heard that one, Ma," I said, finally losing patience.

"Well, pardon me for living."

"Don't get angry. It's just that we heard it before."

"Many times before," Jacob snapped.

"Dad, I'll handle this."

"You never repeat yourself?" she asked me.

"I sure as hell try not to."

"Beryl, you told us that one," Jacob insisted, stoking the fire.

"I don't care."

"But you should care," I said.

"Yes, you should," he bullied. "Because we heard it before."

"Well," she blazed, tapping the table. "I want to hear it again."

This left me speechless. Her small selection of stories was her way of making sense of the chaos of the every-day world. They were more than comforting, they were the oral history of her remembered existence, her way of entering in, having something to offer, of assuring herself she had a life. And yet I was speechless. Not so my father.

"Most people would be ashamed to tell the same stories to the same people over and over."

It was then that the wine and her frustration ignited. Her face knotted in fury.

"No one listens to me. You don't want to hear what I have to say. Like I'm nobody. You interrupt. You change the subject. Well, I want to talk too. I have as much right to talk as anybody. You think I'm stupid. I know what you think. Why is it no one listens to me? The hell with it. I won't speak. I'll just sit here, I don't care. You talk and I won't listen. See how it feels. Oh, the hell with it."

People were glancing at us.

"Shhh, not so loud," we said.

"I'll speak as loud as I want."

"Mom, we don't think you're stupid. Would Jacob give you books to read to get your opinion if he thought you were stupid?"

"Don't bother me."

"It's just this habit you have of telling people stories they've already heard."

"Just forget it."

She wouldn't speak for the longest while. Luckily the dessert trolley came round and we pigged out with strawberry shortcake for my father and Death by Chocolate for me. My mother was finally persuaded to choose one, in fact her favorite: a yellow, sickly-looking lemon meringue pie. With that, and a strong cup of coffee, she became herself again and launched into a tale we had heard many times before.

It was the formative story of her life, all about growing up in an orphanage and, soon afterward, being parceled out to a series of foster homes where, instead of finding love and comfort, she was put to use as a servant. My mother never quite understood the full outrage of this, the true extent of its illegality and inhumanity. As a child, she tried as best she could to do the tasks assigned to her and when asked for the first time, at the age of six, to wash a kitchen floor, she dumped onto it a full pail of water to mop with and was punished by having a full pail of water poured over her head. It was a tale told without self-pity. There was the occasional half smile of pride at having survived it at all. She was quite cheerful now while my father and I were almost too depressed to speak.

"Good restaurant."

"Sure is, Ma."

"We should come here for *your* birthday."

"OK, that's a deal."

"My lemon meringue was very good."

"It looked great to me."

"Next time," my father said, "I think I'll order it myself."

For a moment, for a brief moment, all was well. Then the check came and was snatched from my hand.

"Wait, this evening's on me," I insisted.

"You get it next time," he told me.

"Hey, this is my treat."

Opening his wallet. "It's OK, I'll get it."

Now it was my turn to blaze with anger, remembering all the times I cringed as a child watching my own father behave like an even younger child as he refused to let anyone pay. Once I saw him tear a check in two as he pulled it from somebody's hand. I witnessed Uncle Sol cast into despair because, however often he ate out with us, he never did manage to pay. There were people who stopped having dinner with us. Yet always his argument was the same. "I'll pay this time, you get it next time." Just as he did now, despite my protest. And the struggle to be always the one to pick up the check no matter who he was with, no matter how many times he was with them, no matter how obvious it was that they felt humiliated by it and, in the end, were driven away because of it, this desperate battle which he had to win even if all else was destroyed was his only way to insure that he would never ever be rendered powerless again as he must have been as a child imprisoned by that hysterical, manipulating, insufferable mother of his.

Love (Sic)

It was years before I realized that dating was supposed to be fun. Until then it was a rite of passage to prove one's manhood, except the whole thing had to be repeated next week to escape the shame of another empty Saturday night. My buddies in high school felt as I did: here was a solemn ritual of great importance that we all had to undergo despite fear of rejection and at whatever cost but which otherwise offered few tangible rewards.

In the beginning was the bra. The trick was to unhook the thing with one hand while sitting with a girl in the front seat of my father's car. Success, with its mounting excitement, didn't guarantee further progress and so the unhooking often resulted more in my undoing than hers.

The front seat of a parked car was like a time machine. It could transport you back to the beginning of creation where everything was squeezed into a singularity of such intense pressure that the result was either a big bang or, as luck would have it, not. And so it was in these coy Detroit four-wheel space modules that the initial detonations of early youth mostly, though rarely, took place.

I remember the unnerving sense of inhabiting an empty sports stadium when, for the first time, I had all to myself an entire room with a girl in it. Even more eerie was these fumbling attempts out doors. Lying on a blanket at the beach was like grappling in the very center of the vast and chilly universe.

In childhood, the thought of meeting and then persuading one of those lovely creatures to come away with me to a private place to kiss, to unrobe and perhaps even to lie down, seemed a project so daunting and requiring such delicate and exhaustive effort as to be virtually impossible to achieve in my lifetime. Later, from the vantage point of the front seat of a car, it no longer seemed impossible. Just expensive, time-consuming and unlikely.

Enter, once again, my father who showed me the way. Of all the things he did that I could personally verify he did well, aside from making money, was pursuing his hobby. When I was nine, I often went with him as he struggled with gadget bag and tripod, with sacks of film and a clutter of lenses, with the eye-level Leica and the vertical Rolloflex, plus his ever handy light meter which he aimed at things so frequently and steadily that in the beginning I thought it was this that was the camera. Not for him the frivolous firing of film like ammunition on a shooting range.

He only showed interest in things that didn't move. Even then he took what seemed like hours finding the right position, readying himself, readying the tripod, readying the camera and finally bending over to read the light meter as if it were a book he couldn't put down. Next he peered into the ground glass like Narcissus into a river. Then, at long last, with a sharp, soft *pizzzslap*, a single photograph was taken. Of what, I knew not, for he aimed his camera at puzzling things where, as far as I could see, no picture existed. A fallen tree, a dull sand dune or an abandoned shack. People, never.

Yet, in the darkroom of our basement, when blank paper was slid into a tray of the devil's own brew, there appeared at first a ghostly, then a vivid revelation. Now I saw fascinating rings in the detailed cross section of a fallen oak, or the wind's art work on a canvas of sand, or the sad, round hole of a missing lock in a warped, weather-worn door slightly ajar.

He encouraged me, when I was eight, to try my luck with a cheap

Brownie and my first ever photograph delighted him. It was a close-up of a milkman's horse. The beast stands rock still for his portrait, as he does even now on my wall, forlorn yet regal with a suspicious, world-weary stare. To my amazement, it was perfectly framed with a collection of background clouds matching the furry jigsaw of white and brown between his eyes.

"Frank Capa said if you're not happy with your photos then you're not standing close enough." My father patted me on the shoulder. "That's certainly not your problem. You were born knowing where to stand."

"Who's Frank Capa?"

"Oh, he was great. He photographed the last soldier to die in the Spanish Civil War. I showed you the picture, once, remember? It was taken just as the man was hit in the head and you can see him, with his rifle flung out, beginning to fall."

"Yeah, I remember."

"And he took that famous one of the Invasion of Normandy. Capa got to the beach first and took pictures of our men wading in."

"Did he get killed?"

"Amazingly, no."

So this business of light and lenses, film and focus became my hobby too. Just as classical music became my love, and splitting the check my idea of the perfect end to a perfect meal. The better I became, the better the quality of camera he bought me. The walls of my room were soon crowded with pictures but still my epiphany was waiting in the wings for I was yet to see where all this was leading. In the long term, I had already glimpsed the possibility of making a living with my camera. But there was something nearer to hand that I failed to see. So close, it was out of focus. And then one day my father quoted some famous French photographer who had listed all the benefits of pursuing his free-lance profession. It gave him the chance to travel, to befriend the famous, to make his name, to earn his fortune and, most important, to meet girls. I was hit by an all but biblical annunciation. It was as if an angel had flown in through the window and given me a shtup in the ribs.

I hung a six foot wide roll of blank paper from the basement ceiling that could be pulled down to the floor and toward the camera. This was to eliminate those lines between wall and floor creating instead a formless, seamless space lit by floodlights and in the middle of which I placed that blonde in French class or that brunette I sat next to in cafeteria, and I was able to do so simply by explaining that I was a photographer in training who needed models to take portraits of and in return they would be given, free of charge, 5 x 8 glossies of themselves suitable for framing. They were all eager to help and the prettier ones were the most eager of all.

All this was a prologue to my advanced studies in the ways of a man with any number of maidens. Yet unbeknownst to me was the insight I would be given, against my will, into the most repressed years of the Twentieth Century that I was too young to witness: that squeaky clean, black and white, B picture depiction of the now dead decade, the 1950s. Gone but not forgotten. Not even gone. Tell me about it because still clinging on in the appealing shape of a tiny minority of stubborn girls who saw themselves as the standard bearers of the old repressed America, girls who I had the rotten luck to keep meeting throughout the free, riotous, uninhibited 1960s as if I was still somehow living in that dead decade when sexual titillation was everywhere visible and the moral code the young were meant to adhere to offered about as much release as a short walk in the prison yard. Hollywood, back then, had taught us that the good girl was a virgin who lived happily ever after provided she got safely married, and a bad girl was a wild babe who had a rollickingly time until she was killed in a car crash with a drunken gangster. A good boy, however, was depicted as a roguish lad as bad as any bad boy around. He had a really great time the whole time and then, as a reward, was given the loveliest virgin on offer. Who knows what effect all this had on the poor young souls --or rather bodies-- entangled in it, who wanted nothing better than a stress-free run up to the act which gave the bang that spun the world.

Let me now introduce Hortense Shindlinger. She loved horror films and Mel Torme, wanted three kids, a ranch house in Scarsdale or White Plains but certainly no further than Greenwich and, oh yes, a husband. She had a nose job, migraines and wore a slave bracelet on her right ankle. To use a common expression during those days, she was, for the most part, "a good kid and a lot of fun." But she had a dark side which was a fear, amounting to obsession, that others might discover she and I were "tight," to use another expression of the day and which, of course, had nothing to do with drink. I gave her 12 glossy 8 by 10s and escorted her on three chaste dates, the last to the Loews Valencia and in return she took me to the deep night of her parents' black Buick parked in their closed and windowless garage where she proved to be knowing and skilled while I was a highly motivated quick learner --a bit too quick perhaps-- but finally, deliciously, happily traumatized.

On a number of occasions, when her parents were off enjoying the Florida sun, the Schindlinger residence in Rego Park was the scene of a lively party. At the end, I had to depart as always with all the other guests to make it seem I was going home. I would walk slowly and stealthily around the block to tap with one knuckle on her back door three times and whisper, "Yes," to the muffled question, "Is that you Russ?" I was not so much allowed in as yanked through. The door was quickly shut as if to keep out the contagion of the night. As far as she was concerned, of all the things she did when I was there with her in her bedroom, the most important, the one not to be overlooked on pain of something short of death, was to set the alarm clock so that no matter what successes were reprised or new wonders transpired, she would be sure to eject me well before dawn.

If Hortense and I went out on the town with another couple, I always had to drive her home first, let her out with a peck on the cheek, wave good bye from the front seat as she waved good bye from her front stoop (windows dark, parents asleep) to watch me drive away, stopping in turn at the homes of each of the others to let them out, before making my way back to where Horetense would be standing like a phantom in her dark driveway. She would march out, collar up, head down, as if being led away for questioning, then jump in to be driven to the lover's lane overlooking Flushing Meadows where we huddled in the privacy of the front seat of my father's car which was parked side by side with all the other cars whose occupants were equally huddled in the secret privacy of their front seat. There everyone busied themselves until, as always, a police car appeared. Then would follow the discreet flashing of that NYPD roof light (why were there never burglars to pursue or murderers to arrest?) and all at once, in that secret place, a dozen engines started up, head lights flashed on and we all drove away, anonymous still, but with glimpses in the dark of women, arms aloft, attending to their hair.

Deborah Epps, short and dark, had her hair cut in bangs and her lips slightly parted as if forever ready to bite into something. We met at a party. She worked in an accounting firm in Manhattan and took to the camera like a narcissist to a mirror. Her only dark side, it seemed, was that she lived in New Jersey.

At the end of our initial evening together, I drove her home, a journey of just under an hour, to the apartment house she shared with an airline hostess. I parked, we kissed once, her strict first date limit, then talked. When it came time for me to leave, I tried to start the motor but the poor beast was dead.

My method of resuscitation, when something goes wrong with the engine, is to open the hood to give it air. If that doesn't fix the problem, it's time to send for professionals. At 3a.m. this is difficult. In The Bronx, I could have taken the subway home. In New Jersey there is no such thing as a subway home. I was stuck. Debbie was worried. Ike, when he pondered whether to give the go-ahead for the invasion of Europe, could not have looked more worried. She paced about in a painful frown. Finally, erupting with a flood of words, she announced that I could spend the night at her place but I had to swear solemnly on my word of honor not to touch her. Not in any way, shape or form. Could I keep to the ground rules of such an undertaking? I could. And like a knight of old, I swore.

At last I was allowed upstairs and discovered to my surprise that we were supposed to share the same bed. Before I got in, I was made to swear yet again. I was getting to dislike Deborah Epps. I could see that she didn't trust me. Yes, yes, you are safe, I nearly shouted. In the name of God, you will not now nor will you ever be touched by me again. Finally, and at long last, I was allowed to go to bed.

As I lay beside her in the dark waiting for sleep and worrying how long it would take to find someone to bring my father's car back from the dead, an odd thing happened: she jumped me. She jumped me as if to establish an all time personal best in a rough and ready statewide contest with other couples, to determine, subtly aside, who could fuck the fastest. We went at it like two people on the *Titanic* who chose to die in their cabin rather than join the sing-a-long on deck.

Afterward, I lay there suffering a bruised lip and feeling pleased by her passion and my good fortune at having survived it. I decided to ask Miss Epps what had been the weak link in our pledge of abstinence. While she thought about this, her fridge gave forth a tuneless hum. Then her voice piped up in the dark.

"When I saw that you were good to your word. I mean really and truly. Well, you know, I mean, that changed everything."

Well, I was learning. Apparently I had little choice in the matter. But these lessons were as nothing to the one given to me by a young woman named Sallye Garr, which was how she spelled it for show biz purposes. By then I had acquired my own apartment which convinced me that I had reached something like maturity. We met while she was working in Bloomingdales demonstrating perfume with that blonde, healthy mid-western look as if she had just been newly minted early that morning. As I approached, she sprayed her wrist with some potent stuff from a small vial and held out her hand as if offering it to be kissed. I did just that. She curtsied. I handed her my card. RUSSELL MORGANSTERN: PHOTOGRAPHER.

"Let me guess," I asked. "You're in the theatre."

"I'm a singer. This is what I do when I'm waiting for my agent to find me work."

She agreed to do the standard picture story. Lovely, talented vocalist Sallye Garr seen lounging at home, jumping at the gym, bending at ballet class, having a drink with a friend and, of course, posing for the predictable *non sequitur*, not to mention the *raison d'être* of the piece, cheese cake. It took two days to shoot. She signed a release, I promised to send her some prints, and that was that. Or it would have been except I asked her round to my place for a drink.

It was an astonishingly inexpensive two room pad on Sullivan Street in The Village. I acquired it from a friend who must have been living there since rent control began. Perhaps one reason the others and I paid as little as we did was that the building was owned by the Mafia. So rumor had it. And, in fact, the first four floors were occupied by Italian families. I was on the fifth, and above me lived someone I never saw but frequently heard, a professional pianist who practiced mostly Schubert.

The hallways were depressing but I gave my two rooms a gleaming paint job in life-enhancing, light-reflecting off-white. I covered the second-hand furniture with colorful Mexican blankets and decorated my floor mattress with a crazy quilt and a hill of scatter pillows. I placed on the walls enlargements of shots I had taken: a green and peaceful Central Park, a sunset spill of golden lava high above New Jersey, a father and son fishing through a hole in a frozen lake.

They were hung to give my viewless home splendid vistas of the outside world.

I had a phone put in and the first call was from my father. He was the second and third to phone as well. It soon became clear that he was incapable of calling once. He always called three times running. To hear from him at all was to become locked into a telephonic trilogy. Footnotes, amendments, afterthoughts, came each hard upon the other, as prompt as bills. And I couldn't fail to answer the second and third time he called because I had recklessly picked it up and said hello the first time.

Which was exactly the mistake I made after I sat Sallye Garr on my couch, poured us out drinks and laughed when she stared wide-eyed and spluttered, "Twenty-six dollars a month! You only pay twenty-six fucking dollars a month for this place? That's landlord abuse. What's the catch? Do you have to do hit jobs for the mob or what?"

The phone rang. "Lucky, how are you?" I said. "And how's Mrs. Luciano?"

"This is your father."

"Oh, hi. Sorry I can't talk now. I'm entertaining a friend."

"He's trying to, I'll give him that," Sallye noted to no one in particular.

"I'll call you back later, Dad."

"Oh, OK," he said, deflated, and hung up.

She looked impressed. "That was fast."

"Wait. He'll be back."

A Schubert bagatelle floated down from above.

"My God, low rent and music, too."

"We try to please."

"Does he take requests?"

"Only if it's Schubert."

We listened some more. It was still Schubert.

"Your father hasn't called back."

"Don't speak too soon."

The phone rang. We laughed. It was Jacob, of course.

"Put the clock back?" I almost shouted. "That's not until next week."

"I know, I just don't want you to forget."

"Is he always that thoughtful?" she said, after I had hung up.

"Alas, yes."

She sipped her drink. "He's really very good."

"My father?"

"The piano player."

Three minutes later Jacob phoned again to tell me he had come across a book on Alfred Stieglitz that I might be interested in. "It includes some of his shots of Georgia O'Keefe as well as a painting of him by her."

"Sounds good," I said. "Thanks. Look, I'll call you back later. Or tomorrow."

"Well, which is it?"

"Tomorrow."

"Not too early, your mother sleeps late."

"So long, Dad."

"Put him onto me, next time," she said. "I feel I know him."

"Too late. After three calls his anxiety fades."

"So that was the last one, then?"

"It's just you and me, now."

"And that guy upstairs."

I refilled our drinks and sat beside her. One thing led to another until we became locked in a restless kiss of such deep satisfaction that it seemed as if a smokeless fire had engulfed the room. Trying to stay calm in the face of my personal emergency, I made a desperate suggestion.

"Sallye, you've seen the living room with its photos of the tri-State area. Now is an ideal moment for a tour of the bedroom with its paper ceiling lamp and spacious floor mattress."

It seemed she approved of the idea. She stood up, walked to the bookcase and turned to face me. What took place then was one of the most astonishing things that ever happened to me. She become, quite simply, someone else.

"A bit of groping and I'm supposed to trot off to bed, am I?" Her voice rasped with venom. "You despise women, don't you? You think you can hide it under all that fake charm but you're just a frightened little daddy's boy who wants to dispose of every woman you meet with a quick seduction."

Good God, what was happening? I felt like one of those poor bastards who find themselves on trial for a crime they couldn't even comprehend let alone commit. And she went on and on condemning this person I wasn't with such absolute assurance that for a fleeting moment I feared she was on to something.

"You're emotionally constipated and your anger is so deep you can't even feel it, can you?"

Was she a psychopath? Or one of those alleged multiple personality types; a bus load of women all crowded into one. Whatever she was, she was on a roll. According to her, I had the mentality of a savage who believed that by taking a woman's picture you could steal her soul. Only in my case it was her body I was after. She called me a terrified, selfish, pathetic little fake. A fraud parading as an artist.

"Now, listen to me," she concluded. "I'm going into your john for one minute. Then I'm leaving for good."

She walked down the hall and slammed the bathroom door.

I felt like a man who had survived a bomb blast. A sleeve gone. A shoe missing. Yet sitting upright amid the debris. Today he'd be offered post-traumatic stress therapy. Back then, the most he could hope for was a cup of tea. I considered my next move. To remain seated seemed absurd. I stood up. I had nothing particular to do and, not wanting to sit down again, I folded my arms and remained standing. That, too, seemed absurd. Meanwhile the blast continued to reverberate. I waited, not for a chance to reply, but just to be free of her. The door opened and she reappeared.

"Hello, my love." Here again was the girl from Bloomingdales, offering me a big smile. She came up to me as if I had survived some life-threatening ordeal and she was just so relieved that I was safe. She kissed me.

"Hey, why don't we take that tour you suggested?"

"But I thought..."

She waved all that away. How crude of me to even mention it. It was a silly aberration not even worth talking about. She was unbuttoning my shirt.

"Now you leave everything to me," she instructed. "Does that please you? Just relax."

We crowded into my bedroom which was mostly mattress with a narrow margin of floorboards. I don't remember how it happened but our clothes became like autumn leaves. You never see them drop, yet there they are scattered everywhere. She was tender, I was bewildered. She went at it like someone who hated to delegate authority. I became massage instructor worked on by a student taking her final exam and who deserved an A minus, at least.

Of course, I had no intention of seeing her again. What I yearned for was one of those impossibly romantic love affairs that the French depict in their gloomy, guttural, gauloise-clouded films. Certainly not a psychic mugging followed by an A minus.

But two weeks later she phoned and chatted away as irresistibly as Audrey Hepburn flashing her wide-screen smile to assure the world all was well. Perhaps the psychic mugging was a one-off, just a neurotic need to punish beforehand any man who wanted sex with her, dissipating her guilt and enabling her to bed down with him. Those teeth marks left in me when last we met was what inoculated her against sin, and my hope was that as far as re-engaging with me was concerned, once inoculated always inoculated. Now she had all the freedom she needed.

And freedom was certainly what she exuded when she flounced into the Greek restaurant on Seventh Avenue where we agreed to meet, kissed my forehead and sat down to regale me with her many adventures.

"Last Tuesday I'm at this mental institution up state to sing to a room full of fruit cakes. My agent hates me, you see. Well, I break into my opening number without thinking and the first line is, "They all say I'm crazy..." I freeze. What a blunder. But they're rolling on the floor with laughter. From then on, I could do no wrong."

After ordering our food, she told about her tour of Brazil when she found she left something rather important behind.

"So there I am standing in a crowded drug store, in a country whose language I can't speak, trying to turn myself into a female Marcel Marceau to convey in desperate pantomime to a puzzled salesclerk that what I needed was a tampon."

"Were you arrested?"

"I'll never know why not."

Waiting for dessert to arrive, I had told her of a few of my photo misadventures which she listened to with great attention, staring at me with those lovely green eyes. Then she said, "You think by telling me those lame little stories, I'll jump into your bed again, don't you? I am not on the menu like that bottle of Retsina. Or something you take home in a doggie bag."

"Oh, shit, there you go again, I said. "Drawing blood before having sex."

"There's not going to be any sex, boy-o."

"Don't you know why you act this way?"

"You take me to some cheap little dump and afterward it's open sesame, is it?"

"You, Sallye, have a serious problem."

"That's rich, coming from you, you slick little robot."

It was no good. I couldn't reach her. War had been declared and on she came like Pickett's charge. This frenzied other self hidden inside of her sickened me for I now knew she would always be there, the lady and the tiger both waiting behind the same door. I mimed a quick scribble on the palm of my hand, and the waiter brought the check. As her tirade tumbled out, I left the tip, left the table and walked into the street.

And who should I meet there but none other than Sallye Garr, the blonde from hell, now innocent as a cupcake. She took hold of my sleeve and leaned against me, available as air.

"What happens to you?" I asked her. "Do you have any idea?"

"I climb into your bed, that's what happens to me."

"Look, either we talk about what took place in there, or it's all over."

"Oh, don't be a meanie."

"I'm serious."

"So am I, my love."

"Masochism gives me heartburn. Last chance. Please. Start talking about this or we're finished."

"You're not listening. I am asking you to go to bed with me."

"Adios."

I walked off maddened and miserable. She followed like a puppy. We went up one street and down another as I took care to walk anywhere but home. She looked so willing and vulnerable now that I felt nothing but pity. Though still in denial, she did most of the talking: some trivial incident or other might have happened back there but it wasn't worth discussing. It was unimportant. The important thing was that we stay together, that we go to my place. She followed for quite a while before giving up. When I looked back, she was standing several blocks away, a lone figure wearing a cloth coat staring after me in the windy street.

I went home, opened a good book and listened to Schubert. A week later while doing the dishes, the buzzer hummed. Through the ancient intercom came a squeaky street voice that I recognized as hers.

"Let me come up."

"No," I said.

"Buzz me in, ok?"

"Sorry.

"Why not?"

"Well, the bandages are off now and I look OK again."

"I'm serious. Just for a talk."

"No."

"Please."

"No." I waited. Nothing more came from the street. She was gone except for the penciled note I found next morning in my mailbox.

"Dear Russ: Believe me, it's with the greatest possible concern for your welfare that I tell you that you must get help! And soon!!! I would so hate to see you go through life frightened of everything and running from everything as you ran from me. Please, give serious thought to what I say, my love. Be well, Sallye."

What I gave serious thought to was backing away from bedding down with every neo-1950 toothsome wench that I could get into my view finder, women I seemed to have a genius for picking out of the freest decade ever. Better by far to search for a partner with whom I could be myself and at ease and perhaps even, just possibly, happy.

The Book Collector

"Please do something," my mother said, her cheerfulness gone, her voice ragged. "Talk to him. I can't live like this."

I knew at once what she meant for she had lived like this with my father for as long as I could remember. It was a constant that always seemed to grow worse; first, in their house on Long Island which they still owned and now in their apartment in Manhattan, which my father rented after his heart attack. You entered their apartment and discovered letters, bank statements, newspapers and magazines occupying almost all the chairs and half of the couch. The latest arrivals went directly to the dining table where usually at one end a bit of space was left for them to cluster round for dinner like refugees.

But this was as nothing compared to the books. Books were everywhere yet if you wanted one you couldn't get to it. For in front of many books were piled on their sides, in awesome columns, other books walling in, as it were, the shelved books, which now, forever out of sight, slowly faded from living memory. It was near impossible to sample any of the volumes from these towering structures unless they were near the top. Trying to pull out one of the others made the columns come alive and sway with the real promise of an avalanche.

Upon entering my father's den one arrived at the very epicenter of chaos. In full view was an expensive Hi Fi set that couldn't be reached and an impressive stack of stereo records, lying on their sides, that couldn't be sampled, even if the stereo could be reached, because on top, also on their sides, was a tonnage of art books plus the *Sketches of Audobond* and a boxed two volume tome detailing, with diagrams, Tutankhamen's tomb. The reason the bookcases and the Hi Fi set couldn't be reached was because piles of yet more magazines, thick files and loose papers presented, if you tried to stand on them, an ever moving mass.

There was once a desk in the den. When last seen it was entombed with clutter and could not be used as a desk and so was lost to us in much the same way a damaged nuclear reactor is lost to us when it is sealed up for centuries so no harm can come to those who live close by. Because a work surface of some sort was absolutely necessary, particularly at peak intake seasons when even the dining room table was piled high, forcing us to eat buffet style as if at a crowded party. Clearly something had to be done, so a card table was placed in what little space was left in his den, so he could sit and write a check or open mail or... I almost said read. But he never did. Not books. Chaos is a great time consumer, keeping one busy the better part of a lifetime. And at night, with whatever time was left, there was always TV. No, he never read books. Not any more.

In the beginning he loved them. For what was inside them. The earliest editions in my father's library revealed pencil marks beside ravishing moments in Swinburne or droll arguments of Chesterton or folksy reflections by Montaigne. He bought the first of these volumes with his own money, which he had precious little of, from shabby second-hand book shops in the sub-cellar of the depression, although later he acquired them for free when he became the chief copy writer with an ad agency that specialized in selling books.

"You've got to do something," my mother moaned once again. I said, yes, I would, not telling her, of course, that I had already done something some years ago. The conversation, on that occasion, in the house on Long Island, went like this:

"We have too many books in here, Dad."

"What?" He wasn't deaf but he often didn't hear me.

"Far too many books."

"Why? What do you mean? I need them."

"You never read them."

"I read them all the time."

"I don't see you reading them."

"You're not always here."

"Ma says you don't read them."

"She's not always here."

"Where is she?"

"She goes out a lot. Shops. She's a very busy person."

I spoke darkly of the accumulation of allergy-creating dust from his library and the ever increasing weight they placed on the structure of the house. With that I finally reached him, or reached his anxiety which was the same thing. He said nothing at such moments, changed the topic or wandered away. Two hours later he, with great purpose, came back, a slim, small, frail, fern-colored volume in his hand.

"Do you think we can get rid of this?"

The title said *Abnormal Psychology*.

"Yes, we can get rid of that."

"OK" he concluded, as if his job here were done and now he must ride off to other libraries and help them lessen their bulk. The slim volume was left on the dining room table. The next time I saw it, a year later, it was on one of the living room shelves next to *The Mystery of Mysticism.*

He simply could not throw anything away. He was far too anxious ever to do that. Sometimes I had to remind myself that he didn't invent anxiety, he only perfected it, made it into a way of life that effectively diminished the quality of life. Yet in the real world, which was everywhere outside our home, he flourished. Still, people who flourish because they are driven by demons tend somewhat to over-flourish, becoming increasingly successful and increasingly grotesque.

"When?" my mother asked.

"When?"

"Will you talk to him?"

But she pressed on, too anxious herself to wait for an answer, repeating how impossible it all was. Dust everywhere. Junk everywhere. Can't have guests in. Nothing can be thrown out. There was hardly even space for her things.

"Speak to him."

I said I would.

"I don't understand," she exclaimed. "There's no room any more to do anything."

"Yes, I know."

"Have you looked into his closet?" she asked.

I had, from afar. In his den there was a walk-in, almost a live-in, closet which could well have had above the door the warning: Abandon Hope All Ye Who Try to Enter Here. The way was blocked by gadget bags and tripods, cameras and strobe lights, several old radios and a tool chest with boxes of nails, screws, nuts and bolts, and on the shelves yet more books and in the rear a large, black file cabinet, locked, its key lost. Also a damaged zither, an extra hat rack, some unhung pictures, and boxes of what proved to be black and white film dating back several decades.

"The humidifier is in there somewhere," she lamented.

"And my Staunton chess set. And all my college stuff."

"No, they're in the house in Queens."

"They should be but they're not."

"Yes, in the trunk upstairs."

"That trunk is in the garage and it's filled with *National Geographics.*"

"Is it? When was that put there?"

"Ma, I was too young to remember."

"*National Geographics*? I thought they were in the record cabinet."

"*The Encyclopedia Britannica* is in the record cabinet."

"Oh, oh, oh," she repeated, quickly, as if three small bubbles of revelation had popped pleasurably in her brain.

Whenever we spoke of their house in Queens, that narrow, cheerless, semi-attached, junk-filled, dusk-lit, book-littered, brick-ugly dwelling with a fenced-in back yard four times the size of a freight elevator, I saw again that lovely ranch house perched like a yacht on a green swell of grass which to my young eyes was a replica of the Promised Land.

As I grew, everything around me grew and in the end I moved out of that brick-ugly house because, among other reasons, there was really no longer room for me. When I took that apartment in the Village, it seemed Japanese in its ostentatious emptiness.

"Talk to him," she requested once more, but what I couldn't say straight out was that, in my opinion, the real cause of her distress was something other than his books, or the clutter, or her inability to clean. The real trouble, when you came right down to it, was my father.

This said, it should also be pointed out that he always had with him the catastrophe of his own childhood: the escape from a pogrom in Odessa, the arrival in New York not knowing a word of English and a hysteric as a mother. It had been a protracted assault and what emerged, for all to see, was a terrible fear of deprivation. It went where he went like lumbago.

He didn't change his ways, however. Not only did he collect junk, he also seemed determined to accumulate weight. His bulk mounted steadily, a fact he denied, preferring to accuse the dry cleaners of shrinking his suits. He clung to this argument until good old Sol, whom he hadn't seen in quite a while, dropped in as always without warning, eyed my father and, with his usual delicacy, cried out, "Jacob, my God you're fat!"

When my Uncle left, Jacob asked, "I'm not fat am I?"

"Dad, how often have I told you?"

"You're gross," said my mother.

He sulked and at dinner had two slices of angel food cake.

Soon after that, I flew to Venice with an egocentric journalist to illustrate his travel piece. Poor weather some of the time and his clichéd photo suggestions all of the time put me in the mood to spend a few extra days alone afterward to enjoy the city on my own terms, when I received a knock on the door one morning to be told there was a phone call for me. This, I feared, was a last minute demand for some re-shooting. Instead came a long-distance growl from Uncle Sol.

"Are you sitting down?"

I was standing in the corridor of a cheap hotel with not a seat in sight.

"Yes," I said, my pulse throbbing. "What happened?"

"Jacob's had a heart attack."

"Is he...?"

"He's doing fine."

"Which hospital?"

"Mount Sinai."

"And my mother?"

"As always."

"So Dad's alright, then."

Sourly: "He's himself again. What can I tell ya?"

"How'd it happen?"

"Couldn't find his check book. Got into a real state. House is such a mess, you could lose a Volkswagen in there. Anyway he felt this blowtorch at his chest. Beryl made him lie down until the ambulance came. Why the hell don't you get him to tidy up the place?"

"I seem to remember trying once or twice."

"And to stop eating like such a pig."

"Good idea. Listen, why don't you bring it up next time you speak to him?"

"You're his son."

"You're his brother. Tell them I'm flying home."

"I'll tell 'em."

When I returned, he was sitting up in bed, looking somewhat distracted as if his brush with death had evoked a disturbing image he was now having trouble remembering. For some reason we shook hands which I can't recall us ever doing before.

"Sorry to bring you back," he said.

"I was on my way home anyway."

"They want me to lose weight," he said, as if asking for a second opinion.

"I'm not surprised. Will you do it?"

"Of course. It's important."

"Well, at least you take their word for it, if not mine."

"What are you talking about? If something important is explained to me properly, I understand."

"So you're going on a diet?"

"I'm already on a diet. They feed you slops here."

The doctors also advised him to move to Manhattan so he could walk to his office and then home again each day. This was done. That is they acquired and furnished a lovely three-room apartment overlooking the Hudson. But he never did walk to work. In the morning there was not enough time and in the evening there were too many books to carry.

This was how it came to pass that my parents owned two dwellings in the same city, the larger standing unused most of the year. Their "country home" was convenient enough, god knows, for they didn't have to go out into the country to get to it. I often suggested they sell that house but they hung onto it for safety's sake. If 1929 returned and the stock market crashed again, they could always move back in.

After all, the mortgage was paid off. In hard times, what could be safer? I tried to explain that as they grew older they would be less able to travel out to see if their "country home" was still there but growing older was not part of their plan for the future. The truth was, Jacob really didn't care for the house that much, only for the things inside, though he never made use of them. Still, they were his things and, for a reason only he could fathom, were never, ever, to be parted with.

This meant my mother now had two dwellings she couldn't clean because of the clutter. And keeping things spotless and in their proper place meant more to her than anything. In the past she did a thorough clean three times a week with a diligence, almost desperation, of one who could never quite reach some soiled place, perhaps within herself.

At last it all became too much for her. Those coughing attacks of stifled rage, her endless pleas for reason, her headaches and fatigue, her sense of herself as a failed *housfrau*, her despair. All this, I'm sure, led to her illness. It began with a lump behind the ear that grew into a half grapefruit. The growth was removed from her neck in a three-hour operation. The result was a slight, left-sided face-slide as if an invisible force were pulling at her cheek and her eye that she could not, for the longest time, hold open. My father was marvelous. He was there every day, standing beside her bed for as long as visiting hours allowed and, after he left, winning high praise from the other women in the ward who were puzzled at my mother's less than wondrously grateful response to his devotion. In about seven weeks she was finally back where she had been when it all started, that is ensconced in the very apartment whose massive clutter had made her sick in the first place.

"Talk to him," she said. I said I would.

But how? He had walled himself into a fortress of acquisition which I had placed under siege on several occasions, firing my arguments like arrows, then grew weary, gave up and went home. So I said, rather cautiously: "You know, I think all these books piled everywhere is what caused Mom's cancer?"

"What? You're crazy. It was diet. Bad diet causes cancer, or too much sun, or smoking."

"Mom doesn't smoke."

"And she doesn't sun herself either so that leaves diet. Diet causes cancer. Everyone knows that. Diet is everything."

I kept on for a while, then grew weary, gave up and went home. How on earth was I to proceed? I waited. What for, I didn't know. I achieved, without effort, an almost Zen-like emptiness of mind. Then what I had been waiting for came. It was announced that my parents' building was turning co-op. They could choose to continue living there, paying rent as before, or they could buy. But as rent-payers the apartment could be sold even as they lived in it, sold to someone who must wait, before moving in, until my parents were no more.

"This I don't like," he said. "Our landlord will be someone we won't know, might never meet, and who could choose not to fix things that break. If I fix it, I'll be repairing his place, not mine, and fixing it for free. And what is he doing in the meantime? Waiting around for me to die."

Now, at last, I saw a way to breach the fortress wall.

"Dad, I have the answer. Sell the house and use the money to buy this place."

"Now that," my mother piped up, "is a good idea."

My father said nothing. He was trapped. His fear of having his apartment sold to a stranger with him still in it was balanced by his terrible fear of deprivation, for to put the house on the market he would have to sell, give away or throw out everything stashed away in each and every room. My mother, who never helped in these matters, even when I was trying to do something for her benefit, wanted to know how selling the house would improve the clutter in their apartment. "One thing at a time," I replied. Later, when we were alone, I said, "My hope is he'll loosen up after letting go of everything in Queens so that the thought of getting rid of just some of his stuff in Manhattan won't be that difficult."

I now worked tirelessly to evoke that mythical, free-lance, absentee landlord who would hover like an uncaring god over my father's very existence.

"How will we get rid of all those books?" he flailed, now semi-willing to consider alternatives.

"Any second-hand book dealer will cart them off in a truck."

"The furniture?"

"In a furniture truck."

"How do we sell the house?" he frowned, as if the process was a new concept in real estate.

"We list it with real estate agents. We hand over the key and they do the work."

"I will not give a key to a stranger. That's looking for trouble."

"Of course," my mother pronounced with a wise nod as if considering an abstract philosophical problem.

"Whose side are you on? Look, Dad, I'll drive out there to let them in whenever the agent has a prospective customer. I'll be there to see that everything is safe, O.K?"

He replied a day and a half later. "Maybe."

There were, I knew, Everests yet to climb but this was the breakthrough. The next day I drove him out to Queens to inspect the house I hadn't seen in years. It was filled with silent, soulful mustiness. Childhood memories stared at me like ancient tragedies lived through by others. As I examined room after room of clutter, I arrived at the second floor and my father's den. I pushed, the door finally gave way, and there before me was a lifetime supply of God-knows-what. Cardboard boxes filled the room so that we couldn't even begin to enter. We had been walled out.

"What's all this?" I asked him.

"Books from my office. I had them shipped to Queens."

Evacuating Dunkirk would, in comparison, have been a lightweight exercise in simple logistics. As we left the house several hours later a man in a shirt as noisy as a rock group stepped out of the adjoining house and called, "You hoo!" He was a new neighbor who had moved in three years ago and my father was now laying eyes on him for the very first time. "I vundered, possibly, ven I never saw you, I should maybe write a letter but I never did because I hate writing letters, ah, but there's no need now, is there, cause we meet at last, at last we meet, hello."

As we chattered I longed to get away, my mind bristling with house-selling difficulties, when our new-found neighbor got to the point. "Vud you, perhaps, be considering, ever, to possibly, you know, sell your lovely house?"

"Oh, I'm afraid not," my father replied in his self-satisfied social manner, conveniently forgetting why we were there in the first place.

"We are extremely interested in selling this house," I burst in. "Don't listen to him."

"It is, then, your house, this house?"

"No, it's not my house, it's his house," I said. "He just forgot for a moment what he wants to do with it. He wants to sell it, believe me." And I stared significantly into the neighbor's eye, hoping to suggest that my Old Man was a bit odd but in a lovable way, of course, and shouldn't be judged too harshly.

"Oh, that's right, we might want to sell it, yes," came the somewhat begrudging agreement.

"Right," I almost shouted. "So would you like to come for a drink and perhaps see the place, Mister?... Mister?..."

"Farkas," he said, with a fine spray, and off we went. Needless to say I was reeling from the serendipity of it all.

My father opened some wine as I showed our guest around.

He liked what he saw until he got to the upstairs den where I felt obliged to explain the barrier of books that blocked our way.

Farkus was puzzled. "He took all this here from Manhattan to Qveens? What vill he do ven he gets rid of the house?"

"Oh, sell them. My father works in mysterious ways."

"That's OK for God. He's entitled. For the rest of us, it can cost big bucks."

I found myself explaining, for my own sake, some of the reasons that made him what he was. The last minute escape from a pogrom when he was six, coming to the States at seven, not knowing the language, and there getting thrown into the immigrant meat grinder with a mother whose only talent was reaching for, and attaining, new heights of hysteria.

Sadly he shook his head, as if he knew such tales all too well.

There followed three months of seesaw negotiations during which I was, for my mother's sake, the family adviser, therapist, linesman and cheerleader. My father swung between paranoid intransigence and resentful though discernible action. Still, the great day was coming and this made her beam as I had seen her do just once in an old photograph where, at sixteen, holding a half-eaten apple on a New Jersey rooftop, she was delighted by the warmth of a sun-lit summer and the promise of tomorrow which could actually be seen in the distance in the form of the Manhattan skyline.

Finally all the arrangements were made and the law's delay delayed us no longer. We went out to Queens to meet Mr. Farkas, sip some of his sweet wine and sign the papers, an event second in importance in my mind only to the battleship ceremony that ended World War Two. Now my father had just eight weeks left to empty the house. I helped as much as I could. The furniture, sold as second hand, was carted off. The rugs and the kitchen equipment were left in place, purchased by the new owner. A secondhand book dealer came, made an offer which was, as I gave a sigh of relief, accepted. I took my parents to dinner. The battle was won.

The next week I had to go to L. A. to cover a story about a film team making a drama on surfing. I had never made the trip by car before, so I drove across the country taking eight days to reach the Pacific.

When I returned to New York I phoned to say I was back. My father was in a state about something and I realized it had been a while since I heard the latest in his constant running battle with his secretary whom he continued to employ even in his retirement. But I didn't have the time at the moment to listen to yet another chunk of the saga.

"She's left me," he began.

"Well, get another."

He seemed shocked. "Get another? His own mother leaves me and he says get another."

"Mom left you?" The hubbub of the world ceased. Life twisted into focus. "She left you?"

"Come over," he said, grimly, "and I'll tell you what happened."

When I walked in, he didn't have to say a word. I saw boxes everywhere, just as there had been in his den when I tried to show it to Mr. Farkas. The living room was unusable. The dining table had to be reached via the kitchen. One had to move down the hall sideways. There was even a pyramid of boxes in the bathtub.

"I just kept a few for sentimental value and some first editions," he explained. Then he added, having had a sudden inspiration: "For example, I had to keep your books on photography didn't I? You didn't want me to give those away, did you?"

"What did she say? Or need I ask?"

He gave me a look of painful disbelief. "After forty-seven years, she walks out. Just like that."

"Where'd she go?"

"Is that fair? Is that right?"

"Where did she go?"

"To Selma's, where else?" As always, when referring to his sister in Brooklyn, he waved her away even as he mentioned her name. "You can never trust Selma."

"Do you expect Beryl to live in this... this warehouse?"

"Give me a minute, will ya? You're always rushing me. I have to get rid of some old books to make way for these new ones. Don't worry, I'll clear it all up."

"It took you thirty years to get rid of one slim volume on abnormal psychology," I yelled, "and all you did was move it from one room to another."

"What are you talkin' about? I got rid of it."

"You didn't. I can show it to you right now."

"That's a duplicate."

"Oh, for God's sake. Look, will you call mother? Talk to her."

"You know I can't stand Selma. She wants to know all your business."

"Dad, today she knows all your business."

"What if I call and your mother refuses to talk to me? She's a stubborn woman."

"She'll talk to you. And tell her you'll compromise. You'll work things out."

"What if Selma answers? Or that no good husband of hers?"

"Then give the phone to me."

He was so upset that each time he dialed he had to start again. Finally I took over, then gave the phone back to him without saying a word after Selma had answered and given the phone to my mother without saying a word.

"Where's the Brillo?" my father asked. "I can't find it anywhere... No, I looked under the sink... All right, all right, so I'll buy some more."

I wrote COMPROMISE on back of an old Brentano's bookmark and showed it to him.

"Listen," he said, "about the boxes. We'll come to a compromise,

OK? So just be patient. I'll clear it all up, eventually. What I'm saying is, you don't have to do this. I mean it's OK to come home... Yes, yes, I know about the closets. I'm weeding things out... What do you mean, I'm not weeding things out? I am weeding things out. So, er, when are you coming home?"

My father turned away, and still holding the phone, lifted both hands and dropped them again. "She said she didn't believe me and hung up. Oh, God, that woman is so stubborn."

I suggested we needed a drink and led him sideways down the hall and through the maze of boxes to the kitchen. I uncorked some Chardonnay and put it on the dining room table. I was hunting for two glasses when, displaying his exasperation, he thumped the table with the bottle and sprayed wine all over his jacket. "Damn it. Now look what you've made me do." But when I returned with a tea towel, I saw he was crying.

In time, I was able to get him to sit and sip and listen. I proposed he put all the boxes in storage, then take one box at a time out of storage, empty it of books he wished to keep, fill it with out-going books, sell that box to The Strand Bookstore and then take another box of books out of storage and do the same thing. He said this was expensive. I said he had just sold his house and had plenty of money and, anyway, the expense would spur him on. He said a storage house wouldn't let him do that. I said they most certainly would let him do that. He said storage houses wouldn't take good care of his books. I said storage houses would take very good care of his books. Storage houses, I said, took poor care of expensive furniture and precious porcelain by hiring people to come in at night to scratch the furniture with bottle tops and crack the porcelain with small wooden mallets but that no one in this country, certainly not warehouse people or skullduggery types of any kind, gave a flying copulation about books enough to steal or damage them, and that only bad governments actually burned books and even Senator McCarthy in his maddest moments wouldn't have gone so far as to do that to our collection of James Branch Cabell, James Fennimore Cooper, Conrad, Lawrence and Dickens. His entrenched expression was all he had left by way of argument.

"Shall I phone a storage house now?" I asked.

"How will we find one?" was his last, feeble attempt at a road block.

"In the yellow pages under storage houses."

"All right, go ahead, but hurry."

When, a few days later, I led my mother back into the apartment which admittedly looked as cluttered as it did when she first phoned to say she couldn't live like this, I do believe it appeared somewhat spacious to her now that all the intruding boxes had been removed.

"Isn't it nice?" I asked.

Without comment she vacuumed the carpet. Then she sat down with a cup of coffee. Trying to cheer her up I said, "You know, with all my recent top level experience at negotiation perhaps I should try my hand at missile reduction or maybe the Palestine issue."

"You look tired," she told me. "You should rest."

"I'm fine, Ma, just fine."

The next day I had the flu. Since Beryl was still recuperating from her operation, my father insisted on taking a taxi down to the Village to bring me hot soup as I lay on my mattress with a fever.

"The important thing is one's health," he said, in his attentive bedside manner of light-hearted concern. "Remember, diet is everything."

Mind The Gap

There are few things I hate more than phoning someone out of the blue, without fair warning, someone whom I don't know and don't want to know, especially upon arriving in a distant city for a short stay.

"What harm can it do?" my father asked. "Maybe he'll invite you to dinner."

"I don't want to go to dinner with someone I have never met and who is your friend, not mine and, besides, the English don't ask strangers to dinner, not unless they've known them for at least ten years."

"Don't be silly," said my mother with great confidence although she didn't even know where England was.

"So, if they don't invite people to dinner, you've got nothing to worry about." He drummed the table in rhythmic triumph.

"Look, you haven't been in touch with Mike Guthrie in years."

"That's why I want you to phone him."

"Look, Dad, write him a letter, why don't you?"

"Write who?" Beryl asked.

"A phone call from my son is more personal."

"Which will really make him feel obligated," I said.

"To do what?" my mother asked.

"To invite me to dinner."

"Oh, nonsense." And she waved me away.

“Russ, as a personal favor, call Mike. Say hello. Take you two minutes. Would you just do that for me?”

“All right, Dad. All right. But if you never hear from me again you’ll know what happened. I died of shame.”

Of course, in London, I delayed this assignment for as long as I could, hating myself for promising, hating him for making me promise and hating the phone in the hallway of my cheap hotel that could easily connect me to the desk clerk who, in turn, could easily dial Mike Guthrie. Finally I went off to do the deed. But on the way I became distracted by the beguiling instructions posted on the door of my room. The heading suggested a poem by Keats. ON HEARING THE ALARM BY NIGHT. And it had a list of eight things one must do at once such as “put on your dressing gown” and “shut every window” and “close the door after you” not to mention stopping to read all this before running for your life. Well, the English are famously cool in times of stress except they never had to phone Mike Guthrie. Since there was, alas, not the slightest sign of a fire, I went into the hall and dialed the desk clerk.

“May I be of help, Sahr.”

“Would you please dial a number for me?”

“Certainly, Sahr. What is the number, Sahr? Thank you, sahr. One moment, Sahr.”

I heard ringing.

“There you are, Sahr.”

“Thank you.”

“Thank you, Sahr.”

A young woman’s voice recited back to me the number the desk clerk had just dialed at my request.

“Is Mr. Guthrie there, please.”

“Oh, you just missed him. Daddy left for America this morning.”

All at once, convivial and relaxed, I explained who I was, offered my father’s heart-felt regards, expressed my almost sincere regrets at having phoned too late and, having fulfilled my mission, was about to hang up when she said,

"It's a bit shaming to ask this, but you don't happen to be here on your own, do you? If so, a friend of mine and I are having a party tonight and we're going mental because we're short of men."

Which is how I came to be present, during a frigid English winter, at a party that changed my life. I arrived late, having first gone to dinner with the publicity agent for a Broadway actor whose rehearsal of a play on the West End I had been sent to London to shoot. The meal dragged on longer than planned and it was nearly ten when I arrived at the flat of Miss Guthrie's friend, Anne Chambers, whose bell, I was told, "has packed up so please knock." When the door finally opened (I almost had to kick it down) it seemed that all the sound had been sucked out of the Borough of Islington and pumped into this one thunderous sitting room. Among the booming voices were those of The Fab Four singing about how much they wanted to hold my hand.

Miss Guthrie was as tall and cool as a gin and tonic and her first name was Sue or Sarah or something which I didn't quite catch because she mumbled. I was out of place in a tie and jacket for the men were so dressed down they looked as if they had come to do manual labor. The women were displayed in what was new to me then, either flowing garments or almost nothing at all. Each pair of legs (thighs, to be precise) were fringed at the top with a vestige of what might once have been an actual dress and then, at the knees, disappeared into towering boots. They were less animated than American girls, soft spoken and far more self-possessed and none emitted that all too familiar dissonant, grating sound. The men all looked gay.

I wandered about with a glass of wine (whisky was nowhere in sight) observing this long-legged scene like a delighted anthropologist who had stumbled across a different and perhaps superior species. But soon I began to feel uncomfortably hot. This was due, I thought, to the presence of all those untouchable thighs. Then I noticed a device in the corner of the room which I call a heater and they call a fire but might well have been a nuclear reactor going critical. It gave off waves of stifling heat that threatened a human meltdown though none of the others seemed aware of this. One Englishman, in a leather jacket, stood right next to it and lived. I backed away as far as I could, leaning, finally, against some flowery wallpaper, throat dry, scalp wet. I imagined myself sliding down in a slow faint, trailing a damp stain. Escape was my only thought. There was a door. I stepped through and found myself inside a butcher's fridge. It was, in fact, the hallway. The bathroom was worse. It felt as if I had become gloved in ice. Surely a window was open. I was wrong. Though tightly closed, it wafted a stinging arctic breath. I jogged back to the sitting room that now, to my surprise, was rather comfortable.

Then I saw her. As I was excusing my way through the crowd to reach the bar, I noticed a happy, heart-rending blonde whose beauty made the other young women seem subtly deformed. She was compact, finely-crafted and exuded a discreet and continuous sense of joy. Her gaiety suggested a child-like optimism that she was on course toward a future where life would be better even than it was now and she could hardly wait to get there. More than vulnerable, she seemed positively at risk. I had the preposterous urge to volunteer myself as her guide through the dangerous years ahead to make sure nothing bad happened.

Our eyes met, and perhaps confusing me with an old friend, she smiled. That did it. I had no choice. The covenant was made. Now all I had to do was meet her, win her and stand guard over her for as long as I lived. No problem.

What the fuck had they put in the wine?

I stepped forward and said hello. She answered. I know because her lips moved. But two problems immediately threatened to wreck my destiny. One, was my chronic hearing difficulties that made anything said to me in a crowded room blend maddeningly into the background, which at the moment was that fearsome onslaught called Twist and Shout. Two, her exceptionally soft voice that made it impossible, even when I leaned close, to hear anything but whiffs and snatches. Something about having heard an American was at the party and was I him. And something about herself which I missed completely. Leaning closer, I did catch her name: Hilary Clarke. I felt like an ass thrusting my ear at her mouth each time she spoke. I would have to hug her to hear her which was out of the question. Desperate, I apologized for having to ask but could she possibly speak a little louder. She was happy to comply yet her voice gained little, if at all, in volume.

Then Anne Chambers, as petite and dry as a martini, came up to say that Hilary was wanted on the phone. She hurried off while Anne felt obliged to inquire why I had come to London. When I mentioned photography, she at once introduced me to her brother who, as luck would have it, was also a photographer though I soon discovered he "taught maths to chinless wonders and only took snaps on weekends."

I broke away finally and asked for the phone. It sat on a pile of coats, unused. I searched for Hilary Clarke but she was always in another room until I realized she had left. I spotted Sue (or was it Sarah?) only to be told, "An old boy friend is ill so someone ran her over to his place."

"What's wrong?"

"Oh, I shouldn't think it's serious." Then coyly: "If you'd like to see her again, we'll all be at Westminster Abbey tomorrow."

"You're going to church?"

"Good god, no. The Handel concert. I expect she'll be there."

"Wouldn't she stay with her friend, if he's ill?"

"My guess is he'll be better by then."

"Could you possibly let me have her phone number?"

"Oh, dear, I did that once and she gave me a ticking off. How was I to know he was 'effing bonkers. Kept ringing her up in the small hours. She was not best pleased."

"Suppose I get character references."

"Not to worry. Just let me clear it with her first. Oh, would you excuse me? The record needs changing."

The English are good in adversity. World War Two, for example, or a heavy snowfall. They let it rest where it lands, like an air crash to be inspected later. But then it freezes over and no one can walk on all those unshovelled pavements. As a result,people move single file in the street like pilgrims on their way to a warmer climate. I, too, trudged along at risk of death. From hypothermia, mainly. In Britain the seasons, like prison terms, run concurrently. A spring morning will arrive in December. A shivering weekend might take hold in August. Back in those days, central heating, if it existed at all, was most effective in summer when it had a fighting chance. Otherwise those biscuit-thin radiators gave off, in the dark of winter, only a tepid hint at heat. So I wore two pairs of socks against the ankle-high draft that cuts across the whole country. And, when I ate out, I wore gloves. Conditions that would have been illegal in New York, in London were not even referred to. It's not that winters were colder in Britain. It's that they were held indoors.

When I reached the Abbey I emulated the others by sitting on a kneeling cushion to make the hard bench softer and, like the others, kept my coat on in this grand, spacious but deeply chilly place. I saw Anne and Sue/Sarah who were seated wrapped up like arctic explorers. They waved. I waved. Nowhere could I see Hilary Clarke. A man in church robes came by and slipped on the stone floor. This brought my attention to a plaque embedded in the aisle that read

Thomas Hardy (1840-1928) while towering above me stood the statue of Handel himself. But no Hilary. "Comfort ye," sang a great, clear, deep voice and by the time they were exalting every valley, I became lost in the flood of restorative music that could soothe all ills, at least for a while.

Much later, as tradition dictates, we all lumbered to our feet and while the mighty bursts of, "HAL-le-lujah, HAL-le-lujah," threatened to buckle the walls and lift off the roof, I saw her. She stood at the far end of the row in a fur hat, transfixed. She seemed like an alert child among sullen adults. I willed her to look at me. She looked the other way. Scratching her nose with her rolled program sheet, she fell back into her Handelian trance. When we all sat down, she vanished from sight as a lady down front let go with a lilting rendition of how she knew that her redeemer liveth.

"Oh, hello Russell," Hilary said when the oratorio had ended and I was able to reach through the crowd and pull on the sleeve of her coat.

"How's your friend?"

"False alarm," she explained. "He's fine now."

"Glad to hear it. How about a drink?"

"Good idea," said Anne Chambers who had marched up with a brigade of friends and we all went to a near-by pub that was blessedly quiet. I wanted to talk only to her but it became a communal chat starting with someone asking if I had enjoyed *The Messiah* and someone else pointing out that you shouldn't say the word 'The.' You should just say *Messiah.* There was a general difference of opinion about this.

"But he's right," I said, agreeing with a man whose hair was longer than any woman's at the table. "It's *Messiah* as in, I heard them sing *Messiah* last night. But it's The Messiah as in, I saw The Messiah last night but he didn't see me."

A guy called Drew put a pint of bitter in front of me. I waited for an opening and was about to speak again when a great clamorous ringing filled the room. This, I was told, was the division bell calling MPs back to Parliament for a vote. What with more discussion about the concert and then my offering to buy a round and taking twenty minutes to fight my way to the bar, catch someone's eye, order, pay with a pocket of funny money and return with a tray of drinks, it seemed that I had only just sat down again when the publican started screaming, "Drink up," "Thank you," "Closing time," "Good night, all" "Drink up, now." The lights were dimmed and a barmaid swooped by snatching up our empty glasses. Finally they intimidated us into the street as if we were the sober ones and the staff were all drunk.

I held the door for her as we left. "Let me see you home."

"Bit of a slog."

"I don't mind."

"Super."

We crunched snow as we ran and jumped onto the rear platform of a moving bus. Sitting in the front row on the top level was like rolling through London on wheeled stilts. Every time we turned a corner it seemed we would flatten parked cars or run someone over. I glimpsed people in second storey windows in fixed poses of dull domesticity. We creaked and groaned and I could feel a tremor whenever the driver wrestled with the gears. Speak to her, I told myself. Don't just sit like a boob. Force yourself.

"It's fun up here." This like a breathless dimwit who had reached the summit of Everest.

"Yes it is," she said.

Again I was left clinging above a precipice of silence.

"Yup," I added, pointlessly, beginning to curdle like milk.

She looked at me. "My grandfather was a bus driver."

"Was he? Mine was a sign painter."

"When I was little," she said, "he took me around London pointing out places in Dickens."

"And he was a bus driver?"

"Yep. He loved reading."

"My grandfather didn't read. But he laughed if anyone mentioned WC Fields."

"Oh, that's just as good," she smiled.

"A bus driver. So you come from a, what, a poor, working class family?"

"Yes."

"But your accent..."

"I know. It's a bit posh. I went to a girl's boarding school on a scholarship. Awful place. At table you couldn't ask for the salt. You had to say, Mary, would you like the salt? And Mary had to say, No thank you, Hilary, but would you like the salt? Yes, please. And only then would you get the bloody salt."

"Sounds like hell," I said. "In general, though, I find the English don't ask questions. They don't even ask directions. But especially not personal questions. In the States that's all we ask. Where are you from? What do you do? How much do you make? Can I borrow some? Americans reach out."

"Whether one wants them to or not."

"Exactly."

"The English are terrified of embarrassing each other."

"Some questions are harmless enough."

"Try me," she said.

"What do you do for a living?"

"I've been out of work for five years."

"How's the family?"

"They died in a fire."

"And your roommates?"

"All murdered."

"What are you doing tomorrow?"

"I have to appear in court for sentencing."

"What *are* you doing tomorrow?"

She gave me quizzical look.

"That was a change of subject," I said.

"Ah." She smiled.

"Where are we?" I asked.

"Pimlico."

The name meant nothing. Her building was narrow and shabby. A lady's bike, mangy and rusted, was chained to an iron railing that stood guard over a sizable drop to a concrete area, the size of a room, between house and street.

She agreed to dinner the following day and I said good night at her door like a gentleman. On the tube platform, going back, an ominous mechanical voice warned me to, "Mind the gap. Mind the gap."

When I returned, twenty hours later, Hilary invited me in for a drink. The hallway had an overpowering stink wafting down from upstairs.

"Cats," she explained.

"Tigers, surely?"

"Kittens mostly. The lady has thirty-two of them."

"Good God. Is she a vet?"

"She works as a cleaning lady at Buckingham Palace."

"You're joking? Does the Queen know about this?"

"There are some things they don't tell her."

"How about the Department of Health?"

"Oh, we complained to them."

"What did they do?"

"They did fuck all."

At that moment there began above us a miniature cattle stampede as a tumble of animals moved hell bent from one end of somewhere to the other.

"Does this happen often?"

"Yes, but it's sort of comforting if I'm here by myself."

"Proves you're not alone in the universe. There's you, infinite space and thirty-two cats."

"Exactly."

I was led down to the basement and into a cramped and crumbling kitchen with Belmondo posters, torn linoleum and an ominous dark patch on the ceiling above the stove. I had been warned that her two roommates would be there.

"Are they dangerous?"

"The important thing is not to show fear."

I saw only one roommate, a pretty young woman named Esther who was wearing rimless glasses and making tea. She was dressed like a gypsy. The other roommate, Jeanine, was not in sight. I was told she would be out in a bit. From somewhere in the room a languid voice said hello. Esther handed a cup without its saucer toward a three-paneled screen. "Here," she said. A naked arm insinuated its way from behind and drew the cup out of sight.

"She's taking a bath," Esther explained.

"In the sink?"

"Feels like it," said the languid voice.

"A hip bath," Hilary explained.

"Offer him a drink," the voice suggested.

Esther leaned forward. "Would you like a drink?"

"Actually, I'd like two drinks," I said. "It's been that kind of day. But one would be great. Thank you."

"I'm afraid all we have is whiskey."

"That's fine."

"There's no soda or anything."

"On the rocks will be fine."

Esther looked alarmed and made her way through the debris to a baby fridge. "Oh, dear. All gone."

"How did this get here?" Hilary asked, examining the bottle.

Esther grinned. "All thanks to kind, sweet Drew."

"He just gave it to us?"

"Well, the truth is he left this morning and forgot it."

"So it's not ours," Hilary said.

"Ah, but he rang up to say we could have as much as we wanted."

"Well, he's not all bad, then is he?" said the disembodied voice.

"Oh, shut up," Esther laughed, throwing a crumpled cigarette pack over the screen.

"Come to think of it," I said, to remind them I was still there, "I don't want any ice. I just like the sound it makes. No ice. Please."

They offered me a seat on a wobbly chair at a battle-scarred table covered with dirty dishes. Hilary had her whiskey in a cup, Esther, in a mug. Jeanine said she would stay with her tea. As the guest, my offering came at the bottom of a tall drinking glass. It was either the only one they had or the only one that was washed. That is, I assumed it was washed, the kitchen soap that had been used for it had a sickly, clouded look. Also, there was a deep jagged bit missing. Esther had filled it to the bottom of this V-shaped fissure. As she placed the offering on the table, she suddenly saw it through my eyes. She paused. She reached out and turned it so the gap faced away from me.

"Best to drink from this side," she said.

"Cheers," the screen murmured.

"Cheers." Hilary lifted her cup.

"Cheers," I said, thoughtfully.

"As they say in the States," Esther added, "here's mud in your eye."

The moment we were seated in the restaurant, Hilary got up to "pop to the loo." This gave me a chance to notice yet again, as she wound her way between tables and past the sweet trolley that even the most neutral garment, when worn by her, spoke out and said woman. Lines were traced, secrets whispered, and always the gist was woman. At that party or in the pub after the concert or down in her dismal flat or now as she walked away and later came back, each new posture or shift of weight made something salient, brought forth another annunciation. It was as if she possessed, without knowing it, the awesome power to alter lives.

We talked as two people do who hope they are the converging halves of a great event. Her intelligence made everything easy, her spontaneity made everything new. She seemed to be saying yes, always yes, as if I could not say anything that would displease her. I might lift and carry her out into the street with all heads turning and this, too, would please her. All her expressions and her multiple proofs of beauty whispered "yes" so that the man furthest across the room must surely feel the radiating warmth of her wholesome acquiescence. Yet in none of this was there even the slightest hint of flirtation.

And she even offered to split the check. She wanted to pay *me* for her *half* of our meal. And she meant it, she who lived in that cellar of hell, whose flair for clothes couldn't hide the fact that nothing she wore was remotely new, who worked as a journalist for a pittance and cycled to work to economize, she truly meant to do what no woman I had asked to dinner had ever done before. She took it for granted that she should split the tab. Certainly not, I told her. She protested. I insisted. She wanted to know how much it came to. I snatched the check away. Yet another protest was overruled. And so I paid. She thanked me with a splendid smile. To her I must have seemed demented with gallantry.

She told me about some guy she referred to as "this bloke I was trying to break off with for about a year, the one who rang me up at the party to pretend he was ill." He, who ordered steak when she could barely manage the cheapest pasta, expected her to split the bill fifty-fifty. She though that was "a bit much."

"I'll challenge him to a duel," I told her.

"He'd ask you to pay half his funeral costs."

"Worth it. Pistols at dawn."

"At dawn? He goes to sleep at dawn."
"OK, at midnight."
"He'd be too pissed to stand."
"Damn, he outwits me at every turn."
"Sometimes I think, hey, I don't have to see him ever again. That really cheers me up."
"Me too."

On the way back, she told me something of her life, how her mother walked out when she was eighteen months old, leaving her to be brought up by her horrible grandmother and kind, but weak, grandfather. Her Dad was also on the scene but he worked long hours and was remote even when he was home.

We arrived back at her front steps and while I was trying to decide if I should attempt a kiss or wait until next time, she opened the door and in we went. All was silent. The cats slept; their odor didn't. She led me into the monk's cell of her bedroom. On the wall was a photo of Samuel Beckett looking like the wisest, most weather-worn man alive, also a painting of a careful, kindly, balding gent whose face suggested no great skill or scope or gave the slightest hint that he had written *Hamlet*.

On her night table was a bulbous alarm clock that pronounced each tick with a clank. She wrapped it in a scarf and put it in a drawer. There was also a library book of poems by Larkin. There was a box of tissues. And there was a single bed. In time, we climbed in.

Somewhere, deep in the night, I came awake. New York? No, this was London. A lovely thigh rested on my stomach, a smooth arm lay across my chest. I slipped out into the cold, dead room, found my trousers, shoved sockless feet into unfriendly shoes and tried to remember where she said the loo was. Something about down the stairs and to the right. There was a brown hallway heavy with the dim light of a sepia print. On the floor below I duly turned to the right.

Ah, there. I opened a door and stepped out into the shocking night where there was snow on the ground and the city's business taking place above me on the other side of a railing where people walked and buses towered by. There I stood in a deep, freezing, roofless vault one flight below the street. A man with earmuffs glanced down at me and marched on. The ramshackle sound of a taxi engine idled nearby. I took four steps across what she had called "the area" to reach a clapboard door behind which was a tomb the size of a closet. By blindly slapping the walls and groping the air, I finally touched, lost, touched again, grabbed and pulled an elusive string that made a naked ceiling bulb ignite its wire of light. Somewhere water gurgled softly. A toilet roll on the floor had fringes of damp mounting its sides. Then I saw them, half a dozen of them, there on the walls, moving slowly, some up, some down. An infestation of fat, fuzzy slugs.

"I've got to get her out of here," I said, aloud. "I've got to get her the hell out."

Command Performance

The thousands of lights were like the firmament upside down. Toy cars moved on thin gray ribbons and each street lamp ignited a pale disk of pavement. The stars expanded to become lit windows in squat houses and I saw the dark horseshoe of an empty stadium. Then we skimmed low over a bright parkway as we made a wobbling rush at the earth and thumped home.

An hour later, stepping out into the night, we found ourselves at the bottom of a crushing sea of heat. Our taxi had a busted air conditioner and we drove to Manhattan with the thick soup of hot summer pouring in through the windows. This was Hilary's introduction to New York and a worse one could not be imagined. Half dead already, we were speeding off to meet and stay one night with my parents because the lady who sublet my apartment for the year had informed me at the last minute that she couldn't vacate until tomorrow.

I was absurdly tense about this meeting. As a professional photographer one learns to dismiss embarrassment. Just lifting a camera to one's face attracts attention. To get the job done, one often has to adopt, in front of startled onlookers, all sorts of silly postures: bending, kneeling, standing on tables, lying on the floor, not to mention shouting like a madman to attract the attention of someone entering a police car or exiting a limo. Yet my parents still embarrassed me as they did when I was twelve.

Now that Hilary was at my side, I yearned for New York to behave itself. How I longed to reclaim the story-book charm I remembered from those late Manhattan evenings when, going home from the movies with my parents, I saw a wealth of blankets spread on the grass in Central Park with entire families asleep in the muggy night. And people high above me bedded down on fire escapes amid silence and sirens. Or men in their under-shirts playing cards at a table on the sidewalk lit by a bulb suspended from a wire that disappeared into a window several stories up. How I longed to show her the city bound and gagged by a blizzard as we trudged up the very middle of Broadway in the clean, muffled morning snow, the dysfunctional traffic lights pointlessly winking red and green.

Instead, all we saw now was a rush of humanity in every direction as if the entire population was trying and failing to flee the city. It began to rain and the windshield wipers spread grime everywhere. At last we stood with our luggage at my parents' door and as always I heard the ferocious exuberance of their TV. It was so loud I had to press the bell twice. All went quiet as if we were the police. My mother called "Jacob" loudly and from a distance came his ill-tempered reply. Silence again. There was a long preamble of locks tumbling to the left, tumbling to the right as my mother, in her usual confusion, bolted one as she released another, getting nowhere until I heard the angry,

"Here, I'll get it," and that assertive clash of gears that was my father's handiwork. This swung the door wide and there we all were.

My response to seeing them again was always the same. An upsurge of pleasure, genuine and unrestrained, that lasted until one of them said something. Then I was reminded that they hadn't changed and I hadn't changed and back we went into our holding patterns, circulating at different altitudes for safety.

But here was a new ingredient and my father looked at her and gave a soft, "Ah, lovely," which caused her to levitate slightly if only on the inside. I was astonished that the all too familiar warehouse had been emptied for the occasion and was now, for a while anyway, a living room. In winter, they kept the heat at boiling point. Now, in summer, with all the air-conditioners on at full strength, it was like entering the arctic. But, to my surprise, my father looked better than I had seen him in a long time. Even handsome, with a touch of Toscanini in his face. Jacob said how pleased he was to see me again and how delighted he was to make Hilary's acquaintance. Beryl asked us to sit down. He wanted to know if we'd had a good flight and offered to take Hilary's coat and suggested we were probably dying for a drink. Beryl again asked us to sit down. To her, guests weren't guests until they sat down. As my father saw it, they hadn't been properly welcomed until they were given a drink. So we sat down and he gave us something he hadn't made in years. This comprised a triple bourbon, sugar, angosture bitters, slices of four different types of fresh fruit plus God knows what else to make a drink that sounded safe enough, an Old Fashioned, and which tasted heavenly but was liquid semtex. Hilary said it was delicious.

"You don't get offered cocktails in England," she said.

"But plenty of scotch and gin, surely," my father remarked.

"Not all that much. They're too expensive."

"Here's to us," said my mother, who loved the ritual of offering a toast.

"Cheers," said Hilary.

"To your good health," my father declared.

"Happy days," I added, and there was much stretching of arms and chiming of glasses.

"To us," Beryl repeated. She drank wine and at first was as quiet as my father was exuberant, smiling complacently as if she were the secret architect of this momentous meeting. When we had company, which was rare enough, she let others do the talking. Fearful of having nothing to say, she said nothing. Fearful of drawing attention to herself, her silence did just that. But Hilary went to work with those boarding school skills, gradually drawing her out by praising the apartment and commenting on how cool it was, and how, on the drive from the airport, she'd been "absolutely perishing" from the heat. Soon Beryl was regaling her about my legendary capacity to perspire as a baby. At first, Hilary took this phenomenon as it was offered, as something mystic like stigmata or telekinesis.

"So you found this happened even when you tried putting fewer blankets on him?"

With a frightened look. "I didn't want him to get a chill."

"So I nearly drowned in my crib," I said.

Beryl frowned. "What?"

"That was just his little joke," Hilary reassured her.

"Are you hungry?" Jacob asked, rubbing his hands like a headwaiter.

"We've eaten," I shot back, having told him by phone only yesterday that we would have been fed on the plane.

"I know but to be on the safe side here are some nibbles I got from Zabars." He produced a platter heaped with goodies and Hilary, who in the taxi had told me how bloated she felt, exclaimed, "Oh, how thoughtful." After our explanation of what Zabars was, she dutifully sampled some *kreplakh* and smoked salmon with cream cheese on a bagel, and after each item murmured with pleasure.

My father tucked in as he told her about the many wonderful English people he had met through business over the years and showed her, as if it were a rare archeological find, a photo magazine he subscribed to that came to him all the way from London.

"Have you been there?" Hilary asked.

"I hate flying. I would love to go by ship but Beryl gets sea sick and can only travel by plane." He shrugged, sadly. "So we have never had the pleasure."

Hilary suggested what I had recommended many times. "Why don't you sail and have Beryl fly over to meet you?"

"Exactly," I put in.

"That's no good," he replied with mock solemnity. "That would solve the problem."

"Help yourself to more food," my mother said.

"And to our view of the city," Jacob said, proudly.

"That's right," I said to her, "you haven't seen the view."

We all stepped out onto the twenty-ninth floor balcony into the punishing heat. The rain had stopped. The sky was dead. Before us was the vertical splendor of that glowing firmament, lower Manhattan. To our right was a prairie of stars: New Jersey. Below, a wide swathe of night: the Hudson. I pointed south to a speck of torch-glow: The Statue of Liberty. I pointed north at two flickering triangles above a stream of ink: the George Washington Bridge.

Our guest beamed. "Oh, it's magnificent. If I lived here I might not travel either."

"There," he said to me in triumph. "She understands. She wouldn't travel either."

Just as I was about to object, Hilary put her hand on my arm and changed the subject, as the English do when they sense unpleasantness ahead. "You must have taken loads of pictures from up here?"

I told her about the series of sunsets I shot that had won me a paltry sum from a New Jersey-is-Beautiful contest, and I described the picture story of children playing directly below us that I took with a telephoto lens and which appeared in *Life.* Jacob, who rarely remembered to take an interest in my career, now spilled out an embarrassment of praise over these two accomplishments, mostly because they were shot while he was there to proffer well-intended but unneeded advice.

"Tsh, it's so hot out," said my mother, which sent us back into the chill of the living room. Hilary, who had taken her jacket off, put it on again.

"Sit down, sit down," my mother insisted, as if we might bolt for the door.

While Jacob was off in the kitchen making a second Old Fashioned for each of us and pouring out another glass of wine, Hilary filled the silence with effortless chat as if she and Beryl had known each other, as the English say, for donkeys' years. Hilary, who had never had a mother, was finding the presence of mine a wonder in itself, especially since she appeared to possess only two character traits, cheerfulness and love.

Jacob pulled down an edition of Shakespeare's complete works. It was signed by John Gielgud.

Now Hilary was ecstatic. "How splendid. When did you meet him?"

"Dad's evil brother Sol met him," I explained.

"Pure *chutzpah*. He just walked back stage, book in hand, got Sir John to sign it and then offered to sell it to me."

"Uncle Sol's a wheeler-dealer," I said, in my new role as Greek chorus.

"Did it cost the earth?" Hilary asked.

"No, no," my father said. "As a joke, someone once gave me at Christmas an architect's plans for a fall out shelter. Sol wanted those plans. I wanted this book. We did a deal."

Hilary laughed. "Then you're the wheeler-dealer."

He grinned. "So long as the bomb doesn't drop."

"Is Uncle Sol as worried as all that?"

"He is," I said. "He plans to retire to some safe place where war can't touch him."

"Where might that be?"

"He has his eye on the Falkland Islands."

"We tease him sometimes," Jacob said. "Last year, at a family gathering, we played a game. Sol thinks war with Russia is imminent and so someone suggested we each name a day of the week when we would prefer the bomb to drop. Selma picked Monday claiming that's always a lousy day. Rebecca picked Sunday because with the shops closed it's dead anyway. But Russell had the best answer.

He chose Wednesday for the bomb to fall."

"Why?" Hilary asked, smiling at me.

"Well," I said, "it sort of breaks up the week."

Something was happening and it took a while to realize what it was. I had become relaxed. In fact, I could have slid to the floor like a rag doll. Here was a father I had never seen before. Charming, flirtatious, entertaining. I sat back, sipped my drink and let the good times roll. Jacob was in his element. It was as if he had plugged into a new power source that came directly from the pleasure Hilary took in everything he said. So the secret all along was to do the one thing I always avoided: bring her home to meet the folks. Who would have guessed? And so I smiled complacently and said almost nothing.

Finally jet lag took hold and it was time for bed. My father, having so much fun, didn't want to stop. I had to explain to this seasoned non-traveler that for us it was four in the morning London time, though for him the 11 o'clock evening news was coming on with Johnnie Carson to follow.

I was relieved that my parents had made not the slightest fuss when I explained to them over the phone what I wanted the sleeping arrangements to be. They were self-proclaimed liberals, after all, but of the conservative persuasion who believed in helping minorities provided they kept their distance, just as they were in favor of funding the poor but with other people's money. So my mother took Hilary off to show her where our room was and Jacob loosened his tie and removed his jacket now that his role as host had ended. It was then I realized why my father looked so good.

"You went on a diet?"

"You must be joking."

"But you've lost weight."

"A little."

"A little? A lot."

"Oh, about ten pounds."

"*Ten*? And no diet?"
"It happens."
"Dad, you should have a doctor check you out."
"I just went to a doctor."
"When was that?" I asked, suspiciously
"You weren't here. You were in England."
"Who did you see?"
"Dr Sakorski."
"Dad, he retired three years ago."
"No he didn't."
"He did. Greenblatt took over his practice."
"That was recent."
"How could it be? I went to Greenblatt a year and a half ago."
He looked worried. "Why, what was wrong?"
"A splinter under my nail. Look, I'm going to make an appointment for you to see him."
"What for?"
"For a check up."
My mother passed us on her way to the kitchen. I told her I wanted him to see a doctor.
"I've given up," she snapped, furious at having lost every argument she had ever had with him. "I can never get him to go."
"He's lost a lot of weight."
"I know," she flung back at me.
When she was gone he again dug his heels in. He saw no reason to go to a doctor. I had no choice but to spell it out.
"You realize, don't you, that sudden loss of weight can be a sign of cancer? If they spot it early, you'll be OK." He frowned but said nothing. "Look, Dad, you even take your car in for a checkup."
"I don't know any doctor," he flung out.
"I'll phone Greenblatt."
"I heard he's no good."

"He's fine. I went to him, remember?"

"For a splinter."

"It was a big splinter."

"Where's his office? I'm not going to Brooklyn."

"He's in Sakorski's old place in midtown."

"I hate that office."

"Why?"

"Nothing to read but auto magazines."

"Maybe Greenblatt has a better selection."

"Well does he? You were there."

"I brought a book to read."

"Is that how long he makes you wait?"

"I waited ten minutes."

"Sure, you were an emergency."

"Dad, a splinter is not an emergency."

"It can be. A finger can get infected."

"What the hell are we talking about? If I make an appointment, will you go?"

"Yes, yes, I'll go."

"I ask because I won't be here to take you."

"Where will you be?"

"Boston on a job. Then to France."

He seemed outraged. "France? Why France?"

"To make a living. Hilary has an assignment and I'm shooting the pictures."

"This will make your mother very unhappy. She thought you'd be in New York for a while."

"So did I. But this just came up. So I'll make the appointment and you go. Agreed?"

"I said I'd go. Such a fuss over a little loss of weight."

When I finally said good night and climbed into bed I knew what was coming.

"They're sweet. Your mother's loving and your father has bags of charm."

"Good."

"I mean it."

"I know."

"You all right?"

"I'm fine."

"Love you."

"Still?"

"Always."

I kissed her. She hummed as she did when she tasted the *kreplakh*. I put my watch on the side table and, when I turned back, she was asleep. We had turned off the clattering air-conditioner and the room was warm. Yet the chill I felt, when he removed his jacket, clung to me still. Constant was the running brook of the Expressway. Later I was reminded that I was still awake by the vigorous breathing of the deeply asleep. In an effort to become drowsy, I tried to recall pleasant things but had to make an effort to remember what they were. In time, I became aware of a muffled tapping inside my chest. It was as if something momentarily forgotten was trying, ever so discreetly, to get my attention.

Available Light

New York was an oven, Boston a wind tunnel and when we arrived in Bordeaux there was rain. This was the first time we were given an assignment to work together outside of Britain. But the bad weather didn't budge. Rain won't stop a journalist from describing the joy of exploring vineyards. A photographer, however, needs the sun. Each morning there was the sad hissing of tires in the street and at night, that soft fingering on the window. Once, in the small hours, a jolt of thunder seemed to thrash the sky up and down the length of France. In all of Europe, only the Riviera lay beneath a blue sky, as if to make it blatantly obvious to what extent God favored the rich. In an attempt to hoodwink the rain, we decided to drive to vineyards in the Midi and if the weather hadn't changed by then, to head for the Rhône.

"Right or left?" I asked, leaning on the wheel as we approached a fork in the road.

Her nose nearly touched the map. "Straight on."

"Straight on right or straight on left?"

"Bloody hell, is there a sign?"

"Maybe." Beyond the slap-swing of the windshield-wipers of our rented Dauphine was a distant something. I drove closer. "It says Lannemezan to the right."

"Brilliant. Take it."

She had on her orange T-shirt with the white dove of peace. It was the same one she wore the afternoon she sat on the floor of a phone kiosk near Victoria Station with her spiral note book open on her knees dictating a story to someone in the office of *The Times Educational Supplement*. Waiting for her to finish so we could go to a pub where I planned to ask her to move in with me, I lifted my Leica to sneak a shot of her at work. She waved me away. Cameras were suspect for they played sadistic games creating no end of subtly misshapen Hilaries all modeled by an unwilling and miscast stand-in. Occasionally I produced a truly brilliant portrait, that is to say one she actually liked. Yet, as always, spontaneity died whenever I edged the camera in her direction. She would sit stiff with apprehension as though I had ducked under a black cloth to ignite in her face a tray of flash powder.

"I'm peckish." She crumpled the road map into the glove compartment.

"We have apples in the back," I said.

"I know."

"What could be better?"

"Apples in the front."

"Lazy."

"The more we drive the less I want to move."

"That's why the Romans built so much. They traveled and traveled until one of them said, fuck it. I'm not going a step further. I'm building a fortress and putting my feet up. When I'm thirsty I'll build an aqueduct. When I'm dirty..."

"We'll bung in a bath."

"And do you know why they conquered the known world? To get away from their parents."

"What kept their parents from visiting on Sundays?"

"A moat and a drawbridge. Those were the good old days."

Shaking her head. "Poor Beryl. Poor Jacob. They love you beyond reason and all you want is to be somewhere else."

"Somewhere else with you."

"Careful."

A crouched figure was cycling in the rain, a baguette under her arm.

Hilary looked thoughtful. "It must be amazing to have parents who love you."

"Your father does, no?"

"Not so you'd notice. He phones twice a year and chats for three minutes."

Her grandmother, who treated her so cruelly as a child, was dead as was the one person who did offer love, her grandfather. I squeezed her hand.

We drove past shuttered houses and pastures empty of life. A tractor with its vacant seat had been left on a hill in the rain.

"You should ring him soon," she said.

"I don't know if they got the results yet."

"They should have done. It's over a week."

We stopped among a clutch of buildings and ran through the wet into an empty cafe. I ordered an expresso and a tea with milk. There was a wall phone in back and Hilary, whose French was better than mine, struggled with placing a collect call to the States. She waited with the receiver pressed to her ear, pouted a kiss in my direction and waited some more. All at once she handed the phone to me.

"Where are you?"

"In France, Ma."

"Oh, oh."

"Is Jacob there?"

"He's out shopping."

"Did he get the results of his tests?"

"Tests?"

"The ones the doctor took."

Her voice quickened. "He didn't go to the doctor."

"He didn't? Why not?"

"How should I know? I'm fed up. He went to, I don't know, someplace. Philadelphia."

"Why?"

"A convention. When he got back he was away so he couldn't go to him. Now he has to wait. I tell you, I don't care anymore."

It took me time to extract, from the maze of her explanations, what had actually happened. After we had left New York, my father discovered that the appointment I made for him conflicted with a book conference he wanted to attend. So he canceled with Greenblatt but when Jacob returned from Philadelphia he discovered that the doctor, now on vacation, wouldn't return for a month. Working, yet again, in mysterious ways, my father now became a great admirer of Greenblatt and refused to see anyone else. Furious, I ordered Beryl to make him see another doctor.

"It's important," I shouted.

"I know," she murmured.

"Make him do it, damn it."

A hand rested on my shoulder. Hilary's effort to calm me down. She mouthed the words: *Don't get in a flap*.

"Ma, look, none of this is your fault. I'll call back when he's there."

"Please, talk to him." She sounded helpless.

"Don't worry. I will. You take care now."

"Call soon," came the plaintive voice.

"I will. I promise."

"I should have made him go," I said, at the table, staring into my coffee. "I should have stayed and made him go."

She leaned across and squeezed my hand. "It's not your fault. He's a grown man."

"Really? He ignores the future until it hits him in the face. He'll make plans for dinner but not for death. Not for anything important. Like emptying a house he knew he must vacate but kept putting off doing so until just before the closing date when we were forced to dump all kinds of stuff in the street while neighbors I never even saw before gathered to sift through mounds of goodies and keepsakes. And while we're chucking things out he's blaming me for making him sell the house in the first place which, of course, he had to do because he needed the money to buy the apartment in Manhattan. For him days pass but life doesn't."

"Don't worry. He'll get to a doctor soon enough."

I downed my coffee and waited for her to finish her tea.

She touched my hand. "We'll ring him tonight."

"Yeah, let's do that."

We drove through constant rain, past endless trees. To our right was the dark wall of the Pyranees under the gray roof of the sky. Dusk came like slowly failing sight. Hilary was in the back seat, asleep. I drove, trying not to think about it, of how it grows secretly in one of the rooms of the body, filling all the space it can until the moment when it breaches the door, moves into the hall, intrudes into every part of the house, permanent and lethal. Why hadn't he gone to another doctor? Growing increasingly furious, I lectured him, scolded him, fought with him as if he was looking in at me through the windshield. I finished and started arguing all over again, repeating, adding, revising as the metronome went slap-swing, slap-swing, brushing away the obsessive rain, clearing my view of the road, of the trees, of my father's face.

There was movement all around me. I didn't understand. Didn't care. Movement of something white. They were close to me. There were several of them and they were moving and I didn't care. I was sitting up. It was rather easy. One leg straight out, the other bent. I was resting on my right hand. It was easy. People in white were moving about. They spoke. But said nothing. Something was being done to my head. If I turned, I'd be able to see what it was. I didn't bother. They were all friends and dear to me although I didn't know who they were. I didn't want to know. It was the feeling. The feeling was everything. I felt something on my shirt. It was soaked through. I could tell by the way it clung to my chest. It was all over my trousers, too. It wasn't water. It caused a stain. What could it be that was all over me and caused a stain? I tried to think. They were still moving around, the strangers I almost knew. Odd, that nothing was clear, that nothing stayed long enough for me to get hold of. I was trying to think. It wasn't easy. I looked at the stain again. Blood. That's what it was. Blood. And it was my blood. My own blood. Oh, God.

"Where's Hilary?" I asked.

A nurse was securing a bandage round my head. It felt tight. Another nurse was watching. No one answered. I was sitting on an emergency table attempting to think. I tried to recall the past. It didn't behave. I could see a shining road and a tunnel of trees. That was easy. It came back, as if on film. Always the same and nothing else.

"For God's sake, where's Hilary?"

This time someone answered. She spoke clearly and calmly and I listened with wild attention and could grasp nothing of what was said. I kept listening in the hope that understanding would arrive after the words had stopped. It did not.

"What's happened? Is Hilary all right?"

God, how could I have bled so much?

"Hilary," I called loudly. "Hilary."

The nurse didn't answer. No one did. They didn't even look at me. My friends seemed not to hear. Someone spoke but to someone else. A nurse left the room. The words hung in the air and I studied them. All at once I knew.

They were speaking French.

Boy, I really must have been given a clonk on the head. Four years of it in school and then I don't even know what the fuck it was. Well, here goes. I addressed the nurse in cautious French.

"Good day."

She laughed. "Good day."

So far so good.

"I desire to speak with a person English."

Was that right? Is that the way it sounds? Yet it worked. She didn't laugh or even smile. She replied, "Yes, one moment."

It was then I became aware of a doctor working close to my left side. My arm was being placed in a sling. A dull pain made itself at home in my elbow. It was the only thing that had no mystery. Stiff from sitting in one position, I tried to bend my other knee and was slammed with real pain. It took a moment to recover. Panic closed in like moveable walls. Where the hell was she? I was preparing a sentence demanding to know what they had done with Hilary when someone fraught with concern spoke to me in English.

"For heavens sake, my child, what happened to you?"

Mute no longer, I was free to ask anything I wanted. Except the concern and pity in that loving voice flooded me with hot slush. Had I tried to speak, I would have broken down. So again I was mute

The one who had spoken was a middle-aged, black-robed nun. Avoiding her eyes, I noticed a window. It had been painted black. No, that wasn't it. Night had come. That was it.

"Are you badly hurt?" she asked.

I ventured a sentence through treacherous seas. "A woman... was with me."

The nun spoke in French to the doctor. He mumbled a reply which was translated at once.

"She has a sprained shoulder. She wanted to stay with you but was given a sedative and put to bed. She'll be fine."

I took in and let out a deep breath.

"What else can I do for you?"

"The accident. How did it happen?"

She spoke to the doctor, then to me.

"He doesn't know. We'll find out tomorrow."

"I had camera equipment."

"The police will look after it."

"I can't remember the accident or how I got here."

"That's not unusual."

"How badly hurt am I?"

"Well, nothing's broken."

"Except my car. Except my head."

She shrugged. "God's will."

"So all this is His doing?"

"Who can say?"

A young nurse entered and there was a three-way discussion. The doctor left without glancing at me. "Of course, Sister Marie," said the nurse in French to the nun I had been chatting with and who, in turn, said to me: "It's time to put you to bed. Sleep well. We'll talk again."

A second nurse entered as Sister Marie left. The hallway through which they rolled me was dark and ominous. One of the wheels of the table squeaked incessantly. We moved through a ward lined with beds, the air unclean with communal slumber. Then into a small room where there were two beds. In one of them, hard at work breathing, was Hilary. I spoke her name. A nurse put a finger to her lips. They removed my shoes and out poured sparkling sand. Touching it, I discovered finely ground glass. They lifted me onto the bed and when they removed my trousers I saw, from my underwear, that I had bled there too. A needle jabbed my left arm and I was attached to a bottle of plasma above the bed. My money was in the car out there somewhere in the rain. And our clothes. How could all this have happened? Had it been my fault? So tired.

The two nurses left. The other bed was several feet away. Hilary didn't answer when I called her name.

"Love you," I said. No reply. "You still love me?" Silence. With sleep crashing down, I had time to say just one last thing. "Sorry."

The House Red

At the crack of a whip, an inquisition of light. Bludgeoned into consciousness, I moved. This stirred a cloud of mutinous dust in what had been my cozy tomb and now became a blinding vault of liquid silver. There still was hope. Eternal sleep might yet return. No luck. I was resurrected.

The door stood open. Had someone entered? The whiplash had been the window shade that shot up to let in the angry day. My watch said six. Then I remembered and glanced at the other bed. There was Hilary, squinting at me, head lifted in alarm.

"Oh, good, you're alive," she said.

"Is that what this is?"

She leaned on her elbow to look me over. "God, there was so much blood. They wouldn't let me stay. I so much wanted to. But they promised me you'd pull through."

"When you weren't there, I thought you were dead."

"Shit, didn't they tell you?"

"Finally, they told me."

"How awful."

Reaching out, fingers wiggling, we tried to touch but couldn't.

She winced. "Oh that awful thing on your head."

Touching the bandage. "You didn't complain when Gandhi wore one."

There was a thump in the hall like a broom handle pounding on the floor. It came closer with each rhythmic stroke. When it couldn't get much louder, and as we wondered what in hell it was, a man in a checkered robe with a wooden leg came stamping into view. He glanced in at us, mumbled something like *catastrophe* and marched on.

Hilary, in white pajamas, sat up under white sheets against white pillows in the white room with a flood of window light bleaching her face sickly white.

"How d'ya feel?" I asked.

"Funnily enough, OK."

"They said you'd dislocated your shoulder."

"No, it was jammed or something. I think it's alright now."

"Does it hurt?"

"A bit. Not much. How about you? They mentioned your knee."

"It got a real knock."

"And your poor head. Does it hurt?"

"No."

"I'm dying to hear what the doctor says."

"It's hard to bend the knee, though."

"Oh, dear."

"It'll be OK. Of course, I may never dance again."

"That's a blessing. Ah, look, it stopped."

With effort, I turned and looked out into the free world and locked eyes with a cow. She stood in the middle distance behind a fence, out of sight from Hilary's angle. Further back were three more, all looking intently at something that was out of sight from my angle. Beyond was a dirt road flooded with brown water. Yes, the rain had stopped.

"Terrific," I said.

She hugged her knees and shrugged. "And here we are, stuck indoors."

Slowly, I had worked myself into a sitting position, repressing the occasional grimace. Now it was time to learn the worst.

"Hilary, what happened?"

"When?"

"When? Last night. The accident."

"But we talked about that yesterday."

"We did? No we didn't."

Breakfast was pushed in on a wagon by a portly nurse, smiling as if this was the happiest day of her life. "*Bon jour*," she beamed and asked how we were. We were fine. She was glad. A bowl of warm milk was placed on a table beside Hilary's bed and another beside mine. We were each given two pieces of stale bread and a metal cup filled with wine. "*Bon appetit*." And she pushed the wagon out.

Hilary couldn't believe it. "Wine for breakfast. In hospital? Crikey. They must think it's mediSEENal," she added, pronouncing it as the English do.

"I've always like the French," I said, with a little grin.

"Yes, wine in the morning. Amazing. What must dinner be like?" She paused. "Actually, what I quite fancy..."

"Is a cup of tea, I know. When she comes back I'll put in a request. But about the accident, tell me again."

She stared at the door for a moment. "I was asleep. There was this frightful noise and I was completely disorientated. I was on the floor and there were apples everywhere. My shoulder hurt. When I called your name and you didn't answer, I was so scared. A man in uniform, a soldier I think, helped me out. People came running. I looked in the front seat but you weren't there. I was screaming your name. A woman pointed you out and there you were sitting in the road. You placed a handkerchief to your face and, as if by magic, it blossomed all red like a rose. And there was blood right the way down your arm. When I hugged you, you said, 'Hi babe'. I remember thinking, he never calls me that. I was crying. A car came and stopped. People ped me to my feet. I was so cold. Absolutely perishing. We were driven to hospital and they carried you in on a stretcher and I walked, holding your hand. You kept asking what happened. I wanted to stay by your side but they wouldn't let me. My shoulder was getting worse. Soon it was jolly painful. I don't know what they gave me but soon I was floating. They did things to my arm, then bunged me into bed. My God, was I floating. Incredible dreams. I've forgotten them now."

"But what the hell happened? Was it my fault or what?"

"Please, Russ, I don't know. I don't know."

"OK, calm down."

"You calm down."

"I'm calm."

"You're not calm."

"Neither are you."

"We survived," she pleaded. "The important thing is we're both OK."

"Sure, unless I killed someone."

"Oh, God." With a hand to her mouth. "You don't think... ?"

"Would be nice to know, wouldn't it? And there's the car, our money, my cameras and all those fucking vineyards we'll never get to. Shit."

"Maybe we will. Maybe we'll get there yet."

"And then, of course, there's my father."

"I know." She spoke softly, as if she had hoped to keep this truth hidden a while longer.

My head began throbbing again and I went quiet for a time. A couple of flies had landed on my bed. I moved my good knee. They rose and sank with the blanket but held their ground. Two more joined them.

"Listen," she said.

"What?"

"It's raining again."

At least, she could get out of bed. Later, to prove it, she came over and kissed me. "*Ou, la la,*" said a nurse who came in to collect the breakfast plates and disturb the flies. Hilary went exploring and reported back. "The hospital's sweet." And she was chuffed that some of the staff had complimented her French. "And there's a pay phone on the wall."

"Is there a wheelchair?" I asked.

"There was but it packed up so they sent it off to be fixed."

"You're kidding? How many patients are there?"

"Oh, twenty-five or so."

"And one wheelchair?" I patted the mattress, "I guess I'll be staying here for a while."

"Look, do you want me to phone him?"

"And when he asks where I am, what will you tell say?"

She shrugged. "The truth?"

"You do that and he'll fly here tomorrow. I don't want him to see France. I want him to see a doctor."

At that moment, Sister Marie unnerved me by appearing in her black garb like a compassionate, pale-skinned specter of death. She had nothing new to add except to say that when I was able, I would be taken to the police station to identify our belongings and sign a statement. "Just a formality," she assured me, with an ominous smile. "And the police will have acquired, by then, all the details of this whole sorry affair."

On our second day, Doctor Rossolimo, who had treated me in the emergency room, appeared from the hall and strode up to my bed. He went about his business, hurried and nervous, as though made nauseous at the sight of blood. He removed the "Mahatma," as Hilary called it, so that for fifty seconds or so, before it was wrapped in bandages again, my frail head felt cool in the morning air. Then he disconnected me from the bottle of plasma. "Stay off that knee for a while," Hilary said, translating the doctor's advice and, before I could reply, he was gone. My depression deepened. I couldn't walk or phone my father or find out what had happened out there last night in the rain. And I was itching to get my camera back to shoot a couple of rolls on life in this quaint place so that, with a thousand words from Hilary, we might interest editors in London and New York and, by so doing, recoup our losses. The hospital administration had no objection to this, there was even an office typewriter for Hilary to use, and she already had ideas of what I should shoot. But there was nothing for me to do except lie abed and brood.

Except, as luck would have it, late at night, when all is still, and a special someone gets an idea of how to rid the dark of all its gloom. At the time, I was attempting to follow those disjointed leaps of thought that precede sleep as the cogent world crumbles even as I lie awake and watch. It was then a gentle hand slipped in under the covers to jump start lust. There was a shot of pain in my knee during a maneuver to help her on board, not to mention a resounding knock of heads in the dark. But soon all infirmities were gone as we sank into love like the sea. Moved by its swells and troughs, we were carried submerged yet buoyant toward that ultimate, all-powerful, unstoppable helplessness.

Yet gloom and doom returned at the frightful crack of dawn. Our room was plunged into light and, glancing in at us, the man with the wooden leg thundered by throwing up his arms in a gesture of despair. Breakfast and some flies came and went and by 6:45 the long wait for lunch had begun. At 6:48 Sister Marie appeared. Oh, no, I thought. When the messenger arrives with good news, he is rewarded. With bad, he is killed. But what does the king do when the messenger keeps running in with no news at all? I was wrong. This time Sister Superior had come to ask a favor.

"There is a man now in the hospital," she said, in her slow, textbook English, "who has lived nearby for thirty years and whose wife has recently and tragically died of a stroke. For eighteen months he was inconsolable. Last week he cut his wrists. Sadly his depression continues and our fear, if we discharge him, is that he will again try to take his life." She paused for a moment. "Would you be kind enough to talk with him? You seem a cheerful person. You might do him good."

"Hilary's your man," I said, quickly. "I speak just enough French to get to the john."

The nun smiled. "He's an American."

"He lived near here for thirty years?" Hilary asked.

"His wife was French. She was born here. He liked it and stayed."

"Children?"

Sister Marie shook her head.

Patting the lump of blanket that was my left foot, Hilary urged me to give it a try.

"How? While lying in bed? Sister, I hate to tell you this but I'm the one who needs cheering up."

"Tomorrow," she said, with a sly tilt of her head, "the wheelchair returns and we become once again a modern hospital. A number of deserving patients are longing to be wheeled about. There is Monsieur Beaufret who hates the sound his wooden leg makes when he walks. And dear Madame Souplat has got it into her head that the wheelchair would improve her circulation. And there are even some, like you, who actually need it. So let me just say that it is possible, God willing, not to mention Doctor Rossolimo with whom I will have a word, to have you placed at the very top of the list."

"Sister Marie," I said, treasuring to the full this wonderfully pure and cunning personage, "you've got yourself a deal.

Toys of Desperation

"Russell, I'd like you to meet Archie Wood."

The man grimaced. "No cheerfulness," he pleaded.

"Wouldn't you like to chat with a fellow countryman?" asked Sister Marie. "No? And after all the trouble I went to find him a wheelchair." Her parting look made it all too clear that I had my work cut out for me. She closed the door and left us to it.

He had a pudgy, school-boy's face as apprehensive now as when he was little and bullied. It was as if too much air had been pumped into the balloon of his head producing puffed cheeks, a bulbous nose, extended ears, a mouth that stood ajar and careful, soulful eyes. His was a face for comedy and an off-stage life of sorrow. He wore white pajamas and a ratty bathrobe with the belt loops empty. Both his wrists were bandaged.

Leaning forward, elbows high, I rolled myself closer to where he sat, his back to the window, and held out my hand. He didn't respond at first, then gave me his as if to get rid of it. Not surprisingly, it felt lifeless. While I searched for something to say, he stared at the wheelchair.

"Auto accident," I explained. "Bum knee."

"My wife used one, once."

"Did she?"

"Broken ankle. I had to push her to work. And to church, too."

"When was that?"

"In winter, I remember."

He tilted his head back as if to relieve a stiff neck. I waited as he stared at the ceiling.

"Lots of cracks up there," I said. No reply. "Wall's in bad shape too." He had no views on this. I pressed him with questions. His begrudging answers didn't get us very far. Born in New Jersey, met his wife during the war, works as a pastry cook in a local hotel. Did he enjoy it? He went silent again. My presence seemed to be making things worse.

"Gone back to the States at all?"

He shook his head.

"Things have changed. No one says goodbye anymore. Now all you hear is have a nice day. Someone said it. Now you can't get them to stop."

He nodded sadly and I kept filling the void hoping to push aside his grief at least for a while.

"Hear the one about the little old Jewish lady whose phone rang late at night? I asked.

Archie didn't say if he had or hadn't so I figured, fuck it, and told it anyway.

"She picked it up and said, 'Ha-lo.'"

A man whispered that he wanted to rip off her bra, throw her down, tear off her clothes and have wild sex with her all night long. Silence. Then the little old Jewish lady replied, "Ya got all dat from Ha-lo?"

In the down-draft of his silence, my joke crashed. Why was I tormenting this man?

"Boy, can I cheer people up or what?"

"Please, no cheerfulness. Look, for me, this is the end."

"Or the beginning. You can walk out of here and start again. You can."

"I can't."

"Yes you can."

"How? Sister's got my clothes and won't give them back." Then with disgust: "Says they're being cleaned."

"I meant your life not your clothes. Other men get up and start again."

He glared at me. "What men?"

"Men whose wives have died. You're not alone."

His whisper cut like a scalpel. "I am alone."

"Yes, now, of course. What I mean is..."

"No one understands. I can't stay in France and I got no place to go."

He rubbed his face with his hand. Through the window I saw cars passing slowly in the puddled road. A sparrow sat on a fence and didn't budge. Nor did he. Russ, you are crap at this and I decided it was time to leave. But what do I say to him? How do I ease myself out?

He shook his head. "Been gone too long. Don't know a soul in the States. The people here are all *her* friends. Some of them are gone, too." He looked at me, wondering if I understood. "I had her. I had my job. That's what I had. Me and her took care of each other."

"I know."

"Look, do me a favor?"

"Sure?"

"I'd like to be alone for a while."

"Don't be discouraged," Hilary said, pushing me down the hall as I insisted I wasn't cut out for this sort of work. "Think of yourself as a Good Samaritan. Not a Great Samaritan, just a..."

"Very droll. I keep wanting to say to him, Dummy, life is good."

"That's because you have me."

"If we can only get him to take another look at what's on offer, at this whole chaotic human comedy."

"Did you tell him that?"

"No. I told him a joke."

"A joke?"

"He didn't laugh."

"I'm not surprised."

The wheelchair had stopped at the wall phone near the bursar's office. We had decided to place the call in the late afternoon, which was about 11 in the morning New York time. I waited as she spoke to the long distance operator, waited while the call got put through, waited after the receiver was handed down to me in the wheelchair, listening as it paused and rang, paused and rang. I saw their new white pushbutton phone as it rang on the table near the leather chair in the living room, I saw the old black wall phone as it rang in the kitchen under the cupboard doors where the cereals were kept, and I tried and failed to see the one in his den as it rang under all the crap that was piled up on his desk and, of course, there was the princess phone by their bed that glowed in the dark. All these kept ringing slowly and rhythmically until I began to see, as if through a wide angle lens, the entire apartment empty.

"They're out," I said.

"We'll ring back later. Now let me give you the grand tour."

Hilary pushed me from the poorly lit hallway into a bright dormitory with two long rows of hospital beds. A few men in bathrobes had gathered to talk, others lay reading or doing nothing. The long room was drained of noise as if everyone was in mourning. Several men nodded hello to me until I realized the greetings were for the young woman pushing the wheelchair. We left the stuffy building and went out into the living air. We explored a garden of stone benches and narrow walkways still damp under the obtuse sky.

"It's like the lid of a saucepan," she said, looking up at the gray roof covering us and the distant wall of the Pyrenees.

After dinner, I tried my luck again with Archie Wood. This time, at least he didn't flinch when I rolled in with my salesman's smile.

"Got another joke?" he asked, resting on his side in bed. It wasn't sarcasm. He wanted to make it up to me for not laughing. "Used to like jokes. Could never remember any."

"You sure?"

"I can take it." He crossed his fingers.

"OK, here goes. Two nuns are driving nervously through a dark and stormy night. There's lightning and thunder and they're all alone. Suddenly the devil with horns and green eyes leaps out of the forest, lands on their hood and leers in at them through the windshield. The nuns are terrified. Quick, Sister Mary, says the first nun, show him your cross. In a flash, Sister Mary rolls down her window, sticks out her head and screams, "GET THE HELL OUT OF THERE YOU SON OF A BITCH OR I'LL KICK ASS."

His face, a punch line in itself, lost its cartoon appeal as it ballooned handsomely into a grin.

"Yeah, that's funny," he said, like a cosmologist spotting a distant star that someone years ago had perversely named Funny.

It touched me how hard he was trying and failing to pull himself out of his bottomless pit. And I was failing as well. Time to try a new tack.

"What was she like, your wife?"

He took a deep breath and nodded as if here were the only subject that mattered. Then his burlesque face became distorted in a hopeless spasm of grief.

Hilary couldn't understand why I seemed so low that evening and, not wanting to talk about it, I blamed it all on my father and why the hell not, since he was forever blaming a whole lot of things on me. When we finally phoned him, he was quite carefree about not having seen a doctor and so I had to start all over again, pushing my argument up the mountain of his resistance, knowing it would surely roll back down again just as it had before. When I was finally able to re-infect him with concern over his health, he listened most carefully but, as always, when forced to examine things in my ground glass of reality, it only distorted his world even more, and so back came his old complaint of not being able to find a doctor in the medical wasteland of New York. I instructed him to phone his brother, the pharmacist, who surely had at his fingertips a list of physicians.

"Sol's doctor won't take new patients," he countered.

Slowly, as to a child: "Not Sol's doctor. Just a doctor on Sol's list of doctors. A doctor you could go to, now, for a quick check-up."

"But I have a doctor. You made an appointment for me."

"And you canceled it," I growled, feeling Hilary's restraining hand on my shoulder. "And then he went off for a vacation leaving you minus a family doctor."

"Look, I can't reason with your brain. I can only reason with my brain."

"Great, when are you going to start?"

"Start what?"

"Reasoning. You need a doctor. Phone Sol and ask him to find you one."

"You're always pushing," he complained. "Sell the house, move out, buy an apartment, move in, hurry, hurry. We always do what you want, never what we want. Never. I swear to God, you'll put me in the hospital at this rate."

"You too?"

"What does that mean?"

"What do you think it means? It means I need intensive care every time I talk to you. Now will you phone Sol or not?"

"I'll call him," he shouted. "I'll call him just to get you off my back."

A long forgotten carsickness returned. Our ambulance had filled with fumes and the windows wouldn't open. The vibration of the engine made my innards quiver, stirring the rot that oozed in, filling me like a cesspool. Hilary was just fine. She held my hand as we sat together, her feet pressing on my crutches to keep them from rattling on the floor. They were a temporary replacement for the wheelchair so that we could finally be taken to the police station, a trip I had been dreading all week. But the further we got from the hospital the worse I felt as if that cozy room with its twin beds had become my birdcage of safety, my slow drip of health.

Finally the two rear doors swung open and I was helped down into the gray afternoon carefully carrying my illness with me. Moving across the walled-in courtyard, I stomped forward on two legs, was lifted bodily under my armpits, dropped forward on one leg to stomp forward again on two. In this manner I reached the garage that housed someone's crushed motorcycle and our sad four door Dauphine. The hood had been wrenched open like the jaws of an alligator killed while trying to swallow our luggage. I tore open the gadget bag and examined my two cameras. I checked the shutter speeds, listening to the zip of a 100th of a second, the slap of a 30th of a second and the metallic kerplunk of a 10th of a second. All seemed well. And our luggage and travelers' checks were there, too. We inspected the car. For some unfathomable reason each of the windows had been completely removed. Inside, apples and books were strewn about. The floor was strangely covered with sawdust, thick sawdust, of the kind I remember walking on as a child years ago in butcher shops. Except this powder was white, not yellow, and it was then I realized what happens to windows when the glass isn't shatter proof.

A bored police sergeant, in the main building slowly recited a dozen questions which Hilary translated and I answered while the world around us seemed ominously silent. Yes, I was the driver. No, I don't remember what happened. Yes, the car was rented. Yes, it was insured. Place of birth? The United States. Purpose for coming to France? Vineyards. Elusive, rain-soaked, you-know-what-you-can-do-with-them vineyards. Freely translated by Hilary, my purpose became the fulfillment of a "life-long desire to photograph the beautiful countryside of Le Midi." I then signed a typed statement and that, to my surprise, was that.

"For God's sake," I said, "will you ask him to tell us what in hell happened." Using her charm, she began working him over until the laconic Frenchman finally broke down and talked.

"He says you hit a lorry that was parked well off the road." Having translated this, she turned back for more. "He says our car is a write-off which we know already." He spoke, she listened then, turning to me, said: "No one was hurt. Except us, of course. He doesn't seem to have thought of that. But that's good, isn't it? At least no one else was hurt." Now the sergeant had something to say that took him a while to explain but which finally made Hilary all but levitate. With a great smile, she turned and just looked at me as if I were as lovely as the beautiful Midi.

"What is it?" I asked.

"Oh, Russ, did you hear that?"

"No, what?"

He says a married couple witnessed the accident. They said, in their statement, that the reason you swerved into that lorry was to avoid hitting an old lady crossing the road. They say you saved her life." Hilary's smile flooded the room. "Her life," she repeated. Never had I seen her so happy. "Oh, well done. Well done."

Funny how the ride back didn't bother me. Word of my unremembered heroism had reached the hospital before I did and Sister Marie not only pronounced my action a great and noble deed, for which God would someday reward me, but claimed that Archie Wood was showing marked improvement due to my selfless visits.

Not only had I now become my lover's hero, I was repeatedly smiled at by the staff, held in high esteem by Sister Marie and --talk of friends in high places-- was apparently in God's good books as well. As a result, I received complete co-operation from everyone there. Not one word of complaint as I rolled in my wheelchair from room to room, snapping an assortment of frail patients, shy nuns, pretty nurses, magisterial doctors and a pleased bursar who posed with a wart on his nose the size of a walnut. I was even allowed access to the emergency room when two lads were carried in from an accident similar to ours. While one lay on a stretcher moaning softly, the other sat stoically blood-soaked while Doctor Rosselimo squinted and grimaced as he picked glass out of the boy's face.

I also took a number of shots of shy Archie who now frequently left his room, which he rarely did before, to scrape along the hall in his old slippers, holding closed his beltless bathrobe while giving the camera a wan smile. Later that day when I went to see him he was sitting in his usual state of gloom. But he perked up the moment he saw me.

"That your girlfriend?" he asked, tipping a thumb in the general direction of the office where Hilary was busily typing away.

"Yes, she is."

"Lucky you."

"Yeah, but unlucky her so it all balances out."

He smiled. "Hey, this time I got a joke for you."

"There's a switch."

"Actually, I didn't understand it at first 'til it was explained to me. It's true, by the way. I mean somebody saw it written on a wall in a john in the States. In Latin. Since I don't know Latin, I'll tell it to you straight."

"Go ahead."

"OK, what was written on the wall in the john was this." He paused for effect. "I saw, I conquered, I came."

Prepared as I was to fake laughter, there was no need.

"I think you're going to be OK," I told him.

"Me too," he said, with a hint of regret.

Late that evening, while Hilary and I were in bed and she was reading to me what she had written that afternoon, there was a knock on the door and in came Archie Wood holding his bathrobe together with one hand and waving to us with the other.

"Sorry to bother you."

"No bother," we both said.

"Just wanted to say how much I appreciate all you did to buck me up. Nice of you to do that. Really was. Also, seeing you're a photographer, I wanted to ask if it's possible to buy one of your pictures of me. Haven't had one taken in years. Burned the last one. Figured why not try again."

"Hell, I'll give you one," I told him.

"He'll be pleased to send it," Hilary said.

"No problem," I added. "Just give me your address."

"Jesus, that's real kind of you. Sorry."

Standing at the foot of the bed, he accidentally brushed my bathrobe to the floor. Ducking out of sight, he fumbled about and finally got it draped again over the railing.

"Well, OK then. Good night."

When he was gone, we whispered about his amazing gargoyle face and of how much he had improved of late. Thanks to you, she said. Much later, with our window shade not yet rolled down, and thanks to the moon with its dim, safe-light high in the darkroom of the night, she climbed into my bed where we ransacked each other for all the pleasure we could get.

Hours later, I came awake needing the john. To exercise my knee, as the nurses now encouraged me to do, I limped through the dusk of the hallway, my bathrobe over my shoulders like a cape. A few doors down was the WC with the aroma of a stagnant sewer and its pale bulb in the center of the ceiling. Finished at the urinal, starting to leave, I jumped with fright, gasped for air.

He was hanging from the toilet doorway, turning slightly, head-tilted, a fallen sandal on the floor beneath him. In the hall, and before I could yell for help, I saw a shrouded form striding away in the dusk.

I spoke her name and Sister Marie turned around. When I led her to him, she stood hand clamped to her mouth, shoulders lifted, eyes wide. Crossing herself, she hurried away. Waiting in the chilly room, not able to look at him, I put on my robe. Groping about behind me, trying to find it, I realized that both belt loops were empty.

Breakage

Was that the phone?

I had been listening to the news on the radio while working in the cadaverous light of the darkroom. A statement by London Transport said that yesterday's power failure, causing hundreds to be stranded below ground on the Northern Line, was due to a break in a water pipe near Camden Town. An official of the Water Board claimed a routine inspection had been carried out only last month although plans to install a more elaborate monitoring system had to be abandoned due to recent cutbacks.

Now, with the radio off, I listened with total attention. Yes, it was ringing. "Would you get that?" I yelled, while patterns of black and gray began to congeal into the shape of her impish face as she stared up at me from the bottom of the developing tray. "Hilary, would you get that?" Her features darkened, as did the glass of red wine in her hand. Though one couldn't tell from the picture, she was sitting on the roof of our newly rented Renault and I was standing on the hood in my stocking feet to get the angle I needed to capture her, the vineyard and the whipped cream clouds. We were relaxed for the first time in many weeks for I had made contact in New York, just an hour before, not with my confused mother or stubborn father but with that gruff pharmacist, my Uncle Sol. He, at least, could communicate. At times, brutally. Now, as it so happened, there was some startling news. He and Beryl had just returned from the hospital where Jacob had been given laser treatment on his prostate.

"My God," I said, "I've been trying to get him to see a doctor for months and now suddenly he's in hospital? What happened?"

Sol growled at me from the other side of the Atlantic. "What happened? One morning he couldn't pee. That's what happened. I sent him to a doctor, the doctor sent him to Mt. Sinai and now he can pee. He'll be home tomorrow. They said his prostate's fine."

"So he never did go for a check up?"

"He says a check up is for sick people."

"What about the weight he lost?"

"That's easy. Jacob had a gin and tonic or two every night for years. Then one day he reads that tonic is bad for the heart."

"Tonic is bad for the heart?"

"Of course not. Jacob's problem is he subscribes to a crap publication on alternative medicine put out by a bunch of doctors who got their diplomas at Woolworths. So he makes a decision. Guess what? No more nightcaps. And no more beer at lunch. Says it made him sleepy. Then he starts losing weight and doesn't know why. Jacob's fine. My dog should be as healthy as he is."

"Ah, how is little Brillo?"

Mistake. Sol went on at length about his wire-haired fox terrier who, despite my being a dog lover, I actually hated. The animal was a hypertense barking machine whose forceful greeting was to jump and bounce off people at groin level. Now that he had become too old for this, he used his warm, moist nose to nudge ceaselessly the idle hand of seated guests until they either petted him or got bitten.

Sol was burdened with grief. "I had to take him to the vet again. It's his rear legs. I might have to get one of those, dog-size, two-wheel rear wagons. Then at least he can walk in front and ride in back."

I smiled, though I knew it wasn't meant to be funny. It also amused me that not only did abrasive Sol choose to name his dog Brillo, but if it's true that dogs come to resemble their owners, this pairing might end up identical twins.

"Would you get that," I yelled again, for I could still hear ringing in the bedroom. Using a pair of prongs to transfer the print into the second tray, I remembered the time Hilary stood beside me in this very darkroom watching the blank paper come alive in the developer, unsure of what she would find there, then laughing at the sight of herself in a thigh-tight, rump-cleaving track suit as she came running past me, suspended forever at one five hundredth of a second, while over her shoulder a distant cluster of kites stood aloft in the sky atop Parliament Hill.

As the ringing continued, I thought it was probably my father calling as usual about some nit-picking business of little importance that was worrying him for no good reason. Or perhaps just wanting to hold forth again on how good he felt since his operation, stressing how he hadn't really needed a check up at all. I had decided I was through with the thankless task of being my father's keeper, counting myself lucky to be free of the hassle of forever trying to get him, against his better judgment, to do the sensible thing, if not at once, then at last, knowing of course that he probably wouldn't do it at all. Ah, what a blessing to have an entire ocean between us. I was thinking all this the very first time he phoned after returning home from Mt. Sinai. Then, as often happened when I had finally decided to give up on him, he confounded me all over again by becoming lighthearted, selfless and irresistibly charming.

"We saw that story you did on the vineyards."

"Ah, they've printed it already, have they?"

"She writes wonderfully. Tell her I said so, would you?"

"I will."

"It really held me. And your photos. My God. That one of the farmer helping his little son to decant wine with a candle. Priceless. Also the cooking scene with the wife using a bottle for a rolling pin."

"How many shots did they use?" I asked.

"Five, including a page and a half spread of Hilary outdoors. She seemed suspended in midair. Where was she sitting?"

"On the top of our car."

"And those clouds. So white. You do a bit of fiddling with the print?"

"Spotted that, did you? I masked the clouds and Hilary's white scarf which she borrowed from a tourist. Pretending I was Ansel Adams, I made a slight improvement on reality."

"You fooled Beryl. She asked why the clouds in New Jersey never look as good as those over there."

"Well, for a start" I said, "taxes are higher in Europe. In this world you get what you pay for. Better services, better clouds, maybe even a national health service."

He laughed. "I won't tell her that. It'll damage her faith in all things American. Would you like to speak to her? "

"I'd love to but actually I'm a bit..."

"Hang on. Here she is."

"Where are you now?" Beryl asked.

"London."

"Oh, oh, oh."

"Where'd you think I was?"

"One time I thought you were phoning from down there and..."

"Down where?"

"Your place."

"Sullivan Street?"

"Where?"

"My place in the Village."

"Yes, I thought you were down there and actually you were in Italy or Europe or somewhere."

"What year was that?"

"Oh, I don't no. I don't pay much attention to the years because I'm too busy doing other things."

"I see."

"Well, talk to me."

"Ma, what do you think I'm doing?"

"I mean what's new?"

"Nothing much," I said, detecting a high pitched whistle. "How's your hearing aid?"

"In what respect?"

"Sounds like it's giving you trouble?"

"I know but I don't dwell on it."

"Well, that's good. Tell Jacob to check the battery."

"The battery?"

"There's a bunch in the kitchen drawer."

"The battery for what?"

"Your hearing aid."

"Oh, oh, oh."

I screamed. I was standing at the door. It was closed, locked and light tight but, unfortunately, not sound proof. I could still hear the phone. "Will you get that, for Christ's sake?" No reply. Where the hell was she? When the print had finished its journey and was submerged, finally, in the last tray, I pulled opened the door and dashed, squinting, into a world of dizzying light. Jogging past the bathroom, where the shower was in full flow, I kept on down the hall, dove and grabbed the phone as I threw myself across the bed.

"Yes?"

"Where the hell were -- crysake?" It was Sol's graveled voice reaching me despite a bad connection. " -- about to hang up."

"Say that again?"

" -- about to hang up because -- "

"I was trapped in the darkroom. Sol? Are you there?"

" -- better sit down. Something ter -- "

"Something what?"

" -- terrible happened."

"What?"

"It's your -- "

"I can't hear you."

" -- your father."

"What about him?" My ear was pressed against an immaculate stillness, an impenetrable void. I waited. Nothing happened. Fuck you, I told the phone and started dialing. My finger slipped. I screamed. Started over. Waited. Again, the maddening void. Then I heard a busy signal, rapid, noisy, dysfunctional. Was Sol trying to get me? I hung up and waited, my hand on the phone. Was he waiting too? Both of us waiting for the other to call? Down in the street came the quick, warning beeps of a truck reversing. I removed my hand from the phone. Only then did it ring.

"Sol?"

"God damn phone lines. Can you hear me?"

"I can hear you fine now."

The void opened up again, vast, bottomless.

"Sol, are you there?"

"I'm here," he said, quietly, sounding burdened, tired. "It's your father."

"What about him?"

"He had a stroke."

"Oh, my God. Bad?"

"Not good."

"Can he speak?"

"Somewhat."

"Can he move?"

"Not much."

"Where is he now?"

"Presbyterian Medical Center."

"What do they think?"

"They say it's too early to tell."

"What do *you* think?"
He hesitated. The truck began reversing again.
"Professionally, what do you think?"
"I'd rather not say."
"That's not like you, Sol. Tell me."
"Some recover. Some don't. Most..."
"Yeah?"
"Are never the same again."
"I see... And my mother?"
"Holding up."
"Be there tomorrow. Next day at the latest."
"OK." He paused for a moment. "Russell." He cleared his throat.
"What?"
"Look I..."
"Yes?"
"Just wanted to say."
"Yes."
"There's no rush."

Nothing but Time

When he saw me enter the room, several quick tremors animated his lips. They were meant to be a smile as pieces of glass on the floor were meant to be a goblet. The last time I remembered seeing him lying in bed was when I was small and, in the morning, would run down the hall from my room into theirs where he would make two hills for me to climb by lifting his knees under the blanket. Then he'd let them collapse unexpectedly and reappear just as quickly which soon had me helpless with laughter. Now his entire body was absurdly still and, as he lay there, his eyes looked at me and looked at me. I took his warm, lifeless hand and told him what the doctor had said, that he would recover slowly and to be patient for he was getting the best of care. I assured him that everything possible was being done. And he just looked at me and looked at me.

"I was told you can't speak?" I said.

"No." A grunt more than a word.

"Can you say yes?"

"No."

"Can you say anything else?"

"No."

A nurse entered, introduced herself, checked the chart at the foot of the bed, warned me not to tire him and left the room. After while I said I would come back tomorrow. That Hilary sends all her love.

That together we would help him get well. I said goodbye, letting go of his hand. Smiling, I waved and gave him a thumbs-up. Nothing happened. He lay there and looked at me. From the moment I walked in he hadn't taken his eyes off me.

The first signs of trouble had been pains in his arms and a headache that lingered. He didn't feel well for a few days, then felt well again. He refused to go to a doctor, of course. It was just something he ate. He would be fine.

One afternoon he went down to the basement to stand guard over the laundry. Beryl had set the tumble dryer going only ten minutes earlier by putting in enough coins for the machine to run for an hour and then came back up for a cup of coffee. But Jacob was forever fearful of laundry theft or of someone removing our stuff and leaving it on the table in a damp pile so they could use our coins to tumble-dry their own stuff. So down he went to sit in the tropical heat of the laundry room until the tumbling stopped. When my mother noticed that he had departed without the shopping cart, which he would need to transport their always sizable load back up to their apartment, she went out into the hall, pulling it with her. No one was at the elevator doors located at the far end of the quiet corridor. He was already on his way to the basement.

She pressed the button and waited. They lived at the very top on the 29th floor, actually the 28th since the building had no 13th floor, the elevator going from the 12th to the 14th as if nothing was amiss. She waited and, as always, the wait was a long one. There were three elevators, but due to an electrical hitch that no one had yet been able to put right, when the button was pressed all three came up or none did. Not for a while anyway. Then, in due course, and with perfect timing, all three doors would roll open and, after a brief pause to catch their breath, rumble shut again and down the three elevators would go like Siamese triplets.

My mother waited, not as Jacob would, repeatedly pressing the button and cursing, but calmly humming, listening to the stomach-grumbling sounds in the elevator shaft, perhaps checking her hair in the mirror that faced the doors. Patience was one of her virtues. She could wait at bus stops, check-out counters, doctors' offices, never complaining, contentedly housed in a timeless bubble where she need never strain to follow our conversation or remember instructions or understand explanations. Waiting was for her one of life's greatest pleasures.

At once the three doors on the 29th floor rolled open, revealing two empty elevators. In the third stood Jacob, tie askew, hair disheveled, staring wildly at her as if he had just been the victim of an assault.

"What happened?" she asked.

And my father answered, "No."

An ambulance took him to the hospital and the paralysis didn't take hold until the next day. He was unable to voice a single lament while my mother's complaints were frequent. "You're not trying hard enough," she told him. Greater effort, in her view, would bring a quicker recovery. I took her aside and explained what Dr. Honeycutt had said about the nature of strokes, adding that however long it might take him to recover, one thing was certain, his progress had nothing to do with lack of effort. She was frightened, poor woman. It was hard for her to grasp why this tranquil paralysis that had settled over him so stealthily, couldn't be thrown off with similar ease.

But at least there was progress. A week after I arrived in New York, and while visiting the hospital, I asked if he'd like me to read to him since he couldn't hold a book or even a magazine. We had established a code of communication: one no meant yes, two nos meant no. But now quite clearly and, seemingly without effort, he said, "Yes."

"My God."

Then came another surprise. Wide and bright, revealing crooked teeth and that gold filling, there we were smiling at each other like happy simpletons.

"Can you say anything else?" I asked. "How do you feel?"

"I wheel kay."

"You mean you feel OK?"

"Yes."

"Great. Anything else?"

"Cuss."

"Cuss? That's odd."

"Barrel."

"Barrel and Cuss. Hey, you don't mean Beryl and Russ?"

"Yes."

"Great. Wonderful. Not exactly flattering but what the hell."

"So what's so funny?" my mother asked, entering the room. "What did I miss?"

And I had to explain to her that she hadn't missed anything, that she had come back just in time to hear Jacob give out with his first laugh since all this began.

His speech started to return within days, more quickly than I had thought possible. A week later he regained the use of his right hand and then, a week after that, much of the use of his right arm. Dr. Honeycutt offered encouragement, talked of gradual progress. But then he told me of the results of some recent tests he had taken.

"He can't *read*?" I almost shouted.

"I'm afraid the printed page for him is mostly a blur," said kindly Dr. Honeycutt with a pained expression, offering a second opinion by nodding at his own statement. He was tall and slightly stooped as though from the weight of all that compassion.

"But he can see. I know he can see."

"Oh, yes, he can see. But when he tries to read it's as if he has dyslexia. He can take in people's faces, the background, less well."

"The background's not important."

"If one wants to watch TV it is. That too, alas, is a blur."

"Good God. Will all this get better?"

"We can't be sure."

"Good God."

"Yes."

Still, it was a great day when we brought him home. Though Beryl wanted to take care of him herself, we knew that she lacked the training and the sheer physical strength to see to his needs. So she was made to accept, what Dr. Honeycutt advised, that a home-help professional had to be found and I asked an agency to send over some people. As I interviewed them, Jacob sat in his wheelchair and listened while my mother sat at the dining room table determined to take no part. Several women arrived over a period of days. After each one left, Jacob voiced an opinion. Of one he said, "Not Jewish." Of another, "Too Jewish." A Polish woman was rejected as "sad." Of others, he just said, "No." The only opinion my mother would give was a rapid fire, "I don't care who you get."

Then, one day, in walked a young woman from Trinidad with milk chocolate skin and a life-enhancing smile. Her name was Vida. I explained what had happened to Jacob and stressed that he was improving, that he was quickly regaining his powers of speech and could now move his right hand and arm.

"He's making progress," I said.

"You got that right," she announced. "Patient of mine couldn't do dat much for a whole year. Jacob's doing fine. You got a physiotherapist comin' up here?"

"Yes, we have."

"Good, he need dat. Between you and I, we'll have him walkin' by de end of de year wit any luck. Boy dat's some view you got from dat window. And you got a balcony, too." She looked at Jacob. "Good for takin' you out for a bit of sun. Or we can go down to de park.

Watch de children play. Or I read to you if you want."

"Sounds good," I said. "Doctor said we might need special equipment."

"Don't go buyin' nothin' yet. You know how the hospitals do. Dey tink expensive contraptions is de only way. Dey forget about keepin' the mind alert."

"Not letting the patient get bored."

"You got dat right."

Wearing her reading glasses my mother sat in disgruntled solitude at the dining room table. In front of her was a spread of glossy magazines. She often busied herself clipping out recipes that she would never use, filing them away where they would never be looked at. She, who felt undervalued at the best of times, knew she was being even further marginalized with the inclusion of another woman in her home. It was evident to all of us during the interview that arctic air was wafting our way along with the sound of snipping scissors. Vida glanced over at her a few times while she spoke to me. From such stubborn silence one might have thought it was my mother, not Jacob, who had suffered a stroke.

"When can you start?" I asked.

"Whenever."

"Tomorrow?"

"No problem."

When she was gone I waited for him to speak first.

"Good. She's good."

"Agreed."

"Lots of spunk."

When I turned to my mother and asked her opinion, she refused to give one. Vida had made sure to call out loud and clear, "Good bye Mrs. Morganstern, it was real nice meeting you." The only reply was a cold and careful, snip, snip, snip.

I had sublet my place on Sullivan Street to a friend who understood my sudden need for somewhere to sleep and, to my relief, offered to move out. Chatting long distance with Hilary in London, I told her that sadly I had to stay on for a while to help Jacob settle in.

"Get him to talk to you as much as you can," she suggested.

"But it's my mother who's gone silent."

"Your poor mother. You must make her feel needed."

"I'm trying."

"Or you'll have two problems, not one."

"Ah, like old times."

"Only worse."

"Bed's awfully empty without you."

"Glad to hear it."

In a matter of weeks my father was talking almost as well as he did before his stroke. Now and then a word would elude him and a quiz game would take place with all present joining in until we found the one he wanted. His paralysis, however, remained unchanged. He had the use of his right arm and all the fingers of his right hand. Only slightly could he turn his head from side to side and up and down. Otherwise he was immobile. He could lift a glass and drink unaided, and he could tackle a meal with his fork if someone cut his food into small pieces. But spooning up soup, one of his favorite foods, was much too difficult and then Vida had to feed him like a child. Dr. Honeycutt was clearly concerned with this lack of progress. Still, he continued to offer hope.

Vida was ever cheerful and she managed my mother with considerable skill, questioning her about my father's likes and dislikes and often asking for her help though she could easily have managed by herself. The schedule we worked out, designed to give my mother a sense of being needed, was for Vida to arrive in the morning and get my father out of bed and bathed, shaved and ready for the day. After lunch she would leave him in my mother's care and return in the evening to see him through dinner and safely into bed.

One afternoon we were alone, he and I, after Vida had left and my mother was out shopping. I had pushed his wheelchair to the dining room table and, mostly in silence, we drank tea and helped ourselves to Ruggela. We were sitting by the window, and all the rooftops below seemed coated with caster sugar while black tire tracks left fresh designs in the white road.

"That smoke?" he asked, squinting, worried.

"It's snow."

"You sure?"

"No, the building's on fire. Dad, it's snow. And coming down pretty hard."

He grimaced at the window to no avail.

"Can't you see it?"

"Will Beryl be all right?" he asked.

"Well, all she has to do is walk ten steps from the subway into Macy's and from Macy's back down into the subway."

"She take her umbrella?"

"I made her take it."

"Good."

Now seemed the time to bring up a touchy subject.

"Dad, I'm applying for some credit cards in her name."

He glared at me. "Why?"

"She may need them."

"I can still sign checks if someone holds the book."

"But if the day comes when you can't, we're in trouble."

"She has charge accounts at Bloomingdales and Macy's."

"Yeah, and you get the bills and write the checks."

"So?"

"So she has to learn to do it herself."

"She often does it herself."

"When? I've never seen her."

"You're not always here."

"Dad, no more of that shit. Yesterday I asked her to write out a check to see if she could do it. Thirty four dollars and sixty cents came out three thousand four hundred and sixty dollars. And in long hand she wrote thirty four and sixty dollars."

He groaned.

"She hasn't written a check in forty-five years. She's forgotten how. And she needs her own credit cards for restaurants, shops, gas stations. All those places you and she won't be going to together, at least for a while."

"Ahhhh," he blurted out, as if tasting something terribly bitter, so bitter it brought all discussion to a halt.

We sat in silence for a while. Finally, I reminded him of the times it snowed while we slept and I would come awake as a child to find my bedroom filled with reflected light. Cars would pass in a muffled hush and the rattle of the milkman's bottle cage rang louder than usual, almost as loud as the busy scrape of a neighbor's shovel. One such morning I awoke to the sounds of a tall monster clawing our roof with loud, fierce strokes. Later, out into the street, I saw the huge, snow-laden branch of a tree leaning on our house, raking the tiles as the wind pushed it from side to side. This was the beginning of that glorious day when each glistening tree and bush was gloved in ice, turning all of nature into a glass menagerie.

"You took some great shots," he said.

"As did everyone else with a camera."

"Not as great as yours."

"Spoken like a true dad."

He helped himself to another Ruggela the moment he saw me take one. When he finished it, he managed that perilous balancing act of lifting the cup to his lips and back to the saucer - at which point I relaxed again.

"I want to thank you for being such a help," he said. "Arranging things, finding people, buying equipment." With a smile. "One might almost think you were my son or something."

"Careful now, no family secrets."

Soon he was someplace else, far away and frowning. "There's something I need to say."

"Oh?"

"Involves you."

"Me?"

"Both of us."

The look on his face had me worried. As he took another slow sip, I leaned against the sill and glanced down at the growing complexity of tire tracks in the street. A car, draped in snow, moved from where it was parked, leaving behind a swatch of naked asphalt.

"I'm sorry I wasn't a better father," he said.

"What are you talking about?"

"I was busy with other things, like making ends meet."

"Of course you were. You were the breadwinner, for crysake."

"I did better than most."

"You sure did."

"Voted the best ad agency seven years out of fifteen. Pretty good."

"Terrific."

"But you know what I mean."

"Not exactly"

He took a long breath and let it out. Then shook his head. "How I was stubborn sometimes."

"Who isn't? We all are."

This onslaught of honesty left me scrambling to deny the truth.

"And remember that ranch house at Flushing Meadow? All that crap Sol fed me about gas heating? Remember?"

Reluctantly I remembered.

His face knotted with fury. "Why the hell didn't he mind his own damned business?" He fell silent, grieving over past blunders, heartsick at seeing it too clearly too late.

"There are no perfect fathers," I said. "Or perfect sons."

He looked offended. "What did you ever do wrong?"

"What are we, comrades confessing at a show trial?"

"Can't think of one example, can you?" Tapping his fingers on the table.

"Oh, come on. Did I ever once talk to you about these things? We had fights but we never once talked. That was my fault."

"You tried. I backed away."

"Backed away? I ran away. Instead of facing the problem, I fled to Europe."

"You ran away?" He was shocked.

"That's right, I ran away."

"There's a great father for you. Makes his son flee to another country."

"Oh, come on."

"You said it. You just now said it."

"Look, you weren't a bad father, OK?"

"Well," he conceded, after a moment's thought. "OK, not bad. But I could have been better." Staring for a while at the snow he couldn't see, he added, "There's something else I need to say."

"Oh? What's that?"

"It's this."

"This?"

"This." He slapped his wheelchair.

"Ah."

"If I don't get better..."

"You will get better."

"But if I don't, if I don't, I've decided not to go on."

I lowered my cup into its saucer. He stared at nothing for a while. "I just sit. That's all I do. I sit."

"Now wait a minute." I was trying frantically to think. Far below, children were running about on the white blanket that covered the grass and the two basketball courts. A black dog frolicked among them. In the Hudson, a tug laden with snow moved up river. "You've got to give yourself time."

He frowned. "Time?

"To work things out."

"To work what out?"

"Well, things you can do."

"Like what?"

"Music. Listening to music."

An expression of disdain came over his face. I blundered on. "And people can read to you. Think of all the classics you never had time for."

He didn't reply. Once he read poetry and listened to Brahms. But he hadn't picked up a book or put on a record in years. Was that to be his salvation, then? To pretend an interest where for so long there had only been neglect?

"Is that it?" he asked.

From the window, under the snow, the backless benches in the courtyard looked like graves.

"You mustn't give up hope."

He almost shouted. "I haven't given up hope. I just said if I don't get better, I don't want to go on."

In a quiet panic: "What about Beryl?"

"What good am I to her if I'm useless to myself?"

"Dad, she'd be devastated."

"She's that already. If I'm gone, she might recover."

"Dad, you're all she has."

As if talking to a simpleton. "All she has? All she has? What are you talking about? She has her *life*."

I jumped. The door had slammed. "My God, do you see what it's like out there?" my mother laughed, as she struggled in with her packages. “Oh, boy, I’m telling you. All that snow. That’s really something.”

The Quality of Waiting

The memory of a day spent out west last year came back that night as I lay in bed. I was alone on a vast prairie where there were no people, cars or clouds, just miles of fence surrounding acres of silence. A pick-up truck was to take me, and the suitcase I was sitting on, plus my gadget bag, to the nearest town with a bus terminal. The road I sat beside was endless and empty. To me waiting was hell. It wasted life and halted progress. Yet on that hot day in Nebraska the act of waiting was a revelation. I could overhear the quiet of the earth, float on a sea of stillness, watch where road and sky met. There a distant smudge of dust congealed into a dark speck. This rushed toward me without coming closer, grew in size, yet didn't move. Then all at once a black Ford roared by like a calamity. It dwindled into the future leaving behind a gathering hush.

How different from sitting in a grim bus station among catatonic locals opposite a child chewing a licorice stick beside a man on a bench asleep. Or from the waiting one does at Heathrow with that constant stream of travelers emerging with their luggage to be greeted by exuberant lovers, pleased spouses and grinning friends, all of whom stroll off together while you stay put, your life on hold.

Then a smiling Hilary came into sight with the other arrivals and all the waiting in the whole world ended. I took her across the road to where the car I had rented was parked, the windows papered over on the inside with pages of *The Guardian* held in place with cellotape. We ducked into the back seat, locked the doors and in broad daylight made love. For her it was the first time in a car - ever. For me it was a high school reunion. Afterward we ate cheese and tomato sandwiches and drank tea from a thermos which she called a vacuum flask. Then, holding her hand, I took her back to the terminal where, sadly, we waved good bye as she walked through the door to her connecting flight.

Twelve months later I was waiting for her again, this time at JFK. I had arrived at New York first and went out to the airport to meet her flight from London.

"Hello. Been waiting long?"

Startled, I hadn't seen her approach. "Ah, there you are. How was your trip?"

"A bore, really. Guess what I was thinking the whole time?" She gave me her most winning smile. "When I had just two hours between flights and clever you hung paper curtains in a rented car and made my day."

"I remember," I said, wheeling her suitcase toward the exit, too distracted by angst at home to do justice to last year's conspiracy of passion in the short stay car park at Terminal Four.

Following an awkward silence: "How is he?"

"Oh God, I just can't talk him out of it. Maybe you can."

"Me?"

"Well, he keeps asking for you."

"Oh, dear."

We made our way into the sharp wind and around filthy mounds of snow until I put her suitcase in the trunk of my parents' Dodge Dart and started the engine.

"Russ," she said, seated next to me in her fake fur hat and brown cloth coat.

"Yes?"

"Well?"
"Well. what?"
"Aren't you going to kiss me?"

When we let ourselves in with a borrowed key, we discovered that Uncle Sol had arrived without warning while I was at the airport and had taken command. He had brought with him a motorized wheelchair that operated at the touch of a finger and Jacob, seated in it, was circling the living room looking miserable.
"You doin' great," Vida called out just as he collided with a chair.
"Look out," Beryl warned.
Sol shook his head. "He drives a car the same way."
Vida laughed. "He need a bell to ring like de bike people do."
Grim-faced, my father reversed into a lamp.
"Watch where you're going," Beryl told him.
Jacob exploded. "You're a big help. I can't see behind me, remember?"
"Then go slow."
"I'm trying, damn it."
"Don't worry," Hilary called out. "You'll get the hang of it."
"And he doesn't need a Greek chorus discussing his every move," I told them.
"Well, look who's here," my mother said.
Sol, gloating. "Just in time for my big surprise."
"When did you get here?" Beryl asked as Hilary bent over to kiss Jacob on the cheek.
"Ah, that's what I needed," he said.
"Sit down, sit down," my mother insisted.
Vida waved at us from across the room.
Amid all this confusion, one thing was certain, my father was not pleased with his new wheelchair. As always, whoever handed him a present, received in return a cool reception. Just as he must

commandeer the check, so he alone must distribute all gifts. When handed one himself, his mumbled thanks left the impression he already owned whatever he had now been given. Sol, of course, understood this, gaining profound satisfaction from his expansive act of vengeful generosity. But on this occasion I understood Jacob's despair. What he craved in this vicious world was a full recovery, not greater mobility. Yet the gift so pleased the rest of them that he had little choice but to keep his displeasure to himself.

When asked to stay for dinner Sol never had to be coaxed. Nor did he fear he might be imposing. We were seated, he and I, on opposite sides of the table. I could tell by his attitude toward me, when he managed to take time off from those scenic excursions up and down Hilary's coastline, that he still harbored his conviction that people who free-lanced didn't truly work for a living. He gave me the impression that I had been under surveillance for some time. In his view, I was having too much fun. I was working casually, traveling frequently and living openly with a woman who wasn't Jewish, wasn't converting and, to his amazement, wasn't pressing me to get married. It drove him nuts.

"Working hard?" he asked with mock innocence. A shot across my bow.

"More or less."

"You mean you're working less a lot more or working more a lot less?" He glanced around encouraging others to relish his wit.

"No," I said, "I'm doing more in less time. Leaves me free for other things." I indicated my father whom Vida was carefully feeding soup.

"What you're saying is you can do a year's work in half the time."

"Of course," said my mother.

"No, I'm saying I turn down half the jobs I'm offered and do the rest in half the time."

"Turn down jobs?" My father squinted at me from the far end of the table.

"Yeah, like what jobs?" Sol challenged, as if Jacob didn't fear for my financial wellbeing but, like himself, suspected I was exaggerating my workload.

"Why are you turning down jobs?" Jacob demanded.

"To spend more time with you," Hilary told him.

"That's not right," he said, then lectured me on how I must always say yes to editors or they'll stop phoning altogether.

"I don't see what difference it makes," Sol grumbled, "since he's free to take off as much time as he wants."

But Jacob's fear was in full throttle. I had, he pointed out, Hilary to support. Perhaps children someday, even a mortgage maybe.

"Hilary earns as much as I do," I said.

He didn't hear me. "Are you canceling a job to be here now?"

I was prepared to lie about this but Hilary, who has more integrity than anyone I've ever known, said yes on my behalf and Jacob's fear achieved lift off.

"This has got to stop. Don't worry about me. I'll be fine. You do what you have to do. I don't want you sitting around holding my hand when you've got work to do. Your job comes first."

"Of course," my mother said.

"Vida takes good care of me."

"You got dat right," she agreed.

"What was your last job offer?" Jacob asked me.

"One in London," I said.

"When?"

"In two days."

"The both of you?"

"Yes," said Hilary.

"Then go. The both of you. Go. I want you there by tomorrow." He was in charge again.

My mother frowned. "London? Why?"

"Dat's their job," Vida explained. "It's also where dey live."

“We should all have such a job,” Sol grumbled.
“Go,” Jacob said, “Go,” as if unable to wait another minute.

Alarms and Excursions

It was late spring of the following year when we returned from England. I had kept in touch but each time my father got on the line it was as if he was uncertain what a phone was for. He seemed distracted. He never asked what I was doing, only if we were all right, if I had enough money. That's all he ever asked. In time I stopped inquiring after his health. When my mother answered she said things were fine, as she would to a neighbor in the street. On those rare occasions when I got Vida, she whispered the truth: things weren't good at all.

"How does he spend his time?" I asked.

"He just stare at nothin'."

"Does anyone read to him?"

"I try but he get angry when I say the words wrong. Same when your mother do the readin'. I ask if he wants to hear a record but he say no. He need somethin' to do. He listen to the news but when it finish he turn the radio off. He wants to be doin' all those things he done before. Now he just sit. That's all he do."

"Do they go to restaurants?"

"They go to dat place across the street sometime. But he don't enjoy it like before."

"Why not?"

"I don't know. He don't say."

Often I, too, found myself staring at nothing as I tried, in London, to work out some way to help him in New York. Hilary kept urging me to visit. I didn't see the point of that for I felt I had little to offer. We rarely talked, even in the best of times. So what would he gain by my going there now?

"You'll never find out unless you go."

"If he needs me he'll ask me."

"He never will, for fear of taking you away from work."

"Which means he'll feel guilty if I show up."

"Russ, he'd love to see you."

"How do you know?"

"You're his only child."

"Who doesn't want to make him feel guilty."

"So the solution is never to see him again?"

"Don't be silly. I know what I'll do. I'll..."

"If you phone, of course he'll tell you not to come."

"Oh, great. So what's the answer?"

"OK, phone but simply tell him you're coming. Don't ask."

"I'm not sure."

"Do you want me to phone?"

"Why are you pushing, pushing for me to phone him?"

And at this she laughed.

"What's so funny?"

"You sound just like him."

So I flew to New York and made sure she came too. Another reason to go when we did was our apartment in the Village was free again. My tenant, I learned, had vanished, leaving the security deposit to pay for the last month's rent and taking with him my record player and new floor lamp.

The weather was lovely that June when we landed at JFK. My mother invited us to drive out with them to Long Island for lunch and then, "go and look at the tall boats." As an inducement, she said

Sol would be coming with us. As always, I was determined to avoid getting trapped with my family for an entire day, particularly if my Uncle was there. Hilary pointed out how much Jacob would want me to go. Still I resisted. Instead of going on this outing, we could take them to a restaurant tomorrow night. Hilary said we could do that as well. The discussion got heated but she didn't back down. Finally she hit upon the idea that he might feel less helpless if I, and not know-it-all Sol, helped him with his wheelchair. At that: OK, OK.

But I longed for rain. Never, of course, did a blue morning dawn with such temperate perfection.

Until I walked through the door, I hadn't fully realized how much I'd feared seeing him again. How much I dreaded my helplessness when facing his. He rolled forward, reached out and clutched my hand. He had put back all the weight he had lost and then some. And his hair now was nearly all gray. Hilary gave him a kiss on the cheek. Letting go of my hand, he took hold of hers. I removed magazines, newspapers and a few books from the couch so she could sit down, her hand still in his. "She gets more beautiful each day," he said to me. A flash of his old charm but he hadn't smiled. Not once since we came in had he smiled.

Sol arrived like a top sergeant pushing everyone into action. We used his battle-worn station wagon which even had room for Jacob's folded wheelchair. Lifting my father into the back seat nearly finished us off. As Sol and I struggled, my mother kept saying, "Careful, careful," when we could not possibly have been more careful, and Jacob kept crying out, "Wait, wait, wait," although, in mid-transfer, the one thing we couldn't do was wait. With my mother finally seated in the front and Hilary and I in back, Sol set off to do battle with an army of swiftly moving myopic dolts. Lurking everywhere, determined to slow him down were selfish pedestrians, unnecessary bicyclists and streets that, overnight and without warning, had been perversely torn open for repair. He drove like my father, slowly when in the fast lane of the Grand Central Parkway while, on the narrow streets of Manhattan, in an agitated rush.

It was ironic that in our family my mother was far and away the best driver. Yet when they traveled together my father always took the wheel, frequently making me wonder how on earth he'd passed his test. My mother's parallel parking was impeccable. My father's was a lengthy process of trial and error. He frequently got out to determine whether it was legal to leave the car that far from the curb, and back in again for further fine tuning such as removing the rear tire from the sidewalk. When Jacob was safely in his office and my mother was at the wheel, she drove so skillfully I had nothing to do but watch the scenery. With my father in command, I spent a considerable amount of time contributing suggestions such as, "Careful, there's a car coming," or "He's pulling out, he's pulling out." This was now Beryl's job as she sat beside her brusque brother-in-law offering, from time to time, hurried suggestions on how to avoid collision and death. At last he said, "Who in hell put this back-seat driver in front with me?"

"You tell her," Jacob chimed in, with another rare flash of his old self, never missing a chance to gang up on someone, particularly his wife.

"Look out," Beryl said.

"Boy, are you a Nervous Nelly," Sol said, applying his brakes.

"Like me, she doesn't want to die," I said. "Must be genetic."

"How do they drive in England?"

"Carefully," Hilary said.

"Americans are good drivers," Sol informed her.

"Except," I said, "for the fifty thousand who die on the road each year."

"That's unfair," he protested. "If you have five people in each car and they all get killed, four of them weren't driving. And if they went head on into a car carrying five more people that means out of 50,000 deaths only 10,000 were at the wheel and half of them might not have been at fault either, just unable to avoid the accident. That means there were only 5,000 bad drivers involved and that isn't a hell of a lot in a country of 300 million."

"Sol," I exclaimed, "you should have been a lawyer."

"You're telling me."

"Not *our* lawyer, mind you. Just *a* lawyer."

"But," Hilary said, "if the nine people killed in each head-on crash were better drivers than the man at the wheel and if any one of them had insisted on driving the car instead there might have been no loss of life at all."

In the rear-view mirror Sol looked justifiably suspicious. "Possibly," he growled.

"Which proves," I said, "that only good drivers should take the wheel."

"I'll drink to that," Sol replied.

"Look out," Beryl cried, "look out."

Apart from his dig at Beryl, my father had hardly spoken during the ride. Whenever I glanced at him he was looking away from me, out the window. When we arrived, he steered his wheelchair unaided along the boardwalk as the cool breeze tousled our hair and drew our attention to the spacious sea - everyone but Jacob who looked neither left or right but motored grimly onward until he gave a soft curse when he saw that he would have to be pulled backward up three steps into the restaurant. I managed it myself before Sol could ambled forward to help.

At our table he listened glumly as I read the menu to him. Sol loudly cross-examined the waitress as to which food was best, then ordered beer for everyone and had to call the waitress back to cancel the order because Hilary and I wanted wine, my mother a vodka and soda and my father nothing at all. We tried to get him to reconsider but he refused until we gave up and the waitress shrugged and went off into the kitchen - at which point he changed his mind.

"Careful now," Sol quipped, when a vodka and soda was finally put in front of him. "Remember you're driving." And he swung his laugh full circle hoping to draw us all in.

"What's Bow-eye-la-baa-issy?" my mother wanted to know.

"Where's that?" I asked.

Sol leaned in to see where she was pointing. "Bouillabaisse," he roared. "Bouillabaisse is fish soup."

"It's a very special French fish soup," my father added.

"Then why don't they say so," Beryl said.

"That's foreigners for you," Sol explained.

"Yeah, they insist on talking in a foreign language," I observed.

Sol pressed on. "But Beryl asked a fair question. This is America. Why don't they call it fish soup?"

"Well, for a start, bouillabaisse sounds delicious," Hilary countered.

"Which is more than one can say for matzo ball soup," I added.

"Here's to us," Beryl said, holding her glass aloft as soon as the rest of the drinks arrived.

"To us," Sol repeated, "and to no one else."

My father lifted his vodka and soda as if under duress. After much clinking, I decided to try the desperate measure of telling a joke.

"Dad, you know the one about the blind man who was handed a piece of matzo for the first time? He moved his fingers over it for a while and said, "Who wrote this shit?"

Taken by surprise, Jacob's glum face erupted in genuine pleasure but then that brief flash of his old self was gone. Hilary patted my hand as she often did when she liked something I'd said. Sol nodded with that fixed grin people adopt when they fail to catch the joke. My mother stiffened slightly at the expletive.

Lunch went on and on and then some. Sol harried the waitress by finding fault with his food and how long it took to arrive yet, in the end, insisted we each have a little taste of everything he had ordered. He bragged about all the famous customers who came into his pharmacy, none of whom, as it turned out, we had ever heard of. When the conversation flagged, Hilary, as her boarding-school training dictated, asked him further questions about his business which produced long-winded complaints about how hard it was to find reliable help. I tried to encourage Jacob to tell some of his own stories about incompetent employees, of which he had quite a few.

"Remember the time Lovell insisted the phrase was safe as horses instead of houses?"

My father nodded.

"Or when Jeff phoned in sick and two hours later you saw him having lunch at The Russian Tea Room?"

"Yeah," he mumbled. And that was that.

My mother relished social gatherings but if they included anyone other than my father and me, Beryl was too intimidated to venture a word so she was no help. And my own attempts to lighten the mood died on the wing.

Eventually, Jacob, putting down his cup of tea, lifted his hand, not as of old with a great upward stretch of his arm as if reaching for the sky, but high enough to do the job. The check was brought face down on a chocolate brown plastic tray and my father, sitting immobile in his wheelchair, able to reach out but not lean forward, could not quite take hold of the tray which now was pulled away from him across the table by Sol's quick hand.

"Give me that," Jacob demanded.

"Too late."

"I'm paying."

"That's what you think," Sol replied, triumphant at last.

"Come on. You get it next time."

"Jacob, next time has finally arrived." His crackling voice, softer than usual, was gleefully sadistic.

My father made a noise as if he had just tasted something vile.

Taking out my wallet. "I'll split it with you."

"Put that away," Sol ordered.

"Let me pay the tip, then."

"No way, Jose."

"Well, thank you very much," Hilary said. "It was a lovely meal."

"Yes," Beryl agreed. "We must come here again."

"If we make it back alive," I said, "it's a deal."

My father didn't speak. His face was clenched in anguish. We all rose. Seated, he propelled himself toward the door. I lowered him down the steps and soon we were making our way in the soft sunlight to look at the yachts and sailboats moored along the numerous piers that extended out from shore. Beyond was a jetty to protect the harbor from storms. Everywhere seagulls swooped and squealed. An amateur photographer stood, as was often the case, too far from what he wanted to capture, in this case a cat asleep between two lobster traps. I couldn't tell how much of all this Jacob was able to see.

"Can you make out the ships docked along that pier?"

"A bit," he said.

"There's three, one after another."

"I see a shape with something sticking up."

"That's the mast."

The others strolled on, Sol expounding to Hilary while my mother, her slip showing, stopped to wiggle her fingers at a child in a stroller.

"Shall we follow them?" I suggested.

"No," Jacob said, "I want to look at these ships."

"Why not." And I started to walk out on the pier with him when he barked, "You don't have to trail after me like I'm a child."

"Of course. I just thought..."

"There's people around me all the time. I can't stand it."

"Sorry, sorry." And I turned and followed the others, deciding a little independence would do him good. "We'll be heading this way,"

I called out.

"I know that."

"Where's Jacob?" my mother asked when I had caught up with her.

I pointed and we both saw him rolling along the pier behind a maze of masts and ropes. Sol was explaining something about the "internal carotid artery" and my mother asked if I thought he was warm enough out there in his wheelchair. Hilary was set to reply but Sol's flow of words continued without pause.

A steamship was planted on the horizon. A white gull, like those above the Hudson that often floated past my parents' window, hovered close to the boardwalk as if wondering who we were. Soon he lifted away in an upward glide leaving, as far as the eye could see, the great lethal spread of the North Atlantic. At that moment, an alarm whispered to me in the chilling wind. I turned and saw him at the very end of the pier. He was steering his wheelchair at an open space in the railing where a ladder led down to the dark undulations of the sea. He arrived at the opening and I stiffened, fully expecting to see him roll off, tumble, plunge, splash and, chair and all, sink. But he just lurched forward in his seat and fell back again, a small ridge having blocked the wheels.

I ran. He reversed until he had gone the width of the pier and was stopped by the railing behind him. He was planning another run at the opening. I rounded the turn and raced along the pier as he began to roll forward in his second attempt to throw himself into the sea. We both headed for the same place. My shoes hammered the boards and now I could hear the purr of the engine turning the wheels of his chair. I wasn't going to make it. He was there, ahead of me, bumping against and surmounting the ridge, about to fall, falling, and then I had him, my hands like claws pulling him backward until we both went sprawling onto the rough planks, the empty chair rolling away as if in terror.

Peering Over the Edge

It was much later that evening, after Sol had finally gone home and Vida had arrived, done her job and left, that Hilary and I were at last alone with him. My fear was that he wouldn't talk to me. He had refused to speak during that awful drive home. This is hardly surprising given the way Sol badgered him. What in hell did he think he was doing? Had he no consideration for other people? Was this the way for a grown man to behave? At last my concern for Beryl's feelings, to say nothing of Jacob's, forced me to tell my uncle to shut up.

I brought Hilary into Jacob's bedroom that evening, hoping if he refused to talk to me, he would at least talk to her. First, though, I settled Beryl at the dining room table with a cup of coffee, a pair of scissors and a pile of her magazines. Earlier I had taken Vida into the kitchen and told her what Jacob had tried to do. She widened her eyes and put a hand to her mouth. I warned her not to question him about it and she said, "You crazy? No way." Events had dislodged my poor mother from the surface of things where she was so quick to formulate memorable idiocies. Now she was submerged in a jagged state of serious concern. Finally she decided that the near disaster that afternoon was due to nothing more than Jacob's semi-blindness. He just didn't see where he was going. But her worried look hadn't lifted.

Sol knew exactly what had happened. At first, as we took Jacob back to the car, he restrained himself, then, he turned and glowered at me.

"Why did you leave him alone?"

I took him aside. "Because he asked me to."

"What? Because he asked you to?"

"Yes, and in the same pissed-off tone of voice you're using now. That's why it was hard to refuse. He's maddened by everyone always watching over him and taking care of him as if he were a child. He simply wanted to be alone for a bit."

"To drown himself."

"I couldn't know that any more than you did when you bought him that wheelchair."

He glowered again, a short, bald bull-of-a-man ready for a fight. "You're blaming me, are you?"

"If I am, it makes about as much sense as you blaming me."

Amid the swoop and cry of gulls over the corrugated sea, I walked back to the station wagon where Hilary was standing with her hand on Jacob's shoulder while my mother, a sad, baffled, worried little woman, waited for us to come and lift her husband into the back seat so she could take him home.

It would all settle down and things would be OK again. This was what I told myself. Sol, after all, could drive anyone into the sea. What I had to do was clear. I would take my father in hand and make his life livable. First, though, I must get him to talk to me.

Jacob was propped up against a hill of pillows. I was seated on the bed at his feet, Hilary on a chair by his side. From the window I could see below us the night jewelry of city lights clustered like a bright canopy while the sky above was ink-dark and starless. He saw none of this, of course. I couldn't be sure how well he saw me, just six feet away.

"Listen, Dad, I want you to promise you'll never try that again."

In a sour-faced silence, he gave great attention to the empty space before him.

"Or everyone will be watching you even more carefully than before," I said. "You don't want that, now, do you?"

As if it was a great chore, he drew in and released a deep breath.

"Dad?"

Someone was using a hammer on another floor.

"Do you, Dad?"

Hilary spoke up. "We understand what it's like. You have no control over your life. And no privacy. And precious few pleasures."

"He can be read to," I was quick to remind her.

"What good is that?" he snapped. "Vida gets all the words wrong and Beryl keeps losing her place."

"We can rent cassettes with actors reading novels."

"Vida tried that. They read so slowly my mind wanders. I have to go at my own pace."

To this I found nothing to say for I knew how fast he could read.

"And you don't even have someone to talk to," Hilary added. We were all past pretending that my mother could fill such a role. But her unspoken name prompted me.

"Anyway, Dad, about what happened at the pier... Well, there's Beryl."

Hilary nodded. His face went out of shape as he rubbed it with his one good hand.

"What would she do without you?"

The hammering started again, six quick taps, the last two faster than the others. My father laid his head back, exhausted, as if he had done the hammering. Yet when he spoke again it was in that controlled fury of old when he railed against taxes, anyone who worked for him and Richard Nixon.

"That woman is driving me crazy," he raged. "She still says I'd be walking by now if I put my mind to it. Can you believe that? We fight all the time about everything. I'm sick of it. So bored I could scream. From breakfast to dinner is a lifetime. When I wake up I think, Oh, God, another day to get through. Beryl watches TV all the time and now that she's getting deaf, she always has it top volume. Vida talks all the time about nothing at all. The weather, the Royal Family, the plot of some stupid film. And when the two of them aren't driving me mad and I have a rare moment of peace, Sol drops by. You ask if I've thought of Beryl? Do you think I want to make her life a living hell for the next twenty years? I'm not even a proper husband to her. Do you understand me? Not even a proper husband. With me gone, she'll grieve, get up and go on. People do. Millions have. She won't be alone. There's always you and Hilary. And maybe some day there'll be grandchildren. Of course I think of Beryl. And I think of Russell. And I think of you." He tried and failed to pat Hilary's hand and she quickly took hold of his. Now he was struggling to catch his breath.

"It's all right," she said.

"Are you OK, Dad?"

Another vast intake of air. "I need you... to do something."

She held his hand now with both of hers. "What?"

"I need you to help me end my..."

"*No,*" I answered before he could ask it.

"I want you to..."

"*Wait,*" I flung out.

"Go on, what?" Hilary asked him.

"Get me something to take."

"Oh, dear. Jacob, look. The one thing you don't want is for Russell to go to prison. People have done. You know that. To help is against the law. Maybe it shouldn't be but it is."

He thought about this. "Then get me a gun. Get me a gun."

"Christ, that would really get us in trouble," I said. "Who but me could have given it to you?"

Jacob made that noise as if he had tasted something vile. He rubbed his face out of shape again and took another deep breath. Then he shouted. "Don't you understand, I can't take it any longer."

"Shhhh." I glanced at the closed door.

"Of course we understand," she said.

He looked more deeply in despair than I had ever seen him. "No you don't. You don't give a damn. You don't care."

Hilary looked at me, her face cracked with pain.

Lift us out of this, I thought as we sank into a stifling silence. Say something. But there wasn't a thing in this sad, mad world I could think of to say.

"OK, Dad, tell me how it's done without Hilary and me getting arrested."

"Do I have to solve every problem?"

"No, just this one."

"Get someone else then."

"To do what, go to jail?"

"Don't be foolish," he grumbled.

"Then what?"

"To come up here and..."

"And... what? Kill you gang-land style?"

I smiled at this nonsense and to encourage him to do so, Hilary smiled, as well. But he wasn't looking at her. He was looking at me. His face brightened.

"Why not?" he asked, glancing through the window as if there, almost within reach, was something only he could see: The Promised Land, hovering over New Jersey.

"Yes," he said, more determined than I had ever seen him, "why not?"

Gently Down the Stream

We stopped at the fence with its barbed wire curling along the top and peered through the metal grid at the assortment of yachts and houseboats lying at anchor. No one was in sight. The gate to the fence was locked.

"Could you live like that?" Hilary asked.

"How tough can it be? You pack a lunch and sail off for the day."

"You nit. I'm talking about your father."

"Ah." Beneath a fleet of white clouds, the Hudson River, spread out before us, was flowing down through the center of another splendid day. For a moment I had taken Hilary with me onto its still waters to sail peacefully upstream away from all care. It was a modest daydream. She by my side, me at the helm, we made our way through the shadow of the George Washington Bridge, a hum of cars in the sky above. Then she spoke and like a tooth ache, real life returned. "Could I live like that? I'd have to be in his shoes first to find out."

"I expect you know the answer even now."

"Do I?"

"Yes."

"OK, I couldn't live like that."

"Then how can he?"

We had walked beyond the boat basin where only a low railing separated us from the river.

"People find a way," I said.

"Or they don't."

There were empty benches facing the river and we sat on one to watch a gray tugboat inch its way upstream.

"Is it right for us to force him to live like that?" she persisted.

"We're not forcing him."

"We are."

"Look, in the end everyone is left to his fate. That's life."

As if to a child: "Russ, if we refuse to help then we leave him to his fate. If we step in, we save him from his fate."

We were back again, engaged in our ongoing debate. Did I support euthanasia? Hilary did. I wasn't sure. What about the slippery slope as the young and healthy push the sick and elderly into easeful death to inherit their wealth or simply to be rid of them? Was the possibility of such abuse worse than the surely greater abuse of denying thousands an escape from a life they have found utterly intolerable? Or denying them the comfort of at least knowing that a timely end could be theirs even if they chose not to take it? And then there's the very real chance of going to prison for offering assistance. To be convicted for doing for my father what he's begging me to do? If I refuse, almost certainly it's because I'm afraid to do it, afraid to sit by his side as I hold his hand, waiting for the end. If the law is wrong, Hilary asked, should we continue to obey it? She thought not. I was not so sure. Thou shalt not kill. But this was written in a book two thousand years out of date. And anyway it's a mistranslation of 'thou shalt not murder' which, as Hilary pointed out, is "streets away" from killing someone who wants to be killed, asks to be killed, sees death as a blessing and whose intolerable anguish will be extended indefinitely if he is not given his wish.

"Why," I asked, "did I have to get involved with someone who majored in philosophy?" This made her smile and she replied:

"I'd need a Ph.D. to answer that."

"Well, I maintain my original position."
"Which is?"
"I don't like this argument because I'm going to lose it."
"It's not an argument," she said.
For a moment nothing moved, the tugboat, the clouds, even the river. An alert squirrel stared at us from three feet away. He didn't move either.
"OK," I said. "I know what we should do but I just can't do it. End of story."
A helicopter fluttered towards us like a *deus ex machina* come to save me and then, changing its mind, fluttered away.
"If we do nothing we lack compassion."
"So what do you suggest?"
"I suggest you ask Sol," she said.
"To help? Are you kidding?"
"We have nothing to lose."
"You think because he's family he won't turn me in?"
"You haven't done anything."
"Do you realize what I'm asking? I'm asking him to help me help my father kill himself. Even in *my* family this is an unusual request. He'd never do it."
"He might. He just might."
"Ha!"
Under a lucid sky, she stared across the river at what was a calm, dispassionate but distant world.
"Oh, Russ, I feel so guilty not doing anything."
"Do you?"
"Yes, and so should you."
"There, you see, I knew I'd lose this argument."
"It's not an argument," she said.

Whenever I visit the Upper East Side it's always a revelation. Better dressed with more style not to mention a bit haughty, yet without the rakish character of the approachable, slightly run down Upper West Side where my parents live and where I had just come from. Walking across Central Park, I made my way through the fenced-in Quiet Zone, its carpet of grass strewn with the living as they lay in their bikinis as if practicing for death. I emerged on Fifth Avenue, making my way east for several more blocks until I rang the bell in a small building on a narrow, tree-lined street in the Upper Sixties. Through the intercom, an indignant voice ask, "Yeah, who's there?"

"It is I, Hamlet, the Dane."

"Russell?"

"Speaking."

The door buzzed like angry bees. I stepped into a cool lobby with chairs chained to the walls and I rose, an inch at a time, in a grumbling elevator facing the door that had closed when I entered and each time, at the fourth floor, a door behind me opened instead so that I had to turn around, feeling outwitted and a bit silly because each time there stood Sol to witness my confusion.

His apartment was neat and clean with hideous furniture patched with white doilies. He offered tea which I didn't want but accepted while he proceeded to explain, as he had several times before, how he came to acquire each mind-numbing piece of bric-a-brac that filled the room.

When I brought up Jacob's plight, we talked about him at length with me stressing the hopelessness of it all and Sol up-beat about people's ability to overcome dreadful misfortunes. He mentioned a man he'd read about who could only move his left eyelid and yet managed to dictate an entire novel. I doubted whether this would be of much comfort to my father. Sol demanded to know why. Because,

I shot back, he's not into creative lid-blinking. That provoked a good deal of serious wrangling, each of us trying to pull the other in the opposite direction until Sol, in his immaculate certainty, assured me that what his brother wanted more than anything else in life was to find a way to occupy himself. I blurted out that what my father wanted more than anything else in life was to find a way to end his life. My father had told me this himself, begging me to aid him in the task, and I had come here now to ask my uncle, as a friend, a pharmacist, and someone who surely had compassion for his own brother, if he could possibly help.

Sol looked at me in my new role as a total stranger.

"You want me to help you kill my brother?"

"No," I fired back, stunned that his entrenched opposition had inspired me to launch into a defense of something I hadn't yet convinced myself was right.

"You don't?"

"Well, I didn't. Until I saw what Jacob is going through..."

Raising his voice: "He's not dying, damn it. Euthanasia is for when you're dying in pain. He's not in pain. He doesn't even need an aspirin, for crysake."

Sitting forward in his seat he gripped with each hand the carved lion head at the front of each armrest. In his jaw was the angry knot of small knowledge.

"That makes it even worse," I whispered. "That he's suffering like this and not dying. If he were dying, he'd have something to look forward to."

"You're talking nonsense"

"I'm talking about how his life has become a misery."

He sat back grandly in his chair. "Trust me. People find a way."

My tea was cold. I had a headache. It was time to get the hell out. I was about to stand up when, from the bedroom, came the ticking of a demented clock. Sol's face softened as Brillo emerged like a circus act. The rear of his body was held aloft by a white harness suspended between a pair of wheels that were pulled along unsteadily on the wooden floor by the dog's front legs. Sol leaned down and, with both hands, fondled the long head, scratched behind the long ears and gingerly patted the hoisted rump.

"Finally did it," he said.

"Did what?"

"Made the appointment. Poor Snoogles. Can hardly see. Can you, baby? Walks into things. Doesn't eat. Slips and falls. Yeah, I'm taking him to the vet Wednesday morning."

I stared, too dumbfounded to speak. He looked up.

"This is different," he snapped. "This is totally different."

Shelf Life

The taxi I hired sounded as if it might not make it to the next corner. When it did, I took it as a good sign and persuaded myself to stay put rather than chance another and perhaps even less road-worthy vehicle. We rattled our way through shabby streets, past dingy shops and the occasional empty lot filled with junk. Instead of the glorious multiplicity of grays that gave Paris such color, here in Michoacan, were all the gun metal pigments and ash-colored textures of despair. An old man leading a burro across the street forced my driver to apply his brakes. At least, now, I knew he had brakes. In a doorway stood a woman silhouetted by a red table lamp. Behind her was a double bed. Young men seated on the curb scowled at us as we went by while down the street an old woman carried a basket on her head.

Much later, in the hills, the road climbed to a great height with a wall of rock on one side and a sheer drop on the other. We passed a number of wooden crosses indicating where a car had gone over the edge and the occupants killed. The driver blew his horn at each curve. Reaching a plateau of flat scrubland we gained speed with an alarming increase of knocking and rattling. The relentless vibrations made me bob and weave as if in a prize ring. An empty beer bottle kept rolling against my left shoe while the rosary hanging from the rear-view mirror danced and snapped in the air. I was about to ask the driver to slow down when we were stopped by a congestion of cows.

In any case, he was prepared to drive no further because of the conditions of the roads up ahead due to the earthquake. He had warned me back at the airport. Beyond a certain point he would go "no mas." This was clearly it.

I paid him and climbed out with my gadget bag and knapsack. The taxi drove off and I was left in a vast nowhere amid colossal mooing. Only then did I notice I wasn't alone. Barefoot peasants seated on a hill watched me with an almost sadistic lack of concern. It had been a relief to be given an assignment that got me out of New York, even if it did take a miracle to arrange, but waiting now in the sun, thirsty and abandoned, I was not so sure.

I'd been told that a bus came this way on some days and on some days not. I took it as a good sign that there were peasants waiting as I was, unless they weren't waiting but just sitting. In Mexico it was often hard to tell the difference. Half an hour later a junkable wreck appeared and, with a grinding seizure, stopped. On top were crates of live chickens and someone standing in back holding a goat with a rope. The peasants bestirred themselves and climbed in. They gave the driver money. The driver gave them money. When I climbed onboard, the same exchange took place. I found a seat beside a man whose beard was like frost and who occasionally mouthed a pint bottle of tequila. There was a grinding reverberation and the wreck belched forward. The driver gave gutteral yells as he leaned from the window and slapped the side of the bus with his hand. The blockade of cows gradually parted and we reverberated on our way.

A car jammed with people came toward us with a mattress roped to the top. Another car appeared with people seated on the roof, clinging to the luggage rack. A number of donkeys ambled into sight, laden with goods and led by their owners. Without exception, everyone we met was traveling in the opposite direction. At last, when we finally saw the town, it was all too clear why they were fleeing from it. Most of the buildings had been shaken to pieces. We in the bus stared at the wreckage. No one spoke.

I spent two whole days photographing the ruins of that place as people milled about or sobbed in grief. Here and there, walls were missing and the inside of houses had spilled their pathetic secrets into the streets while, elsewhere, entire buildings were hollowed out by a collapsed roof. The Red Cross had set up tents for the injured and at night we all slept outdoors for fear of further tremors. In the evening, as I lay in my sleeping bag, I heard *Old Man River* played, one slow note at a time, on a twelve string guitar. Yet, with so much misery all around me, I kept conjuring up, as I drifted off, a vision of my father in his wheelchair tumbling into the deep.

It was warm even in the small hours, which was a blessing, until there came a sweet, nauseating smell. I had shot five rolls by then and was ready to leave. The odor became so foul that instead of walking through the center of town to get back to the road and the bus, I took the long way through the outskirts.

Amid rusting junk and wooden shacks and naked children, I came to a graveyard half of which had slid away in the quake. Coffins were exposed, some had split open and their occupants thrust into the light. I didn't want to look yet I shot another roll.

In Mexico City, preparing to leave for the airport, I phoned Hilary to tell her I missed her but never got a chance because she told me at once that my father was more depressed than ever.

"And your mother's in a state," she said, her voice stressed and with a touch of anger, "which doesn't help Jacob at all. We must jolly well do something. I don't know what. But something."

Anyone meeting my father now would assume the stroke had deprived him of speech. Most of the time he remained perfectly still like someone sitting for his portrait and clearly displeased at how long it was taking. Beryl couldn't get him to speak and had given up trying. Vida was able to extract a few words but doing so only seemed to deepen the depression. When Hilary sat beside him and spoke of England and her childhood, he would nod from time to time. Nothing more. Me, he refused even to look at. And I knew why.

My haven from all this was our three room apartment in the Village and it was there we retreated each evening. The pianist had long since done with Schubert and these days he sent down to us the ceaseless, glittering clatter of Scarlatti. We loved few things better than sprawling on the couch, after dinner, with a glass of wine, listening. But it was in this very place, in this most inner of sanctums, where I kept deluding myself into thinking I would somehow get free of a decision I was determined not to make but knew I couldn't avoid, that Hilary produced a surprise. It changed everything. After much hesitation, she took from her shoulder bag and put on the coffee table, next to a circular stain in the unpolished wood, something she had found in my mother's medicine cabinet. A bottle of Nembutal. It had a large, white, child-safe cap. The design of the label was all too familiar. There were many such labels on the far too many bottles in my parents' apartment. They all came from my uncle's pharmacy. This label said there was still some shelf life left. I didn't touch it.

While I was in Mexico, Hilary had researched and written an article on an American porno queen who had become involved in a sex scandal involving children. As a result of the world-wide publicity, she ended her life by swallowing a large number of these very same pills.

"I guess we didn't have to ask Sol after all," Hilary said.

"She used Nembutal?"

"That's right."

"I thought you couldn't get them anymore."

"Oh yes you can, even though some doctors and pharmacists pretend you can't."

"Well, well."

"Do you want to know how many she took?"

"No," I said. "How many?"

"They're not sure. The coroner said she swallowed the contents of a bottle. But it may have been half empty. When full it held twenty pills."

"Like that one?"

"Like that one."

I still didn't touch it.

"Look," she said, pointlessly straightening a magazine on the coffee table. "When I saw that bloody bottle, it simplified things. The whole problem changed. Or at least it changed me. Russ, I've decided I don't want you to do this thing. I thought I did but then I became truly frightened. You see, it's real now. Look, I don't want you to go to jail." She took my hand. "Let's not do this."

"And my father?"

Looking wretched. "I don't know." She glanced away, then back again. "Maybe, after a while, he'll change his mind."

"He's never done that, ever."

With her reversal, my desire to do the right thing, if it was the right thing, collapsed.

"Look, don't *you* get depressed now." She moved close and put her arms around me. "Have I let you down? I'm sorry."

"No, no, of course not."

"You sure?"

"Positive." I kissed her.

"Ummm," she said, when our lips parted, "not a moment too soon."

"It's just that..."

"What?" She looked worried again.

I smiled. "The time is out of joint. O cursèd spite..."

She nodded. "It certainly is."

The sudden lifting of mood let in an idea I hadn't thought of before.

"You know something, we're wrestling with a decision and having all this trouble and the reason we're having all this trouble is it's not our decision."

"You mean it's his?"

"Yes. It's not a matter of 'That ever I was born to set it right.' It's his decision. So let him decide. Now it'll be real for Jacob, as well. So that's what I'll do. Fuck it. I'll show him this." As I lifted the bottle it felt terribly light in the palm of my hand.

"Oh, God. I hope you're doing the right thing."

"Look, the pills were in his bathroom. He might have found them himself and swallowed them without anyone's help. Maybe now he will. It doesn't have to be the right decision. All it has to be is his decision."

"But we're deciding something, too."

"Yes, we've decided to let him make the decision."

She thought for a moment. "Maybe then things will change for him as they did for me."

"Let's hope so."

"Yes, lets."

"Then we're agreed?"

Softly she said, "Agreed."

It was only then I became aware that, for a while now, the music from above had ceased.

Closing Down

"Please do something," Beryl pleaded. "Talk to him. I can't live like this."

Holding a mug of morning coffee in one hand and the phone in the other, I said we all knew how awful it was for her. He's hit a low point but he'll pull out of it. In time, he'll come to realize that although he is trapped in a wheelchair, the important thing is he is still alive. Hilary winced as I said this. I shrugged in return, not knowing what to say to my mother except to deceive her with hope at least for a while longer.

"All right," I said, finally. "I'll talk to him. I was planning to go up there today anyway... No, Hilary's doing a story on air-traffic control. She'll be on the phone all day probably... They're like traffic policemen of the sky. They see to it that two planes don't land at the same place at the same time... Yes, Ma," I said, glancing at the bottle of Nembutal that was still sitting on the table. "I said I'll talk to him and I will... OK, OK, I'm on my way right now."

The taxi I hired went straight up Fifth Avenue. Seen through my side door window, the glossy shops and busy pedestrians seemed as remote as some city in Spain. In the rear-view mirror, my driver's eyes caught mine. He had gray hair and was the color of milk chocolate. "Eyes got good news," he said, when we were well into Central Park. "The sweet Load, Jesus, loves ya. He dad fo yo sins. All he axed is confess yo sins and accept his love and yo will live for-eber. That's all he axed. I found religion and I want to share it. I want to share it wit de hoe world."

When I finally climbed out in front of my parents' building and gave him a big tip, he said, "May de Load bless you and keep you. An tanks for listening to my little talk."

"A few more blocks," I said, "and you would have converted me."

With a tooth-gapped laugh: "Maybe next tam."

"How is he?" I asked Vida, when I entered the apartment.

"Not good. I try to feed him and we're at war."

"Won't eat?"

"No way. You better talk to him."

"Ah, there you are," my mother said, emerging from the bedroom and taking me into the kitchen. "Vida's stealing things."

"Oh, god, not again."

"Yes, again."

"No, I mean you're not starting all that again."

"I tell you she's stealing. I had five umbrellas and they're gone."

"You didn't have five umbrellas."

"I did so have five umbrellas."

When she first accused Vida some months ago, my first thought was that it might be true. But when she told me what was missing, I pointed out that no one steals toilet paper. And sure enough we found the six rolls in question on the top shelf of their bedroom closet. The missing earrings were more worrying and I again became suspicious of Vida until they turned up in Beryl's sewing box a week later. When this in no way lessened my mother's distrust, I realized that my father's condition was beginning to affect her. Or was it old age? Or both.

"So if she didn't take them," Beryl insisted, "where are they?"

The walk-in closet in the living room was, as usual, too cluttered to enter. I removed several boxes and rolled out the four-wheel coat rack. Inside, among suitcases and file cabinets, I poked about until I found, in a small wastepaper basket that had somehow been pushed behind a trunk, five ladies' umbrellas. When I emerged into the light holding them up as proof, she said, "Sometimes she moves things around, puts them in the front closet so she can take them out."

"Take them out?"

"Of the house. When I'm not looking."

"I don't think so."

"Tsh, you never believe anything I say."

"Look, they're still here."

"For how long?"

"Forever, if you hide them behind the trunk in the closet."

"Oh forget it."

I followed her into the dining area.

"So tell me, how are you doing?"

Angrily, she waved me away. "I had to go to doctor what's-his-name two times last week."

"Has the infection cleared up?" I asked, greatly doubting it because of the rosé tint in the white of her left eye.

"So stupid."

"Who?"

"Doctors. Two times I had to go to what's-his-name and for what? Such a waste of time when I could have been home doing something important."

"Like what?"

"Like keeping an eye on Vida."

When I entered the bedroom, Jacob was seated in his wheelchair looking through the window and not seeing the river or the flatlands of New Jersey nor the distant hills of Pennsylvania. Vida had just finished combing his hair. Late for her next job, she just had time to look at me, look at him, raise her eyes imploringly to heaven and make for the door.

"How are you, Dad?"

No answer. I sat on the windowsill and said I had something to tell him. He didn't respond. I explained that Hilary had found something of interest in the medicine cabinet. Still no response. I told him what it was. For the first time in I-don't-know-how-long, he looked at me.

"How many are there?" he asked.

"Twenty. It's unopened."

"Is that enough?"

"I think so."

His eyes were furtive with doubt. "Are you going to give them to me?"

"Are you certain you want to go ahead with it?"

"Would you like something to eat?" my mother asked, standing in the doorway.

"No, Ma, I had breakfast."

"Will you stay for lunch?"

"Perhaps."

"Say yes."

"Yes."

"That's better." She came into the room and started hunting through a dresser drawer filled with a tossed salad of under things.

"Ma, what are you looking for?"

"Scissors."

"Would they be in there?"

"Could be anywhere."

"Here." I snatched them up from where they were standing with a number of pencils in a drinking mug and handed them to her.

Jacob waited to be sure she was gone. Then his eyes found mine and he nodded.

My stomach dropped an inch. "Are you saying... are you really saying you do want to go ahead with it?"

Fraught with impatience as if forced to converse with a dim child, he managed a small, hard yes. I could only sit and stare at him. A shadow flicked across his body. I turned and saw a gull floating away.

"Will you help?" he asked.

The intrusive sound of the TV assaulted us from the living room. There was canned laughter, loud mumbling and brazen trombones followed by the onslaught of an orchestra. I went to the door and discovered it didn't shut properly. A large clothes bag that had hung for years from a hook, permanently blocking a full-length mirror, had warped the door with its weight so that it no longer fitted the frame. I went into the living room and reduced the sound to a reasonable level but Beryl said that now she couldn't hear. I went back and slammed the bedroom door a few times in vain, finally leaving it ajar.

"I shouldn't have asked," he said, when I returned to the window sill.

His face wore a fixed grimace of loneliness and fear. The plan to free ourselves as accessories by letting him decide his fate and, if he wished, close out his own life, fell to pieces.

"I'll help," I said.

"I don't want you to get into trouble."

"I won't, don't worry."

"If anyone finds out..."

"Look, either you let me help you or the pills stay in my pocket. That's final."

"You sure?"

My mouth was dry. "I'm sure."

He reached for my hand. I leaned forward so he could take it and he clutched the ends of my fingers and moved them up and down.

But then the unexpected happened as it unfailingly does whenever I'm certain of what's coming next. His spirits lifted. He sent Vida in a taxi down to the Princeton Club to bring back a bowl of vichyssoise which he claimed was the best in New York. Then he had Beryl order a hot pastrami on rye with mustard from *Fine and Shapiro* and, the day after, for breakfast Vida had to stop off at *Zabar's* to get him cream cheese, lox and bagels. There were letters he had me write to old friends saying how fondly he remembered them and how he hoped all was well. Then, at his request, I read aloud from Swinburne and Rupert Brooke and that same afternoon he wanted me to open a volume of photos by Henri Cartier-Bresson and describe each shot until he was able to remember what he once loved but could no longer see. He asked me to do the same with a book by Alfred Stieglitz, and when I came to that famous one of a docked steamship with a crowd of people on deck pressed against the railing, he reminded me that before releasing the shutter, Stieglitz had waited half an hour until the man in the straw hat looked down. This enabled sunlight to bounce off the disk of crown and brim, giving the picture a much needed center of interest.

Because the bottle of Nembutal was not referred to again, Hilary and I became hopeful that this savoring of favorite food and revisiting old interests would make him realize enough remained of the pleasures of life to make him think twice about death. I didn't know if it was a good sign or not but next Saturday Jacob wanted us all to be present at a family dinner for which I was sent to buy expensive bottles of wine.

Most of the seven assorted relatives who attended that evening felt certain he was his old self again or why else would he go out of his way to throw a dinner party? What they failed to realize was the Jacob of old might throw a dinner party but never for relatives. When I was young, a few such rare events were held in our house on Long Island. But only for businessmen and their wives who came all the way from Manhattan, providing jokes and laughter which I greatly enjoyed. Those memories still reach me as does the light of distant stars that have long since burnt out. But this hasty gathering, for family only, was highly unusual and so it seemed to me that Jacob was most certainly not his old self.

Of course he did instruct Vida on how exactly to cut up his meat and, refusing help, groped, flat-handed, along the tablecloth each time he wanted to find his wine glass. The rest of the time he peered with effort at whoever was talking, trying to make out their features.

Selma had been invited which surprised me for he always professed to dislike his sister due to a number of unspecified but never forgotten slights and disloyalties. I found her loud but amusing and her husband, Nat, careful, well-groomed and someone in whom the flame of spontaneity had long since blown out. Selma saw herself as, and perhaps once was, a sexy lady. This was why she still wore revealing tight slacks which now, unfortunately, disclosed what almost anyone else would wish hidden, and whose side pockets were permanently pulled open like mouths gasping for air. Sol, of course, had been invited and was insufferably self-congratulatory, referring frequently to the prediction, which no one remembered him making, that Jacob would soon recover his good spirits and all would be well. Each time he said this he gave me a knowing I-told-you-so smile.

My mother had cooked what, for her, was a surprisingly edible meal. She offered us a weight-watchers version of sour cream for our baked potatoes, claiming it was fat free to which a skeptical Selma replied, "Yeah, the fat's free to spread all over."

"You got that right," Vida agreed, patting her not exactly flat stomach and eliciting a disapproving look from my uncle who thought hired people should not speak unless spoken to.

"Is there anyone not dieting these days?" Sol asked.

"Yeah, the Queen of England, from the look of her," Selma replied.

Hilary and Selma now got into a discussion about Queen Elizabeth while Sol told my mother about the personal tragedy he had suffered in having to put down his poor little one.

"Who?" she asked.

"My dog, Brillo."

"Oh, oh, oh."

"He wanted me to do it. I could tell by the way he looked at me."

"You put him out of his misery?"

"Yes, I told you, I put him down."

Beryl nodded approvingly. "Good."

"It broke my heart."

"Of course."

"What?" Selma asked, having overheard from the other end of the table. "You killed that little dog? Oh, you cruel man."

My uncle flared up. "He was sick, blind and paralyzed."

Selma, proudly: "I fed my cat with an eye dropper to the very end."

"Maybe Sol didn't have an eye dropper," I said.

"You're the cruel one," Sol growled. "You made your cat suffer."

"I did not."

"You did so."

"Do they put animals to sleep in England?" Selma wanted to know.

"Yes, they do," Hilary answered.

"You're joking? I thought they loved animals in England."

"Funnily enough that's the reason they do it."

"Do what?" asked my mother.

"When I was small I had an Airedale," Nat said.

Everyone looked at him.

"And you put him down?" Sol asked.

"No, no, he ran away finally." Nat subsided into another long silence.

"We show more kindness to cats and dogs," my father said, with real feeling, "than we do to people."

An uncomfortable pause was broken by Hilary saying, "True."

"Very true," I added.

"Well, I'm against killing," Selma insisted. "Man, beast or whatever."

"Oh, there's so much crime these days," Beryl lamented, shaking her head.

I seized the chance to lighten things up. "Did you know that in New York we have more criminals than there are people to steal from. It's awful. Thieves get into each other's way breaking into the same house."

"Thugs," said Hilary, "are reduced to mugging one another."

"Pickpockets lift each other's wallets."

"Murderers," she continued..."

"Do each other in," I added. "How sad when a big city can't provide enough victims to go around."

"How shaming

"It's a scandal."

"No joy there."

"Only in America."

My father was smiling. For the first time in I don't know how long, he was actually smiling.

The next morning, while I was having coffee, my mother phoned again. This time the TV wasn't working and she asked if I would come and take a look at it. I did. The battery in the remote control needed changing. The smell of coffee was seductive and I stayed and had my second cup of the day.

Jacob had moved his wheelchair up to the table and was squinting his way through the family photo album with my mother attempting to help. I joined them and we all peered into our black and white past. Some were taken before I was born. There was my teenage mother so young and pretty as to be unrecognizable. She was sitting on the ugly tar roof of a building in New Jersey with Manhattan skyscrapers in the distance. There was my bald and impish grandfather, delighted with life as he stood by a fence in some unknown backyard. My dreaded grandmother, about to climb onto a trolley car, glanced back at us like a grim puritan setting off to squelch the pleasures of others. Uncle Sol, in his army uniform, glaring firmly into the camera, was at his combative best. My surprisingly thin father in white shirt sleeves looked up from his office desk, awash with papers, where he was sitting in front of a window magically aglow with underexposed light and through which one could see, across the street, pigeons on the roof of the 42nd Street Library. And there I was as a callow youth wearing an awful paisley, short-sleeved shirt and having recently suffered a near scalping at the barbershop. Like romantic trophies from a long forgotten knife fight were the forceps scars near each eye received in the battle of birth. There I sat in a crib with a one-eyed teddy, at a beach on a cardboard suitcase, and at the Cloisters, as a blond six-year-old in a dark beret, standing straight as a soldier and looking insufferably cute.

My mother named the person in every picture which was no help to my father and so I described each photo in detail. A few Jacob not only remembered but offered revealing details like which garden Grandpa was standing in (his next door neighbor's) and why Beryl was sitting on a roof in New Jersey (visiting a school friend) and that my awful paisley shirt was a birthday present from (guess who?) Uncle Sol.

While reminiscing, Jacob tried to draw Beryl into their shared past. He held her hand and asked if we still had his favorite shot of the two of them together on the boardwalk in Coney Island. But my mother had thrown it out, insisting it was a horrible picture of her.

"Remember," he asked, "when we walked barefoot along the sea shore?"

"When was that?"

"Years ago."

"We never did that."

"What are you talking about? We had to run from a big wave."

"I was there?"

"Of course, who else?"

"You're making it up."

"Try another memory," I suggested.

"How about the time we took a rowboat out on Candlewood Lake," Jacob said.

"That was in Central Park."

"We did that, too. This was a different time."

"That was the only time."

"Selma was with us and she lost a brooch in the water."

"That was in *Central* Park," she stressed.

"Oh, for crysake."

When we at last put the album away and had our coffee, Jacob told a story I had never heard before. It was about the trouble they had had getting married. The original plan was to have a proper ceremony. My grandmother, however, opposed the marriage because my mother wasn't Jewish. This spurred my father into attempting a *fait accompli*. A Rabbi they went to said: "Don't you know this is the Sabbath?" A minister asked if they had been baptized. Several others tried to talk them out of it because my mother was so young. The Registry Office was closed on Saturday. They spent hours going through the Manhattan phone book. For one reason or another they were turned down by everyone.

"I didn't know what to do," Jacob said.

My mother seemed annoyed by being reminded of it. "The four of us wasted all day at this. I tell you, it was really something."

"Who were the other two people?" I asked.

"The Feldmans," Jacob said.

"Who?"

"Our witnesses."

"Where'd you find them?"

He seemed surprised by this question. "They were friends."

"You never mentioned them before"

Beryl said: "We never saw them again."

"What was his first name?" Jacob asked her.

She waved the question away. “Oh, who cares.”

I was transfixed. “Well, what happened?”

About to sip his coffee, Jacob paused. “A French priest finally agreed to do it.”

“A French priest?”

“He was going back,” my mother explained, unhelpfully.

“Going back?”

“To Paris,” Jacob said. “He was leaving the next day and I think he liked the idea, in a mischievous way, of marrying someone he really shouldn’t have. We were lucky to find him.”

“I put my foot down,” my mother said, grimly. “I said, no more. If he don’t marry us, I’m goin’ home. I have better things to do.”

Beryl’s less then romantic response stunned me. She burned with smoldering outrage as if she had been involved in an atrocity instead of a wedding. Afraid to ask further questions, I kept still. The silence was like a glaring light on what I had once assumed was a happy occasion. Jacob looked grim and also said nothing. My mother took the plates to the sink and stacked the dishwasher. Then she went into the bedroom and in a short while we heard, from time to time, the rumble of her sewing machine.

“You still have those pills?” he asked.

Down below, people were sunning themselves on benches. Some lay on blankets on the grass. The exhaust pipe of a car was making a shadow line along the gray surface of the street. When I didn’t reply, he repeated the question.

“Yes. I have them.”

“Where are they?”

“I took them home.”

With some difficulty, he turned and looked at me.

“Tomorrow,” he said. “Tomorrow.”

Lost Ending

That evening was the absolute worst. At first we tried to talk then we sat in silence. Hilary didn't fancy making dinner so I went out into the rain and brought back a pizza and a bottle of wine. All that day I had felt so light-headed with fear, it was as if some cowardly part of me was straining to escape into an out-of-body experience. A constant vibration seemed to be emanating from the center of the earth.

When Hilary is under stress, any frightful possibility, however slim, becomes an imminent certainty. The future was clear: I would go to prison. She hated my plan even though she had agreed to it when I phoned from my parents' place urging her to decide quickly because my mother was wandering the apartment again, searching for god-knows-what and my father was a near catatonic again. She hated it because she was sure I would be spotted by someone and almost certainly be incriminated. Yet I squeezed out of her an agonized yes and I then told my mother that Hilary was happy to accept her offer of the two of them going shopping together. While they were looking at dresses in Macy's, I would avoid the doormen by entering the building through the underground garage, assist my father in his last act on this earth, leave unnoticed by the same route, and wait out of sight across the street for their return. Then, under the pretext of arriving to join them for dinner, admittedly two hours too early, I would bump into them at the elevator to be certain to be with my mother when the terrible discovery was made that Jacob, alone and unassisted, had ended his life.

Actually, I didn't care for the plan that much myself. It was simply the only one I could come up with. Of course, if Hilary now backed out that would be an end to it. But we were in this together and she didn't let me down. She just let me have it. I was bloody wrong, she said. And if this bloody plan proved to be a balls up, which it was almost certain to be, it would jolly well be my fault.

Neither of us got much sleep that night and the next day we had another fight when I told her if she didn't hurry, she would be late for her appointment with Beryl at Macy's. "I will not be late," she screamed, "and besides your mother has never been on time in her life." Then she added, "Oh, bother, I've lost a shoe." Five minutes later there was another explosion as I pressed her again. I was quite irrationally worried that Beryl might give up and go home. "Why are you getting at me?" she raged. "I'm going as fast as I can. I am not late. I am fucking on SHEDule." But when she pronounced the word as the English do, my overload of angst quickly dissolved making me an innocent bystander to our head-on collision. She was right, of course. She would be there on time and even if she was a bit late, what did it matter? When she left, finally, I wanted to run and bring her back because now, for the first time in my adult life, and more than anyone on earth, I was enormously alone.

The Seventh Avenue subway took me uptown much too fast. The first stop was 34th Street where, above ground, if all had gone according to plan, Hilary and Beryl had begun shopping. Next came Times Square but this express train didn't wait, as it often does, for the local to arrive. Then, after one long dash, I was at 72nd Street. For me, the end of the line.

The wind off the river made the legs of my trousers flap. I walked to the bottom of the road and around the side of the building to the garage. There was a window at the entrance through which I could see one of the bored attendants sitting at a desk reading a newspaper.

I hurried through a concrete chasm filled with parked cars to a locked door which I opened with a key. The hallway led past an empty laundry room with several machines churning softly. Then it happened. An elevator door opened and out stepped someone I knew. Mohammed, one of the maintenance men, without looking in my direction, walked the other way. I jumped in, hit button 29, rose to the lobby and stopped. The door rolled open and I heard the voices of two women chatting out of sight in the mailroom.

"Must dash," one of them said, "there's the elevator. See you Tuesday."

"Wait, Tuesday is pottery. Friday good?"

"Think so. I'll call you. Hold the door please."

It started rolling shut. I didn't move. Didn't breathe.

"Please hold the..."

Too late. I was on my way and the chances now of running into someone I knew were slim. At 28 my ascent slowed and at 29 stopped. I walked out, and there, to my left, was my mother. She wore her blue jacket and was holding a black handbag. As I stepped out of one elevator, she stepped into another. Both doors rolled shut. My mouth stayed open. I closed it. And breathed again. I waited for a while, gazing down the long hallway with its doors like prison cells. With one step after another I finally, softly, much too quickly, reached their maximum security cell and undid all the locks.

"Beryl just left," my father called out with alarm. "Did she see you?"

"No."

"Are you sure?" He looked doubtful.

"I'm sure."

"Because if she saw you..."

"She didn't see me."

He was seated in the wheelchair with his back to the living room window, listening to a cassette. Not in decades had I known him to put on music.

"I want you to do me a favor," he asked. "Will you make me, make us, an *Old Fashioned*?"

Though I knew how, he gave precise instructions anyway: in each glass three dashes of Angostura bitters, two shots of bourbon, one lump of sugar and wedges of three kinds of fresh fruit. At last I sat on the couch and he rolled into position, facing me. I held up my glass but, considering the occasion, couldn't think of an appropriate toast. He lifted his glass and said, "To happy endings."

"To happy endings."

He wore a dark blue sport jacket, gray slacks and an old pair of white slippers. Since his eyes were now all but useless, he no longer used his thick framed glasses.

"Did you bring them?" he asked.

"In my pocket."

"Good."

The music coming from the sound system was something by Delius, a composer who, for me, at his best, created works of genial insignificance. And this particular piece I had heard before. Yet now it was oddly compelling as if it had been rewritten by the composer since the last time I heard it. Impossible, of course, since he died in 1935.

"What's this called again?" I asked.

"The Walk to the Paradise Garden."

How unnervingly appropriate. It threw me for a moment while Jacob seemed embarrassed as if I had caught him in a secret romantic indulgence.

"It's lovely," I said.

He nodded and we listened together for a while as the afternoon breeze came though the window and turned a few pages of the dictionary lying open on the book stand.

"You must look after her when I'm gone."

"Of course I will."

"And be there if she needs you?"

"I promise."

"I wanted to have a last word with her but she was in a rush to leave. Last night I talked about the day we met. She said all that was in the past. I must now concentrate on getting well. She still thinks I don't try hard enough. So stubborn, that woman. She simply won't accept..." He looked miserable. "I was just trying to say goodbye."

"I know."

"I'm worried about her."

"How can you not be." I took another sip. He did too. "Look, Dad, you've shown, of late, a new interest in life. Why not give it a bit longer?"

With the hand he could still move, he clutched and rubbed his face.

"Why not go on for a while and see what it's like."

"I know what it's like. Look at me. I'm helpless, humiliated, frustrated, bored. If I have to live another week like this, I'll..." The music had stopped too, depleting the room with its silence.

"I do not want you to go."

My stomach knotted and the threat of tears mounted like a groundswell.

"You know what I found in a book of quotations?"

Unable to speak, I shook my head.

"I asked Vida to read out what they had on death. She came up with this... let's see now, how does it go? Something like... if God was suddenly condemned to live a life which he has inflicted on me... He would kill himself."

"Who said that?"

"Alexander Dumas."

A door slammed in the hallway.

"Would you like a refill?"

"No, we're losing time," he said. "Let's go."

"Now?"

"Now."

"Why the rush?"

"Because I have no idea how long it will take."

There was nothing I could think of to say. In the bedroom, he rolled into position beside the night table where a glass of water stood on a coaster under the lamp. He was squinting. I adjusted the Venetian blinds to close the bars of sunlight across his face. He had that expression I had often seen when he was cramped in thought over some small matter. Yet his calm amazed me. I wasn't managing half as well. I had a moist forehead and a dry throat. I sat on the bed, stood up, removed my jacket and sat down again. A few deep breaths didn't help.

"Are you all right?" he asked.

"Not too bad if you consider what I'm doing."

"What are you talking about? You're not doing anything. You're an assistant, that's all."

"Always trying to lower my standing."

"Always trying to raise a smile." Patting my knee. "There's valium around here some place. Help calm you down. Go on. Look for it. I'll wait

Amazing. Even now, he was the father, I was the child. I felt like a tourist visiting old battle grounds. Never had he quite believed I could go forth in the world and win. Once out of his sight, I would surely sink. And his job was to rush to my aid. When I brought home good news, he was just able to find it in himself to be pleased. Bad news was what he was made for. It brought out the best in him. He would come to the rescue whether he was needed or not. The smallest of worries were always large enough for him to want to help. Even now, at the very bottom rung of life, facing the abyss, he wanted to help.

"I'm fine, Dad, really. The important thing is how do you feel?"

"How do I feel?" He studied me with soulful eyes. "Sorry to be leaving you."

I took his hand. It was warmer than I had expected.

"And Hilary. Damn, I wish I had said goodbye to Hilary."

"I'll tell her. I'll say it for you."

He rubbed his face, then lowered his hand to the armrest of the wheelchair. "Some day --this is very important-- some day, when she's herself again, explain to Beryl why I did this, will you?"

"Yes, I will."

"Good."

Through the tilted blinds I could see, well beyond the river, a column of black smoke that rose and bent southward.

Turning to look at him, I blurted out, "I'd like to tell you what you've meant to me."

"Not now." The wind sent slight, sibilant gusts along the wall of the building.

"But there'll never be another time."

"I must do this now," he said, with some of his old petulance. "I don't want to go all soft. Let's start."

A police launch was moving up the river. A car horn sounded in the street. I slowly took the pills from the pocket of my jacket that lay folded beside me on the bed. Something dark with wings slipped by the window. I looked up and then down at the bottle again. Twenty yellow capsules. He asked to see them. I held them up.

He nodded. "OK, go on."

"I suppose it's no use my trying to..."

"Open it."

"Sure." I was just about to, then he stopped me.

"Wait. Let's see if I can do it. You're not supposed to be here, remember?"

He took the bottle, put it in his useless hand and pressed his useless fingers into a fist. The cap twisted off with a snap. He looked pleased. He picked out a wad of cotton and threw it away. After dumping the contents into the breast pocket of his shirt, he placed the empty bottle on the table. He had planned every move. Reaching into his pocket, he lifted out a single yellow capsule and put it in his mouth. He took the water from the table, looked at me, and before taking his first sip, lifted the glass in a silent toast.

Mortal Coil

I stayed to the end, frightened to the end, yet the entire experience, when I look back, was resolute and valiant. If he was frightened, as he took yet another pill, yet another sip, he didn't show it. If I showed it, he was careful not to notice.

We began by sitting in silence waiting for him to be rendered silent as well. This wouldn't do at all, I realized, this agonizing pause at the edge of an abyss. So I started talking and kept talking. I reminded him of the many things we had done together. With genuine bemusement, I spoke of how all my major interests in life were his, as if I had been somehow unable to find any of my own. I described the first time he took me on a photo jaunt when I couldn't make out what he was aiming his camera at or why. Only later did I learn that a toppled tree has its secrets and the chainsaw that cut through the rough-hewn log exposed to his camera the delicate rings of all its years. That a forgotten sand pile I wouldn't even have noticed had been sculptured by the wind into abstract art. That an abandoned shack, gutted and useless, could be rendered as poignant as music.

"Only if you move close enough," my father said.

He was quoting Frank Capa who had taken such chances photographing the invasion of Normandy and, years later, was killed in Vietnam.

As I talked he continued taking pills, but at longer and longer intervals. I had no idea how many were left for I had lost count. While I was describing the little photo studio I had constructed in our basement with two flood lights and a roll-down backdrop, he reached out in my direction. I at once took hold of his hand and held it. I fell silent. Time edged by. With his eyes shut, he tilted his head against the back of the wheelchair. He didn't move. With my free hand I felt his shirt pocket. A few pills remained.

"Dad?"

He grunted from far away.

"Dad, there's some left."

No reply. Silence. He became blurred. His face swam in a hot cloud of light that filled the room, flooding my eyes. Unable to see him, I gently removed my hand from his.

In the bathroom I washed and dried my face. His toothbrush hung in its slot beside my mother's. When I returned, his mouth was open as if in amazement. I leaned closer. He had stopped breathing. I took hold of his wrist, pressed the underside with my fingertips and felt nothing. It was over. The road from Odessa to Delancy Street to the Upper West Side had ended. I leaned forward, kissed him on the forehead, walked into the living room and refilled my drink.

The plan now was for me to leave, make my way to the basement and exit through the garage. But there was a problem. I couldn't leave. Not yet. I played the tape, hearing once more what we had listened to together. When it ended I didn't move. He had left me and I was free to go. Yet somehow I couldn't leave. Just could not tip toe away. So I didn't leave. I poured myself another drink and sat down.

When it finally came, the snap of the door lock startled me. Then the second lock was turned and in they came, carrying bundles. When she saw me, Hilary gave a yelp.

"Ah, there you are," my mother said. "Good, you're early. We can eat soon. Boy, I'm tired. Would you like a cup of coffee, honey?"

Hilary didn't answer her.

"Why are you here?" she demanded, barely containing her fright.

"He came early, that's all," Beryl replied on my behalf, having put her bundles down and dropped her coat over a chair. "How is Jacob?"

Hilary glanced in panic first at her, then at me.

"Napping," I told her. "He's napping."

"That's good." She went into the kitchen, calling out: "Coffee? Yes, no?"

Hilary stepped up to me, desperate for answers.

"I couldn't leave him," I whispered.

She, wide-eyed with fright, "Is he... ?"

"Yes."

"Then why not?"

"I'm sorry. I just could not walk out on him."

For a moment, she flared with the anger of terror. "Why not? Why not?"

"You have no idea what it was like."

"Leave now."

"Too late."

"Why?"

"Why do you think?" And I glanced toward the kitchen where a perky voice called out: "Who wants coffee?"

"No thanks, Ma."

"Hilary?"

Again she didn't answer, perhaps didn't hear. Leaning close to me again. "What do we do now?"

"Don't know."

"Oh, God."

She looked so forlorn, I was about to put my arms round her.

"The water's on," Beryl said, as she re-entered the room. "All that walking. Boy, I'm telling you. They should have chairs in Macy's." She sank onto the couch and looked at me. "So, what's new?"

Knotted with fear, Hilary walked in a tight circle, returning to where she had started.

"Sit down, honey," Beryl suggested, "sit down."

She seemed unaware of the tension in the room as she talked about her day on the town, what fun it all was, how they must do it again and how next time I should come too. Hilary finally subsided. She took tea while Beryl and I had coffee. We sat at the dining room table and talked. I couldn't focus on anything now except my mother. A bomb was about to decimate her life. Everything would change. Indeed, had already changed. And there she sat, chatting about dresses and prices. Though she was smartly made up, she looked far more drained than would have resulted from one day's exertions. Her chronically worried look, developed since Jacob's stroke, seemed more deeply etched than ever. Then all at once the vacuous monologue ceased. Reaching out she tapped my right hand which was what she did when she particularly wanted to get and hold my attention.

"He needs to find another doctor. This one he has is stupid."

"Honeycutt? He's a good doctor."

"Don't be silly," Beryl snapped. "When you call him he doesn't call back for days. Jacob can't see. He can't walk. She agrees with me. She says he's not getting better."

"She?"

"Her. What's her name? Vida. I want him to walk again. I tell you he's no good. We need a better doctor. I'm worried."

As gently as I could I reminded her that when I spoke to a specialist at the hospital he had told me that if a stroke patient didn't improve early on it was almost certain he wouldn't improve at all. Physiotherapy had helped a little but nothing more could now be done.

And then I found myself saying, "He'll have to live that way for the rest of his life."

"What Russ is telling you is true," Hilary added.

"In another country," Beryl began, then coughed, "maybe they know more. Maybe in England..." She kept looking at us, moving her gaze from one to the other.

Hilary took my mother's hand and told her that life was hard, that sadly bad things did happen to good people. Softly, like a piece of metal breathing in and out, the doorbell went ding dong. No one moved. Hilary looked at me with alarm.

"That's Vida," my mother said.

"You've got to open it," Hilary told me, as if I might refuse.

Scraping the chair back from the table, I got up and walked to the door.

"Hi." As always, she bustled in ebulliently. "Hi, Beryl. Hi, Hilary. Ohhhhh my, somebody's been shoppin'."

"They just came from Macy's," I explained.

"You too?"

"Not me."

"They use your money and leave you behind. Ha."

"Something like that."

"Sorry I late. Got held up wit my other job. I go right in now and see to Jacob."

She hurried off. I couldn't move. Hilary's face was stiff with dread. Beryl sat with her back to me, shaking her head sadly. From where I stood, I could see the gray river and the twin towers and the rush-hour traffic building up on the Highway.

There was a scream. Vida hurried back with a hand to her cheek. "I didn't touch him, didn't do nothin'. He just went and threw up all over hisself."

And from inside we were just able to hear an anguished, "Damn. Oh, damn."

Lifting the Gloom

There was the almost forgotten matter of making a living. I was able to start hunting again toward the middle of the hottest summer I could remember. The newspapers were filled with the usual trauma and trivia but nothing I thought I might shoot and sell. When I phoned editors here and abroad whom I knew by name and to whom I hoped to present a few ideas, they were all on vacation in Maine or on holiday in Devon.

Hilary had better luck. She was given several books to review and a job that involved over-the-phone interviews with several fashion models, all of whom had once suffered from anorexia. Finally, early in September, she was given an assignment for an English broadsheet to do an article on the Staten Island Ferry. But the travel editor intended to use old photos pulled from their files and didn't need my services. It was just after Hilary broke this news to me that our phone rang and for an irrational moment I thought it was London calling to say I could do the job after all.

"Vida stole the watchyamacallit. Our banking thing. You know, the one with all our money. And don't tell me she didn't do it because she did."

"You mean the savings account book?"

"She took it. And now she's gone out with Jacob."

"Out? I thought he was too depressed to go out."

"Well, they went out."

"Sounds like good news to me. Where did they go?"

"I don't know. But she stole it from the drawer."

"Did you put it back the last time you used it?"

"Yes," she hissed.

"It's not in your handbag?"

"Tsh, no."

"Did you look?"

"Yes, I looked."

"Has anyone else been up there?"

"Just him. You know."

"No, I don't know."

"Oh, what's his name? Vida's boyfriend."

"Moke?"

"Yes, Moke."

"When was this?"

"Today."

"Why was he up there?"

"Jacob wanted to see him."

"Jacob wanted to see Moke? What on earth for?"

"How should I know?"

This was Saturday morning and a bakery van would soon arrive filled with cakes and canapés and a cupid's heart molded out of chopped liver. The driver would take me in air conditioned splendor to Greenwich, Connecticut where I had offered to shoot (free of charge) the wedding of an old high school friend who had done me the great favor of vacating my Village apartment on the spur of the moment when my father had his stroke. So I told Beryl I couldn't come today but that I would be there on Sunday morning. My hope was that by then the bankbook would reappear and I wouldn't have to, which is what happened. It had been in Jacob's possession all along.

"He says he likes to keep it with him," said my disgruntled mother on the phone the next day.

"So it wasn't Vida."

"But it was her all the other times."

"Well, this is more like his old self, keeping a grip on the money."

"I don't like it."

Was it his old self resurfacing or did he intend to do something drastic with all that money? And I just couldn't stop puzzling over my father wanting to talk to Moke Johnson of all people. I had met him only once, a year ago, and once was enough. Vida was scheduled to appear in court as part of the process of becoming a U S Citizen and she asked her boyfriend, who worked in a supermarket several blocks away, to fill in for her until she returned. That was the very day, as luck would have it, that I attempted to brighten my father's life with some goodies from *Zabar's*.

When I returned, the door was opened by a grinning giant. He wore a shirt with bits of thread where the sleeves should have been and he had a large tattoo of a writhing serpent decorating each bowling ball bicep. His laugh was like the repeated snort of a kazoo. He had a tooth missing, and he was the first person I had ever seen with rings and beads embedded in his face as if he had been caught in a bomb blast in the jewelry department of *Woolworth's*. Moke had obviously been told about me by my bragging parents because much later, when he was leaving, after having shaved and dressed my father, he said he didn't have a camera in Nam.

"I coulda got great pictures there."

"I'm sure."

"Like choppers flattening the grass before they land. And you know what's really cool?"

"What's that?"

"The way those babies come in low and splash the hills with napalm."

My mother, of course, liked him. Her hunger to socialize made her overlook how odd or even deranged people were so long as they were friendly and there was a chance she could induce them to sit down.

Perhaps asking Moke to help had to do with Vida's new found determination to keep an even more careful surveillance on Jacob. All this took place after that awful afternoon when, to my shock and relief, I ran into his bedroom and there he was, outraged at finding himself alive. Not surprisingly, he felt miserably ill and had to be put to bed. Later, when Vida and I were alone, she informed me, with a professional calm that seemed almost brutal, of what my father had tried to do. Luckily he hadn't swallowed all the Nembutal at once, she said, but one at a time over an hour or so, and it was this that had saved his life. She breathed not a word to my mother who had decided that Jacob was made sick by food poisoning. Nor did Vida ask where I had been while my father was slowly downing those pills. She studied me carefully as I carefully said nothing since nothing had been asked of me. Her brown gaze, acorn-hard, was unnerving. Did she suspect? I had no idea and yet her steady stare made my aching conscience worse.

Hilary appeared to be in shock. There was little for her to do except to tell Jacob she hoped he felt better and to agree with Beryl that the mushroom pâté had gone off and that this was the culprit. They also found in the back of the fridge not one but three half empty jars of mayonnaise that Hilary, with her economizing Englishness, thought were useable; but Beryl, "to be on the safe side," dropped them in the trash bin.

When I went into the bedroom that evening to say goodnight to my father, he was still nauseous and had a pounding headache. Despair blighted his face like a wound.

"I'll never try that again," he groaned. Gloom lifting, hope unfurled, I quickly asked: "Never try to end it again, you mean?"

"Never try with pills again," he countered.

In the next couple of months I saw him as often as I could bear it. Once more he had slipped into that mineshaft of gloom where we had all to do to get him to speak. Once more he was imprisoned inside his crippled life, suffering each hollow day, one slow minute at a time. Once more Hilary said we must help him and once more I said, yes, but how? Which was as far as we ever got while our days, too, filled with gloom like smoke.

So I began searching for work again. Our money was drying up as if in the summer heat. Then I was told that a great change had taken place. Moke reappeared in Jacob's life, lifting his spirits and I knew that my father only cheered up when death was near. Once more the task of making a living was postponed as I hurried off to my parents' place to see what was up.

"Well, Dad, I hear you're feeling better."

"Somewhat."

"I'm glad."

"Good."

"The future looks brighter, does it?"

"A bit.

We were out on the balcony in the morning shade, the heat made manageable by the river breeze. It had blown away yesterday's smog to disclose, in the great distance, a barely discernible Statue of Liberty.

"Do we have Moke to thank for cheering you up?"

He looked at the blur that was all he saw of my face, said nothing, then asked, "Moke? What are you talking about?"

"I don't know. That's what I'm trying to find out."

"Moke helps Vida sometimes."

"That's it?"

"That's it."

"Yet something lifted your gloom."

"Who knows. It lifts and it settles again."

"That's all you have say?"

"That's all I have to say."

When it was time to leave and I was saying goodbye to my mother, who was sorting the laundry in the bedroom, I noticed his jacket hanging over a chair. The flap of one of the side pockets was half in, half out. I bent to adjust it and felt something inside. Out came the famous savings book that hadn't been lost, just commandeered. I opened it amid a whiff of guilt but this vanished the moment I saw that last Friday $3,000 had been withdrawn. I put this chilling evidence back where it had come from. Evidence of what? I wasn't sure. I hurried to the balcony.

"Dad, why did you take out so much money?"

"What are you talking about?"

"From the bank."

"That's none of your business."

"Does Beryl know?"

"It's none of her business."

"That's not true."

"I look after the cash in this house."

"Not since you've been ill."

"Than it's time I did."

"But why three thousand?"

"To spend on things."

"Like what?"

"Different things."

"Like what?"

"Damn it," he shouted, "why do you keep sticking your nose in my business? Can't I have some privacy, for crysake? What do you care? It's my life. Keep out."

A duel of car horns clashed in the street. Serene and unhurried, the Goodyear Blimp floated high above the Hudson.

"Well, you're certainly your old self," I said.

An insect was bothering him and his one movable hand wasn't able to reach high enough to flick it away. I did it for him.

"It's hot out here," he grumbled. I helped roll the wheelchair over the ridge of the doorway and into the living room where my mother had turned on the air conditioner.

There was nothing more I could think of to do. I said goodbye and turned to leave. At that instant came the toy-soft dingy-dong of the doorbell. This time it was I who opened it.

"Hey," Moke exclaimed, grinning as though at some obscure joke of which I was the punch line. He wore paint-stained sandals, a pair of jeans that had been torn in half and were now a pair of shorts. No shirt, just a skimpy undershirt with thin white straps over his tanned, mountainous torso. With arms and tattooed dragons akimbo he stood in the doorway as if waiting for me to guess his weight.

"Moke, well, well."

"Snap any good ones lately?" he grinned.

"I suppose you're here to see my father."

"Yeah, dropped by for a chat. Great guy, your Dad. Tops."

As he stepped into the room it shrank.

"Hey," he said to my father.

"Well, look who's here," my mother exclaimed, pushing a shopping cart filled with laundry.

After some pointless chit chat, and after Moke had several times politely declined my mother's request that he sit down, Jacob suggested that they could talk in private in his den and off he went with Moke behind him pushing.

"What does he want here?" I asked. "Vida's come and gone already."

"They talk."

"What about?"

"He works in the A&P."

"They talk about his job at the supermarket?"

"I don't know what they talk about. But it gives him something to do."

"They are jolly well up to something," Hilary said, when I got back to our apartment.

"I know."

When I returned from the kitchen with two glasses of Root Beer, I sat beside her on the couch where she had kicked off her shoes.

"Wish I could have been there," she said. "He must look a treat."

"Jacob's buying something from him, I'm sure of it."

"Drugs?"

"Christ, I never thought of that."

"Might do him wonders."

"You think he's on something already?"

"Perhaps."

"And that's what cheered him up?"

"Could have done."

"But three thousand dollars worth?"

She was lying on the couch, her now bare feet on my lap, with me gently kneading them like dough. Moonlight came down from above in the form of a sonata. We listened for a while.

"What do you think it is?" she asked.

"Beethoven, of course."

"No, I mean with Moke."

"Hope I'm wrong but I fear he's selling Jacob a handgun."

"To shoot himself with in his bedroom? He wouldn't do that."

"OK, outside then."

"And you think we should stop him?"

"Should we stop him? I don't know. Yes. Think of afterward. Think of my mother."

"I know." She paused. "But three thousand dollars to buy a gun?"

"Some to buy it, the rest to pay the man who buys it for you."

"I see." She grimaced. "Oh, God, now what do we do?"

Taking the Sun

What set me thinking, even before I became aware I was giving it any thought, was a casual question I couldn't remember Vida ever asking me before. I went back often after that day Moke dropped in. I hung about and tried to be of help. Then, when no one was in sight, I made a quick search of whatever room I was in, plunging my hand into the back of dresser drawers, some almost too stuffed to open, groped blindly in the treasureless trove that made each closet nearly impenetrable. I even got down on my hands and knees to inspect beneath his wheelchair while Jacob was being given a shower. No weapon. But since one could camouflage a cannon among the jumble of junk my father refused to throw out, a small hand gun could be safely hidden until finally, like most of his things, it faded from memory. Searching seemed pointless and I finally gave up. After all, if there was a gun no one else would be able to find it either.

Then late one afternoon I phoned, my mother answered, we chatted and afterward I asked to talk to Vida, as I usually did, for it was she who was best able to fill me in on what was really happening.

"Jacob's OK now," she told me. "He don't joke or nothin' but he's not depressed. Not like before."

"You and Moke went with him to the bank," I said, deciding to confront the issue. "He took out a lot of money. Do you know why?"

There was a pause before she said, "I don't."

"Where's the money now?"

"He put it in his pocket and we took him home. That's all I know."

"So he still has it."

"I guess he do."

"Is it still in his pocket?"

"I don't know."

"What's going on between Moke and my father?"

"Moke talk about hisself in the army and your Dad, he talk about when he was poor and in school and all dat."

"So they just chat."

"Dat's right."

"And we have Moke to thank for cheering him up, do we?"

"You got that right. People like to talk to Moke. And he enjoy to talk to your dad."

"Does he?"

"And your Mom, too."

"Ah, huh."

"Moke wants to be a success and live high up as him and your Mom do."

"I see."

"He really like your Dad."

"Good."

"And your Mom too. Uh, oh, Jacob callin' me. Got to hang up."

"Well, thanks, Vida. See you soon."

"You comin' here tomorrow?" she asked, as an afterthought.

"No, tomorrow it's back to the old grind."

"Ok. Say hi to Hilary. Bye, bye."

From the outset, I had been impressed with Vida. She had the resilience and determination of someone who had come up from a long way down. Having escaped from a brutal marriage arranged for her in Trinidad when she was seventeen, she made her way to New York with the help of an uncle who put her to work, illegally, at slave wages. She broke away, lived with friends, worked nights and trained by day to be a home help professional. Street wise and resourceful, she also had good business sense. Having recently bought a house in Brooklyn, she planned to open a speciality shop on the ground floor.

Her cheerfulness also impressed me. To Jacob she chatted away with happy detachment, never seeming to be moved by his plight, however tirelessly she tried to be of help. Whether my father was in that terrifying state of rigid gloom or in his somewhat improved, though equally heartbreaking stoic mode, Vida behaved towards him as I'm sure she did with all the others in her care, like a frisky porpoise among shipwrecks.

Yet something niggled at me. Each time I brushed it aside it bobbed up again. That night, in the bedroom, after getting up from making love, feeling warm and moist and glowing, I went to the fridge to get us something cold to drink, and as I stopped to inspect my two recent photos of Hilary, even then it niggled at me. The wide-angled, 35mm, hand-held Fujicolor shots, sprayed and bleed-mounted were not, however, displayed on the wall of my choice --"to put them in the sitting room," was, in her view, "cringe-making"-- but were hung above the radio in the kitchen as a compromise. One was taken at a birthday party for which she had made herself bone-breakingly beautiful, something she could do when necessary, conjuring up all that age old ruthless glamour-magic, while the other caught her off-duty from the rigors of enticement as she sat unintimidatingly pretty atop Primrose Hill.

It bobbed up and niggled at me again as I stood barefoot on chilly linoleum, running the sink water to fill two glasses stacked with ice, niggling at me even though, and perhaps because, it was such a casual question that Vida had asked: "You comin' here tomorrow?" It was the sort of thing she never concerned herself with. Maybe it meant nothing, and all this business about a gun was just so much nonsense, and perhaps the money he withdrew from the bank lay unspent and safely hidden and was just part of his reawakening obsession with regaining control, staying top dog, being the boss. But I didn't buy it.

Nor did Hilary. She blazed at me louder than need be in our small, dark bedroom. "I don't want you to go up there. First you help him and now you want to stop him again. Whatever he's up to just jolly well let him get on with it. Stop pressurizing him. It's his life. Keep away. Stay out of it."

"I know what you're afraid of."

"What?"

"That I'll get shot."

"*YES*." Her voice splashing like hot fat.

"Oh, come on."

"A gun is a gun. Last time you could have been jailed, this time you might get killed."

"I'm not the one he wants to shoot. Look, he's my father. I just can't wash my hands of the whole..."

"God almighty, not again. I can recite that off by heart. Look. Will you leave. The poor man. Alone?"

Silence inflated that night-filled room as if it were as vast as all of space. I closed my eyes. Galaxies of iridescent fluff, micro bits of nothing, floated about.

"Well?" she demanded.

"I'll try."

"Try what?"

"OK."

"OK, what? You'll leave him alone?"

"Yes, I'll leave him alone."

Early that morning, as Hilary lay asleep, I went there once more. It was a gentle September day except on subway platforms where remnants of the recent heat wave had been driven underground.

Usually I rang the bell holding the key at the ready and, if no one heard its dull ping-pong, let myself in. On this occasion, my mother opened the door at once. She was pleased. Not at seeing me, as it turned out. Pleased at Jacob having asked to be taken downstairs. He wanted to sit in that part of the building complex that was all grass, had a view of the river and, in the past, had been a favorite of his when the balcony was too windy. In the past he would carry down a beach chair and a manuscript and read in the sun. The spot he chose was nowhere near the gray, backless stone benches that lined the walkway and it was far removed from the fenced-in basket ball court. All this could be seen far below if one stood at the window. The plan was for Vida to take him down there as soon as she returned from the laundry room. After telling me all this, my mother, humming tunelessly, went to work in the kitchen, washing the morning dishes. Left to myself, standing at the window, I scanned the open river and, in the other direction, watched a traffic jam on West End Avenue. And waited.

There was the sound of purring in the room. I turned and he was coming toward me, a finger on the controls. Prepared for his outing in the autumn sun, he wore a bright orange short-sleeve shirt, tan trousers and white slippers. There was no ominous bulge where a weapon might be, a weapon I no longer believed in but kept looking for.

"Russ? Did I hear Russell's voice?"

"Over here, Dad."

He changed direction until what he could see of me came into view.

"What's wrong?" he asked, as if upbraiding the family malingerer. "Why aren't you off somewhere working?"

"I've come to see how you are."

"You come too often. You have a life to lead. Get on with it."

"How can I? I'm worried."

"Oh, for crying out loud. I'm OK. Stop worrying. All this watching, watching drives me crazy. I'm fine, so stop it. Now, look, before you go, sit for a minute. You had breakfast? You sure? OK, there's something I wanted to say. Kept forgetting. About you and Hilary.

We really like her."

"I gathered that."

"So I want to ask you something."

"OK, shoot," I said, and winced. Was it my imagination or did he, as well?

"It's a simple question. Are you planning to have children? Beryl wants to know."

"Beryl."

"Yes."

"She wants to know."

"That's right. She'd love to be a grandmother. Make her very happy."

"Having a child is a hell of a commitment."

"You won't regret it."

"Can I have that in writing?"

"You really won't. I didn't. Anyway, that's what I wanted to ask you."

"Well, you asked it."

"It was Beryl. She wanted to know."

He glanced toward the kitchen. I tapped his knee to get his attention. He didn't feel it. He looked at me when I said,

"OK, Dad, now I would like to ask you something. If we decide to, should we agree to try, would it give you a reason to hang around for a while?"

He flinched as if, at that moment, I had placed the baby in his lap.

"Can't promise," he said, quickly.

"Wouldn't you like to be a grandfather?"

As if I had needlessly wounded him. "What do you think?"

Nothing happened for a moment. He rubbed his face. Then suddenly overwhelmed, he reached out as he had when I sat watching him swallow those pills. I gripped his hand with both of mine. He pushed and pulled, pushed and pulled as if, unable to speak, he was reduced to some primitive ritual of showing despair or offering love.

"Might make the difference as far as Hilary is concerned," I said,

. "to agree to try."

"To try?"

"To have a baby."

Vida burst in through the front door. "You ready?" she asked, as if with an arrest warrent. Then startled: "Oh, hi, Russ."

"Don't stay in the sun too long," Beryl called from the kitchen.

"Can I go down and sit with you?" I asked.

"No, I'm never left alone, not ever, damn it. I want to be by myself. To think. To consider what you just said. Get your camera. Go back to work." Agitated, he rolled himself across the room. "Going out for a while, Beryl. Let me give you a kiss."

"A kiss?" came the embarrassed voice from the kitchen. "Maybe, when you come back, if I'm in the mood."

Never had I seen her show affection to my father. Once, years ago, I recall him putting his arm around her as they sat on the couch. Beryl, embarrassed and unbending, acted as if someone she didn't care for, at a party she wished she hadn't gone to, had taken hold of her for a photograph.

Jacob paused, as if trying to remember something, then swiveled round so I could see him again. He waved more at the lamp than at me, his palm up, rocking slowly from side to side. I lifted my hand in return though I knew he couldn't see that far. He gave the lamp a broken smile, his face, for a moment, like crockery poorly glued back together. As he rolled out into the hallway, Vida, carrying a magazine and the house keys, held the door for him and guided him through it.

To Cross the River

It began quietly enough although I still couldn't work out what, if anything, was about to happen and what, if anything, I should do about it. As I stood by the window, Beryl came out of the kitchen and surprised me by recommending a new restaurant just up the road. She couldn't remember what it was called but the desserts were very good. I should go there sometime.

"Yes, that's it," she smiled, when I supplied the name, but frowned when I reminded her that we had eaten there a few years ago.

"I was with you?"

"Yes."

"Never."

"You were. You said the food was too spicy."

"Me? No."

"And you didn't like the clientele."

"Huh?"

"You said only old people went there."

"Oh, come on."

"Anyway, it was a long time ago."

"What was?"

"The last time you went to that restaurant."

"What do you mean? We were there yesterday."

"You and Jacob? I thought he refused to go out anymore."

An ominous feeling spread through me as she explained how he had insisted she phone Vida to ask her not to come until later because they were going out to dinner together.

"He talked about the old days, didn't he? And when you first met each other."

She blinked at this display of magic and my hope of being proven wrong vanished.

"He drank a toast to all your years together and reached out to hold your hand."

This made her lips part.

"Am I right?" I asked.

"How did you know?"

Quickly I opened the door to the balcony and stepped into the tepid sunlight. The tall city buzzed and hummed. The wind, tangling my hair, made the day chillier than I had remembered. Below, far below, I saw my miniscule father in his toy wheelchair parked on the lawn in his orange shirt. Vida? Ah, there, on one of the stone benches with her magazine held open. Except for a young woman lying face down on a blanket in her bikini near the basket ball court, there was no one else there. The children of the Lincoln Towers complex were either in school or still at home, their mothers or *au pairs* not yet ready to bring them out to play.

I hurried back in and asked for the binoculars. Beryl hadn't a clue and went off to look in Jacob's den. When she was gone I noticed them on top of the dining room cabinet. They were next to a cardboard box that had once housed a three volume set of Proust and in which she now kept newspaper clippings.

On the balcony again, I pressed the binoculars to my face and focused the circular blur until the milky granules tightened into a seated and sharply visible Vida holding, but not reading, her magazine. She glanced at Jacob, then away, at Jacob again, then away once more. I slid the circular enlargement of life along the grass, past a candy wrapper, a crushed beer can, a bent straw until I found the large wheelchair in which Jacob sat like a stone Lincoln in his memorial throne, peering in the same direction in which Vida had been glancing. I moved my optical circle along the grass toward where their mutual interest lay. It slid over a low mound of shrubbery to the sidewalk, over parked cars and into an empty street. Beyond were railroad tracks, an open field, the elevated motorway, the glistening river. Shadows of clouds were like smudges on the water.

Back to Jacob in his loud shirt. The look on his face reminded me of the expression of heroic defiance that Karsh, the great portrait photographer, tried but failed to summon up on Churchill's face until, in desperation, he yanked the cigar from the Prime Minster's mouth just before releasing the shutter. I stopped using the binoculars and peered, unaided, at the miniscule figures thirty floors below me: Vida on one of the many benches that circled the area, my father alone on a mound of grass, facing the street. A lorry drove past. Eyeing that shirt again, remembering his fixed and bold expression, I finally understood and nearly cried out.

Tossing the binoculars onto the couch, I ran past my mother who reappeared to say, "They must be here somewhere," just as the front door slammed behind me like the starting gun for my forty yard dash down the hallway. Light cast a yellow rectangle on the carpet. One of the three elevator doors was standing open and about to close.

I yelled, "Hold it, hold it," reaching maximum sprint as I stumbled in to find short Mrs Blaug calmly pressing the hold button and eager, as we descended, to conduct yet another of her elevator interrogations.

"Your father, poor man, how is he?" she rasped.

"Fine, just fine."

"And you mother, such a nice person, is she holding up?"

"Oh, yes. Yes, indeed."

"And that lovely lady friend of yours from England, is she here?"

"Here?"

"In America."

"Yes, she's here."

"You still living, where? With your parents?"

"No, in the Village."

"Oh? In Greenwich Village? Really? Oh, that's nice. But very expensive."

"Could be."

"I mean, I've heard. It's what I've been told. My cousin Norma whose wonderful son lives..."

On and on she went, impaling me with her atonal sound box piched half way between Stephen Hawking and Ethel Merman, until we reached the lobby and I left her in mid-sentence as I ran past the mail drop, turned the corner, pushed open one door, then the heavier, rear exit door, still running until I was standing outside on the grass at the bottom of a towering blue day, so much warmer than on the balcony.

He was facing the river, sitting with his back to me, the sun gleaming on the silver spokes and rods of his wheelchair. I hurried, further flattening a beer can, and kept going until I stood in front of him.

As if thunderstruck: "What are you doing here?"

"Trying to find out what's happening."

"Nothing's happening. For crying out loud why won't people just let me be. Go away."

"Not until we have a talk."

Now Vida was there, as well, having placed herself just near enough to listen. Behind her, at the bench, her magazine lay open where it fell. She said nothing while everything about the woman screamed at me.

I called out to her. "What's happening here?"

"Nothin' happening. Can't you see he need to be by hisself?"

"Whose side are you on?"

"His."

"Is that you Vida?" Jacob asked, unable to turn his head. "Tell her to go away." Raising his voice. "Vida go away."

"What's the plan?" I asked him. "Come on now, tell me."

In whispered fury: "Leave. What must I do to be left alone?"

"Just tell me."

"And *then* you'll go?"

"Come on, why don't you want me here, Dad? The truth."

He wouldn't speak and that anguished look marred his face again. I watched until I couldn't take anymore.

"OK, let me tell you," I said. "It's because you're afraid I'll get shot."

"No," Vida protested from a dozen yards away.

Jacob rubbed his cheek and said nothing. I lowered my voice. "Dad, that shirt is for a purpose, isn't it? The plan is for Moke to drive by out there and with his newly bought rifle..."

"Not true, not true," Vida yelled.

"Pardon?" This to my father who had spoken at the same time she did.

"What if it is?" he whispered.

I looked at him.

"What if it is the plan?" he asked, louder.

Squatting beside his wheelchair, my hand pressed on soil that was still moist from a recent rain. "This is crazy. Innocent people could get hurt. That girl in the bikini."

Disgusted. "She's nowhere near us."

"There's a lady pushing a pram."

"She way over on that side of de park," Vida said.

"Go back," Jacob yelled, as he sat facing away from her. Twice I had to wave before she threw up her hands and walked off. "Has Vida gone?"

"Yes, she's sitting on the bench."

"I don't understand you," he growled. "You break the law, find me pills, hold my hand and now you're what, saving my life?"

"A gun is different. It's terrible."

"I have no choice."

"Think of Beryl."

"I always do."

"Dad, she'll have to *look* at you afterward."

"Vida will keep her away."

"You mean she'll try."

"If she said she will, she will."

"Oh, sure. And Moke? He could go to prison."

"He's getting paid. It's a job."

"You're paying someone to kill people!"

"Not people. Me."

"You're asking him to do a terrible thing."

"You tried to do it."

"You didn't ask. I offered."

"So did he."

"Oh, Christ. Is he a good shot? Suppose he just wounds you?"

"He was trained in the army. A marksman, first class. He intends to press off three shots."

His use of this military term jolted me. We were hurtling away from each other at such a rate soon all contact would be lost.

"The wrong person could get killed. Or get killed as well."

Jabbing a finger at my chest. "That's why I want you the hell out of here. He's due any minute."

Glancing at the road, then back at him again. "Leave? I don't think so."

He exploded. "Oh, get away from me. I don't want you. I don't need you. Get the hell away."

Nothing more was said for a moment. The abrupt dismissal of his own son so wrung him with anguish that I could see in his face a glimpse of the child he had once been. With his features threatening to come apart, he added a single trembling word.

"*Please*."

"Oh, Jesus..." I grabbed his hand.

"It's OK, Russ. It's OK." He pushed and pulled as my hand clutched his, pushed and pulled and said, "Don't worry." He managed an encouraging smile. "Just move away. Now."

I stood up. Things sparkled as the moist earth went out of focus for a while until, with a few desperate blinks, it all slipped back into place. Vida was perched on the edge of her bench, peering at me. A double blur of birds flashed across the lawn. The girl in the bikini took a drink from a bottle and, turning face up, lay still. I was hemmed in by tall buildings, each with balconies like book shelves. All was calm. I wasn't at all sure I could get myself to move from where I stood. Then I jumped at the murmur of a car as it rolled with slow stealth along the road. It kept going and was gone.

"What happened?" he asked, aware of my little dance.

"Someone drove past."

He said nothing.

"How will you know?" I asked.

"Vida will tell me."

"Ah."

"You've got to go, Russ."

The final good bye took me by the throat and I went mute. With a squeeze of his shoulder, I walked away

Once out of his range of vision, I stopped and leaned against the rough brick of the building. I was as far from him on my side of the grass as Vida was on hers. Like worthless sentinels, we kept to our posts in the mounting heat. My father, in his wheelchair on that slight elevation of ground, had a panoramic view of which he saw nothing. A Circle Line vessel carrying morning tourists up the Hudson and around Manhattan came into view. Traffic moved slowly and endlessly along the West Side River Drive while much closer, just beyond the last slope of grass, was the empty street with its central faded yellow line. A silver Toyota appeared and I braced myself for the world to explode. When the car continued on its way, I went slack and felt sick. Vida had watched it with something like calm since only she knew what to look for, had been a passenger when Moke was at the wheel, knew the color and make. But how would she let Jacob know when the moment had come? What would the signal be? I had to find out.

Pushing myself away from the wall, I strode along the cement walkway that curved through the enclosed park to her bench. Some movement off to the left caught my attention. People were coming out of the exit door at the side of the building. They were heading in my direction toward the circle of grass. It was my mother and Hilary, each walking in a happy hurry to tell me something. Beryl's slip was showing. Hilary smiled and waved.

I ran forward. Vida popped up like a puppet, the magazine splashing to the ground. She jogged toward them in bright sneakers, her breasts heaving.

Hilary laughed and said loudly, "They can't find the pictures."

My mother called out. "Isn't that wonderful?"

"You can shoot the story after all."

From my expression, Beryl thought I hadn't understood. "The ferry," she explained. "Staten Island."

"Good news, isn't it?" Hilary said when she reached me.

"Look, take my mother upstairs right now."

"Why?"

"Oh, there's Jacob," Beryl said. "A letter came for him this morning." Holding it in her hand, she headed toward the wheelchair.

"I'll take that," Vida said.

"Give it to Vida," I insisted. Again to Hilary: "Now. Take her away, now."

"What is it? What's wrong?"

"I'll explain later. Just do it."

"Wait," Vida demanded, but my mother was not about to take orders from someone she considered a menial. On she went, shaking off the hand that tried to restrain her. "Wait. He want to be by hisself."

"Mom, come back." I ran to stop her.

"Oh, look, look," Vida called, as if to a child. She ran in front of her, still pointing.

Beryl turned, squinted. "Oh, my soul."

I looked round and there, striding toward me from the gate that opened onto West End Avenue appeared Uncle Sol. He wore a big smile. But even more amazing, he was pulling and being pulled, dragging and being yanked, by a young, manic, black Doberman Pinscher to whom he was helplessly chained.

"Name's Rocky," he grunted, dancing sideways until his feet could get a grip to halt the thrust of the beast who had now seen a squirrel.

I tried to be everywhere at once, running to Hilary to implore her to take my mother away and to Beryl to implore her to go with Hilary, then calling out to Sol, informing him that we were all going upstairs and to follow us.

"What are you doing?" my mother complained, as I stopped her after she had crossed the walkway and was heading into the circle of grass.

"Now's not a good time."

"For what?"

"Jacob needs solitude."

"Oh, nonsense."

"We're going upstairs. Come on now."

"Tsh, oh all right."

"Aheeeee," came Vida's startling intake of air.

Her cold fright ran right through me. I swung around and saw an old Chevy barely moving up the street, heading north, edging slowly forward as if about to stop and then stopping. Its front fender had been scraped clean of paint. A side door was badly dented. Nothing happened for several moments. What looked like a thin pipe emerged through the open passenger window. My hand flew to my mother's arm. With a dull yet compelling voice, more an announcement than a query, Vida said, "You OK, Jacob?" He raised his hand just high enough for her to see and lowered it.

We were too many and too close. All I could think of was to run and stand in front of my father and stop it from happening. "Hold it," I yelled, but before I could sprint forward, I was hit, knocked down, stepped on, my face affronted with a hellish breath and licked hard with a rough tongue.

"I'm trying but he's tough to hold," my uncle said, grunting with effort as he yanked the beast away from me and, in turn, was yanked away himself. "Sorry."

Hilary asked if I was OK, and just as I got to my feet a loud pop like a bursting balloon echoed among the buildings, emptying a tree of birds, jolting the wheelchair and turning it slightly, then a second pop and at the same moment something punctured solid flesh with a stricken, gasping, gulp of sound. Beneath a moving cloud of sparrows no one moved. The girl sunbathing on the blanket stood up, puzzled.

I ran to my father's side. He looked at me.

"What happened?" he asked, as I noticed at the top, an inch from his head, a missing piece of wheelchair.

"*Oy, gevalt*," Sol cried out, clutching his head. The beast lay on the grass, a rear leg twitching, my uncle kneeling. And this made me look toward the street. The Chevy was backing up for a better view, for another shot. Vida and I yelled, "No." As the car reversed, it ran into a taxi that had stopped behind it. For a moment, nothing. Then, with a searing screech of tires, the Chevy was gone.

Deadly Virtues

More than at any time since his stroke, more even than when he was trying to die swallowing pills in my presence, I feared for him. Though he was unable to turn and view the splintered wood next to his head, he grasped that the ordeal had ended and with it the agonizing tension of stoically taking the sun while waiting for what he couldn't see and couldn't hear to come rolling by and kill him. When he finally understood, he came apart. Beryl thought it was the shock of being targeted by a passing madman and that he would soon recover. He didn't. It took until he had downed his third straight scotch back in the apartment that the trembling lessened. But then what she couldn't grasp was why the bottomless depression returned, deeper than before, with that familiar dull-eyed silence.

After the shot was fired, many things happened to which I paid little notice. Almost all my attention was on my father. Sol, a man of action when events gave him little choice, marched into West End Avenue and brought back a puzzled policeman. He pointed at the road, the blighted wheelchair, his dead dog, then stood arms akimbo impatient for justice. The officer produced pad and pen and proceeded to take down names. My grief-stricken uncle then marched into the building and reappeared with a four-wheeled luggage cart into which he lifted the dead animal.

Vida told the officer that the man who fired the gun was driving a green Volvo. I offered a quick confirmation of this lie. Hilary hadn't a clue but my mother insisted it was a blue Chevy for she remembered a neighbor owning one just like it. Vida disputed this sighting rather too forcefully while I lied again and said that Mr. Kobylka, the one time next door neighbor to whom Beryl was referring, actually had a Volvo, a blue, four-door, second-hand Volvo. Outvoted, Beryl shrugged, too distracted to argue the point, having only now realized the narrowness of Jacob's escape from death.

An escape Sol had no sympathy with since he had suffered a great loss. Back in the apartment, he marched up and down, raging at the demented scumbags who drove through the city shooting at any poor dog they happened to see, killing a harmless pedigree Doberman who had his whole life ahead of him. Stupid, mad, sadistic scumbags, that's what they were.

While Sol raged on, Hilary pulled me from my father's side and into the bathroom. She wanted to know what had happened before she arrived. When I told her, she sat down on the edge of the tub as if weak in the knees.

"What he's been through doesn't bear thinking about. And, yes, you could have been killed. If they arrest Moke will Vida be in trouble? Bloody hell, she's supposed to care for people, not arrange to have them shot."

"She cares too much. She knows I gave him those pills. She knows he's desperate."

"But if the police catch up with her, will she implicate you?"

"We'll have to wait and see."

Two detectives came the next day to ask more questions. But the police never did find the man who fired that shot. As the weeks passed Vida became less tense. Moke never reappeared. Sol considered a law suit against the NYPD for inadequate street protection but his lawyer talked him out of it. Jacob's condition stayed the same. He rarely spoke, even when spoken to.

My mother always referred to the forces of evil in this city as "they," saying things like, "You know what they're doing now? They're mugging everyone in Central Park." When *The Daily News* reported that a man was shoved in front of an in-coming train, she told everyone that, "It's terrible. Now they're pushing people off subway platforms," as if at each station rows of passengers were being toppled onto the tracks. After our own private, drive-by shooting, the dreaded "they" posed a new danger. She advised us to stay indoors at all times and not venture out except under cover of darkness.

It wasn't long before we realized that Jacob's condition was worsening. He refused to take any of the anti-depressants Dr. Honeycutt prescribed for him. He lost his appetite and would eat a little only when Vida and my mother both insisted. I used the excuse of having to make a living as a means of escaping for a while.

I shot four rolls capturing for English readers something of what it's like to ride on the Staten Island Ferry and my god was it good to get out onto the water, refreshed by the coolest breeze we had felt in months. Yet each time on the return trip as we again approached the skyscrapers crowded together on lower Manhattan, growing taller as we churned nearer, all I could think of was him.

Another job involved going to Block Island and still another took Hilary and me to a children's fashion show in Boston. For three whole days I didn't phone and I didn't write. Yet we had to return in the end and when we did there was no getting away from what I had to do. So the next day I left Hilary behind and took the IRT uptown to see how things were.

It was late afternoon of a starched autumn day. When I arrived my mother was out, her sewing machine on the dining room table, part of a skirt trapped in its teeth. Vida, who was spending more time in the apartment, was trying to persuade my father to let himself be given a shower. "Get away from me," I heard him rage. "Get the hell away." Soon she came into the living room, and without saying hello, told me how despairing she was about getting him to do anything at all. And she said how awful things were for my mother who now seemed almost as depressed as he. I asked if there was anything we could do that we were not doing and she just shook her head.

Walking firmly on the parquet floor of the hallway to alert him that someone was coming, I went yet again into that musty bedroom to find him, as always, in the wheelchair, the back rest and its missing chunk of wood covered by the Mexican blanket I had brought back for them after shooting the earthquake story. I gave him a cheerful hello and was burned by the silence. His eyes stayed shut as if trying to locate a sound no one else could hear. He still wore his robe and slippers and hadn't allowed himself to be shaven. He looked like a peasant I had seen somewhere once, his beard like frost, who seemed to have reached the nadir of a grueling life.

The river was gunmetal gray and seemed as fixed as mud. A red convertible, its top open, was abandoned in a lay by on the motorway.

For no apparent reason, he opened his eyes. I hoped for a smile. It wasn't there. Nor, in any meaningful sense, was he. Just his features marred by the erosion of grief. All at once it was as clear as glass. He and I were alone in this world, sutured together as father and son. An ancient taboo had lost all meaning. It galloped away, riderless. I was commanded to release him from a suffering past all endurance.

"Dad, listen. Let me do it for you now. Did you hear me? Dad?"

"Do what?"

"End it. Now."

"My life?"

"Yes."

"How?"

"Not sure yet."

"Use a pillow."

"A pillow?"

"Yes. No, they'll arrest you."

"They won't."

"Twenty years in jail."

"Listen. I spoke to Dr. Honeycutt and he said if anything happens to you he's prepared to say it was due to natural causes."

The stilted tone I detected in my voice surely betrayed the obvious truth that what I said was a lie.

At last those lifeless eyes looked at me. "He said that?"

"I was in his office today. A last try. He all but gave me the go ahead."

Jacob rubbed his face. He reached out and took a sip of water.

"You'll be safe, then?"

"Absolutely."

"Is that certain?"

"Yes."

"Really?"

"Yes."

He considered this for a bit. "Give me your hand."

"Here, take two."

"They're cold," he said, frowning.

"So are yours."

"What will you tell Beryl?"

"I don't know. A heart attack. People who had one often have another."

"If I struggle," he said, "don't stop."

"Understood."

"I'm grateful to you."

"I hope I can do it."

"You can do anything you put your mind to, Russ." He was pumping me up with hot air as he sometimes did when I was small. "You really can. I've seen it many times. And that damned Honeycutt, he'd better do what he said."

"He will, don't worry."

Jacob pushed and pulled at my hand, pushed and pulled until

suddenly, worried: "Let's do it now. Right now. Or the moment might pass."

I stood up and walked about fighting an urge to run, thinking how fine it would be to get out into that autumn air, walk under that motorway and take that foot path beyond the boat basin to where the river is so close you could reach down and touch it.

There were a number of pillows on the bed. I picked one up, light, feather-filled, terrifying.

"Ready?" he asked.

"If you are."

He sat still for a moment. "Go on, then."

First I squeezed his shoulder, which was all the goodbye I dared risk. He hardly noticed, his fear was too great. His five usable fingers gripped the hand rest while I stood behind him. He was ready. I was ready.

I faltered. Couldn't get the hand with the pillow to move.

He became a coach. "Come on, now. Do it." Then he became a father teaching his child. "We'll do it together, OK? Here, give me your hand."

I was trapped. How could I face him again, having come this close and then fled? Here I stood, the dutiful, caring, cowardly son. And he sat with his expression of implacable resolve.

A noise in the living room. My mother returning home? No, just Vida in the kitchen.

"Let's go," I said. "Ready?"

He reached up and we clasped hands, my right holding his while my left clamped the pillow over his face. Nothing happened for a moment. For several moments. Then his hand fought to get free of my grip. I held his firmly, ready to use all my strength. But he had almost none. For an immeasurably agonizing length of time, I stood behind him, holding him, killing him. The door opened and someone came in. Vida took one look and bit her knuckle. I didn't move. She came closer.

"Let go his hand."

I did. His arm fell into his lap.

"Is that it?" I asked.

She told hold of his wrist, adjusting her grip several times. "He gone." Gently she removed the pillow and put it on the bed. She closed his eyes. I recall her asking if I was OK and I said yes. But a secret trembling had begun. I felt cold. She considered for a moment, then asked if Jacob had agreed. I nodded. Now I forced myself to look at him. Eyes shut, head back, mouth agape, he seemed fixed in a state of shock as if struck by a revelation he had not expected.

The heavy door to the hallway banged. Vida's eyes met mine. I walked into the living room. Into the kitchen. "Oh, you're back," Beryl said. "Good." She was emptying the shopping cart. I helped. There were the Oreo cookies my father used to take with his coffee, the marge he spread on his morning toast, the ice cream he ate after dinner. These and many other things she had bought, hoping to renew his interest in food and, with food, life.

"Mom, there something I've got to tell you. It's an awful thing but, in a way, it's also a blessing." When I told her that Jacob had died of a heart attack, she stared with her ravaged, up-turned face as if pleading with me not to let this be true. "Oh, my God," she said and then, "Oh, no. Oh, no." She went to the table and sat down.

"He die peaceful," came Vida's voice from behind me.

My mother rocked slowly in her seat. "Oh, no. Oh, no."

Vida asked if she wanted to go in and look at him. "Not yet," she mumbled. We sat with her for a long time. I held her hand. Vida put an arm round her shoulders. I tried to explain how it was all for the best. Vida made her a cup of coffee which Beryl found too hot to drink. While we waited for it to cool, Vida said to me, "We need a death certificate. While I watch your Mom you better call de doctor."

I went into my father's den which was filled to overflowing with all those things he had promised to sort through and get rid of and now never would. Because I didn't feel up to facing the coming crisis without her, I phoned Hilary, but only then remembered she had gone uptown to interview someone. After a deep breath, I called Dr. Honeycutt and his secretary said he had been called to the hospital on an emergency. She didn't know when he'd be back in his office. Perhaps not till next Monday. Since this was Friday, I explained why we couldn't wait that long. What to do next? My mother looked up from her position of hunched grief to ask what was wrong. I explained that we needed a doctor's certificate before we could get Jacob safely into a funeral home. Dial 911, my mother said, as though she had been through all this before. Since getting in touch with the police was the last thing I wanted, I pretended to ponder the idea while dismissing it altogether. A welcome distraction was the plink plunk of the doorbell.

Hilary entered, her interview over. She exclaimed at what a lovely autumn day it was and how much she was dying for a cup of tea. Vida put the kettle on while I took her into the den to tell her that my father had just died. Heart attack. Her response was predictable. Sorrow at the loss and relief that he had been spared further suffering. I nodded, relieved that she suspected nothing.

"I must go to her," she said, jumping up at the very moment we heard Vida calling out, "No, Beryl, no."

We rushed into the living room as my mother was saying into the phone, "Yes, that's the address. We're on the top floor."

Vida grabbed my wrist. "She phone 911, that's what she do. Police is comin' now."

I grabbed the receiver. "Hello?"

"Who's that?" a voice barked. I told him.

"You're what, the son?"

"Look, it's not necessary to come up here..."

"A 911 cannot be cancelled."

"All we need is a death..."

"Stay put. Someone'll be there in five minutes." Click.

"What did you say to them?" I asked Beryl.

"That Jacob died, that's all."

"What I tell you? Police be here soon."

"What does it matter?" Hilary asked.

"Dey is for when somebody do a crime," Vida said, like an oracle warning me against an unavoidable fate.

"But there wasn't one," Hilary asked, "so what's the problem?"

"No problem," I said, a bead of sweat slipping like slime down my back. "No problem. Just a lot of needless fuss."

Twenty minutes later the place was filled with cops, plus two paramedics with a stretcher. "Where is he?" asked a boyish officer who followed me into the bedroom where my father sat upright in his wheelchair, head back, mouth open as if hoping to quench a final taste of life.

"Died of a heart attack," I said.

"It just stop," was Vida's contribution from behind me.

In groups of twos they came in, glanced at him and left. A paramedic felt his pulse and left. By turns, no matter what room they were in, they gazed out the window commenting on the view. The young officer, assisted by a lovely black policewoman, questioned me at length in my father's den. We all sat within arm's reach of each other and, trembling beneath a pretence of calm, I proceeded to lie about the heart attack and to explain the problems concerning the death certificate, the absent doctor, and our mistaken belief that 911 might be able to advise us. They scrutinized my every word with the professional impartiality of people convinced I was the killer.

The boyish officer used our phone to contact his superior. He explained the impasse. He listened to what I hoped would prove to be wise advice. Then he hung up and informed me that before funeral procedure can commence, the law required a certificate of death to ascertain exactly what caused the deceased to die. He seemed quite satisfied with the result of his inquiry. The lady police office said the sunsets must be amazing from up here. I said they were. The boyish cop nodded in agreement as he sat staring out the window.

"What happens now?" I asked.

"If no doctor is found," he said, "there would have to be an autopsy."

My fear, which they still hadn't noticed, covered me in sweat.

"And I suppose you have to remain here till this is resolved?"

"That's right."

"Well," I said, "now I know why there aren't more police on the streets. They're all up here with me."

The policewoman, a holster on her right hip, a nightstick on her left, emitted the tight smile of an unstable gunslinger. The boyish one nodded as if my little quip held more truth than he cared to admit.

Hilary beckoned to me from down the hall. The doorbell had rung. It had been plink-plonking for the last hour as yet more members of the NYPD, some in uniform and others in drab street clothes, came in and out, as if for the express purpose of admiring the view. One of them even offered his gruff condolences to my mother who was still sitting near the sewing machine, unable to get herself to go into the bedroom. Hilary beckoned again.

"I'll be there in a minute," I called. Not to be put off, what I saw next yanked me to my feet. There he was, Dr. Honeycutt coming toward me, tall and slightly stooped as if under the weight of a great suspicion. We met and shook hands. He said he was sorry to hear the news. "How did it happen?"

"Heart attack," I said, quickly. "We were with him when it happened."

"We?"

"Me and him," Vida added, from behind us.

We went into the bedroom. Honeycutt bent close and with his thumb lifted an eyelid. My father glared out at the world in alarm. He pressed into Jacob's throat with his fingers. Felt his good hand, then replaced it in his lap. He told Vida that he would like to talk to me alone. She went out, closing the door.

"Why all the police?"

"My mother dialed 911."

"They have enough men here to arrest the Third Reich."

"That's New York for you. No half measures."

He tipped his head toward the wheelchair. "So you were with him when it happened?"

I nodded. Dr Honeycutt looked at me as if studying something under glass. He stood up straight. "Your father was suffocated. Probably with a pillow." He stooped again.

"He died of a heart attack," I insisted.

"No, he didn't."

"What happened is what he wanted to happen."

"He's not here to confirm that."

"All he wished for was to die."

"You came to my office about this. I refused."

"He's my father. I had to help him."

"Did he ask you to?"

"Yes, but he was afraid I'd go to jail. So I lied. I told him I spoke to you and you promised that however his life ended you would say it was his heart. Only then did he agree. But all he wanted was to die."

"People say that and change their mind. They get depressed and recover. They want to die now but later they think again. I've seen it many times. How do you know what he might feel next year? Or the year after next?"

"You realize that he tried to throw himself into the sea?"

"Yes."

"That he tried to end it with pills?"

"I know."

"I sat by his side as he swallowed them. He never once hesitated. You should also know something you're going to find hard to believe. He was so desperate, he arranged for a drive-by shooting which he hoped would kill him while sitting out on the lawn in his chair."

"When was this?"

"Last month. You can check with the police. He sat there, a human target, without flinching for twenty fucking minutes. The bullet missed by half an inch." I removed the Mexican blanket to reveal the ugly bite that had been taken out of the wood. "Is this a man who didn't know his own mind?"

Honeycutt stared at and then touched the shattered wood. After a moment he said, "You put me in a terrible place."

"Some doctors would support what I did."

"Most people would not."

"Most people wouldn't know enough about my father's life to have an informed opinion."

He winced. "Why did you do it like this? It's not even assisted suicide. It's murder."

"The pills made him sick. Took him weeks to recover. He couldn't get himself to try that again. He didn't have the strength to lift a handgun. What was left? I saw what I had to do and did it."

He frowned. "Doctors struggle with this more than you realize."

"I'm sure they do."

He stood there for a bit, stooped with the weight of it all. Then he went to the door and paused with his hand on the knob. A moment later he made his way into the living room. I followed. He looked around and asked who was in charge. The young police officer stepped forward.

"Coronary thrombosis," Honeycutt said. He signed a death certificate, gave my mother a prescription for sedatives and, without looking at me, left the apartment.

I caught up with him in the hallway to offer what I knew he didn't want, my thanks."If you need help, phone me," he said.

"Help?"

"When the reality of all this kicks in."

"Don't think I'll need to but thanks anyway."

While the police were filing out in twos and threes, I made myself a stiff drink.

"Aren't you offering any to us?" Hilary asked.

Soon I phoned the funeral chapel. Later two men in black suits arrived with great solemnity and disappeared into the bedroom. In time they rolled my father into view on a hospital wagon. He had been zipped into a black bag. As they were heading for the front door, my mother asked me if she could say a last goodbye. I stopped them. Reluctantly, they unzipped the bag and waited. Beryl came up to Jacob who now looked calmly asleep. She touched his cheek. She tousled his hair. Then she astonished us all by bending over and kissing him passionately on the mouth.

The Speed of Darkness

The future was out there somewhere, slightly blurred, in the middle distance. Finding it was the problem. With each attempt, all I did was reinhabit the past. Though I longed to return home, we stayed where we were for my mother's sake. In a month's time, when she seemed somewhat herself again, we disentangled ourselves and flew to London. But the future wasn't there either.

Autumn became incandescent that year with the trees in Highgate feathered with gold. Soon it was too cold to drink outdoors at The Flask and some of the tennis fanatics in Waterlow Park wore gloves as they played. We were pleased to be there and I felt OK. It was just that everything I did took a long time because nothing I did was easy to do and wherever I went the past was waiting like a chore I had forgotten about. Hilary had a solution. We should have a child. It would send us in a new direction and leave the past where it jolly well belonged. I agreed, we tried and nothing happened. But that was all right. We were in no hurry and it would happen in the end. I was OK. Then I began to feel less so. It began like a headache without the pain. And there was constant, soundless static. Everything took effort. I slept badly and slept late. I still shaved each morning but it wasn't easy. I started talking in my sleep, talking to my father, Hilary said. When I awoke in the night, like a boat run aground, I was afraid to set off again. The dreams grew worse. It was as if trauma had gravity as does a planet, able to bend light and hold things in place so they couldn't escape.

He was always berating me for bungling the job of killing him, asking me to do it again and properly this time. In one of those dreams I'm sitting in my mother's living room. The couch is uncomfortable. I get to my feet, remove the cushion I'm sitting on and there is his face, gasping for breath. Now I'm gasping as well which brings Hilary awake. "Oh, no, not again," she says, or holding me: "It's all right, Russ, it's all right."

Soon I couldn't listen to the radio or watch TV for then the soundless static worsened and became psychic pain. The only relief was a Chopin Nocturne or the slow movement of a Mozart concerto.

Hilary insisted I see our GP. "No," I said.

"Why not?"

"It'll pass."

"And if not?"

"It will pass."

"Russ, you are ill."

"Just a bad patch."

"I'm making an appointment with your doctor."

"Don't."

She marched into the bedroom with mutinous strides and soon I heard her voice abruptly calm like a trained receptionist. Not trying to hear what was said, I busied myself emptying the dishwasher. The conversation went on longer than I had expected and finally Hilary returned and leaned against the fridge as if trying to remember a half forgotten recipe.

"That was a nurse at the surgery," she said without looking at me.

"Oh?"

She stared at nothing for another moment. "I'm wondering if you're ready for this."

"Ready? Did she give a diagnosis over the phone?"

"No, of course not."

"What, then."

"I'm not so sure I should tell you."

"What do you mean?"

"In the condition you're in."

"You're making it worse."

"OK, then." Her smile lit all four corners of the room. "I'm pregnant, that all right?"

I didn't know it at first but from then on things began to improve because now I really had something to worry about.

Nine months later we found ourselves cheerfully astride a runaway horse called parenthood. It was a decision made without illusion. Or so we thought. Instead of living happily ever after, we had a child. What we weren't told was that the gallop never ceased and each morning began with a mad dash that ended at the starting line for the next day's race. Jessica transformed our lives in ways we could never have guessed. She freed us from certainty and self-obsession and opened up a complex world where we extracted great pleasure from the simplest of things. She deepened at a stroke our understanding of life and renewed, as never before, our acquaintance with dread. She was always with us even when she was somewhere else. And when she was somewhere else, the dread was worse. My wife and I thought the other worried excessively because we each had different fears. When flying, she was engrossed with death, I with the cost of the flight. When eating, I was obsessed with cholesterol, she with calories. But separately or together we worried about Jess.

My mother, to everyone's surprise, was doing fine. She and Aunt Selma, now also widowed, spent their time eating out, going shopping or seeing the latest film. Beryl liked best those with the least cursing and whose stories were easy to follow. Selma loved any movie with explicit sex.

One evening while doing the dishes and listening to Radio 3, I was transfixed, once again, by my father's favorite Delius. I learned afterward from the announcer that *The Paradise Garden* was actually the name of a pub.

"Did you hear that?" I asked Hilary who was putting leftovers in the fridge. As I spoke, the wineglass I was washing broke in my hands. Jess, aged six, saw blood and ran off. As Hilary dropped the larger pieces into the bin, Jess came running back with the First Aid Kit.

"It's OK, Daddy, don't worry." She dabbed at the wound with a paper towel, wincing at every touch. Then she applied what I called a band-aid which she called an elastoplast.

"Does it hurt?" she asked.

"Not any more."

Days later I found her eyeing a framed photo on a side table beneath a lamp.

"Did you take that picture of Grandpa?"

"I did," I said, bending to study Jacob's casual stance in Selma's backyard, dressed in a windbreaker, holding a beer. Teasing, I once said it made him look like a godfather at a gangster cookout minutes before the Feds closed in. Actually, it caught one of his rare moments of good humor and contagious charm. He had been holding forth on Tennyson, as I remember, and even quoted a few lines.

"What's that on his shoulder?" Jessica wanted to know.

"A camera strap."

"Did you teach him to take pictures?"

"No, he taught me."

"Did you ever bandage his finger?"

"Never."

"But I did yours, didn't I?"

"You sure did."

The next morning I said to Hilary, "Last night I had another dream about him."

"Oh, God."

"No, it wasn't like that. He was in his wheelchair in our sitting room asking to be introduced to Jess. I went looking for her but she was nowhere to be found. I even went into the back garden. Then I heard her calling, "Daddy, Daddy," and there they were rolling toward me, Jess in his lap manning the controls. She drove the chair every which way and he was holding her tight and laughing. That's all I remember."

For about an hour I felt wonderful. Then the phone rang. It was my mother calling from New York. We went through the usual what's-new-nothing-much-what's-new-with-you? routine but her voice was tentative and distracted. Finally she said:

"I want to ask a question. Did you ask Sol for something?"

"For something?"

"To end his life."

My wife looked quizzically at me from the doorway. With a hand over the phone, I whispered, "Beryl." Losing interest, Hilary disappeared.

"To end whose life?" I asked, wanting to flee from her answer.

"Jacob's. Is it true?"

"Is it true? Yes, it's true. Dad asked me to do it. You know how unhappy he was. So I asked Sol for some pills and Sol being Sol he said no. But we found them in the medicine cabinet anyway,"

There was a pause. "He said something else."

"Go on."

"He thinks you helped him die when the police came."

I wanted to scream, to flatten his face. "He's wrong, Ma. Dad's heart stopped. The doctor said so. Ask him."

Plaintively: "Then it *was* his heart?"

"Yes. His heart."

"Good." Again, relieved. "Good."

"And for god's sake, why in hell is he tormenting you?"

"Who?"

"SOL, who do you think?"

"Oh, he's so suspicious. One time he asked me if we were legally married."

"You and Jacob?"

"Can you imagine?"

"Well, were you?" I asked, smiling.

"Of course," she snapped. "What kind of question is that?"

In the summer as usual we went back to the States and as usual Beryl urged us to take a vacation and leave Jess with her as if she had a pressing backlog of grandmothering to do and was eager to get started. This time we relented. My wife, of course, was uneasy about the plan. Jess would be spoiled rotten by Beryl's permissiveness and, in general, made unhealthy by America's glorious god given democratic freedom to make themselves, and all who visit here, obese. But the real fear was that Jess would almost surely be put at risk by my mother's famed incompetence. Hilary was annoyed that I didn't share this view. I reminded her how good Beryl was with children. "Ha," she exclaimed, "look what a cock-up she made of you."

But we went anyway. Drove upstate to a hotel I had seen on a job long ago. Toward the end of our first day we bought a bottle of red wine, borrowed two stemmed glasses from the desk clerk and drove to a ridge above a long valley that led down through forest to a glittering lake. As the sun lowered and the distant mountains were set aflame, we lay on the dry grass and drank.

Why that moment rather than another? I felt content as never before and so very close to her as we shared the wine on that high hill above such a splendid view that I thought, yes, now, do it now. It was there inside me anyway, pushing, always pushing to come out, to speak, to be heard and so I let it emerge, finally -- the last secret.

"I know it's a bit late to bring this up now," I said, "but when my father died..."

She looked at me, worried, yet resolute in her neutrality.

" ...of a heart attack," I continued. "Well, the truth is it didn't happen that way."

Her hand went to her lips to hold in something that had already escaped.

"I offered. He agreed. Even insisted. So I did it. I had to."

"How?"

"A pillow."

"Oh my god. That wasn't assisted..."

"I know."

"It was..."

"I know."

She turned towards me, aghast. "You could have ruined our lives. Ruined everything."

"I didn't think so."

"Years in prison."

"Doubtful."

Something small and terribly alive lurched in the undergrowth. The glittering lake had gone dull in the enveloping dark. She tore up some grass and threw it away. Without looking at me, her voice almost normal again.

"That's why you went through that bad patch."

"Yeah."

"How awful." She leaned closer and took hold of me. "To have to do such a thing." Her arms tightened. "And the courage."

"Yes. His, not mine."

There in the near dark I felt her full, warm lips.

By the time we got back and parked in the dirt road behind the hotel and climbed out of the car into the solid night, the Milky Way had overflowed its bank. We stood and marveled as it flooded all of heaven. What a tonnage of light is dispersed throughout the darkness. It was as though a great and shining perfection had been shattered into a million fragments in an urgent need to signal a message we have yet to understand.